JEWELL

KRIS MICHAELS

WWW.KRISMICHAELSAUTHOR.COM

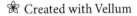

CHAPTER 1

O ne year ago:

He leaned back and took in the systems he'd linked together. Millions of bots running innumerable variables to find a chink in Guardian's armor hadn't yet found a vulnerability. He'd worked for over three months before he got lucky with the undercover operative the Bratva had found. Guardian's operative used a cell phone for check-ins, and that access point cracked the shield. When he admitted his success to the bastards that paid for his services another godsend was delivered. He didn't know how the head of the Bratva had the information to gain access to the heart of Guardian, but with the combined access points his system was data mining the unbelievable amounts of information he now had access to. He'd identified the key players, and when he had the time, he'd search further. It was the highest point of his career, and he planned on capitalizing on the coup... after the leaders of Guardian were six feet under.

Present day:

Jewell King glanced over her shoulder. Again. The large, black leather chair she'd ordered for *him* mocked her with his absence. Not that she cared. Zane Reynolds was a royal pain in her ass, and she was better off with him gone. His forced presence in her life was nothing more than an inconvenience. Well, that was bullshit. He was way more than a simple inconvenience. The protection detail "Guardian" had subjected her to was a thorn in her side and an intrusion on her privacy. *Protective Detail? Bullshit. He was a babysitter. Someone her brothers paid to watch her.* He was gone, and she was happy to have her freedom. No more turning around and running into a six feet five-inch wall of muscle. Damn blond haired, brown eyed gorilla.

She grabbed her energy drink and downed the last of it. She could drink as many as she wanted now. There was nobody to limit her intake or force her to eat 'real' food. She worked the hours she wanted and slept when she crashed.

Jewell tossed the empty toward her over-flowing trash can. She'd take her trash down to the collection point. The cleaning staff wasn't cleared to be in her wing, so the people who worked here cleaned their own areas. She'd get around to it—later. Zane would freak out if he saw the condition of her office. Jewell sneered to herself. *Whatever.* The man was her shadow for months, almost a year actually, and then he simply… wasn't. She knew exactly when he'd left. That day had been insane. Not only had the organization been working the aftermath of the Bratva mission, but her brother, Jacob's division, executed four simultaneous overseas operations which when run alone were labor intensive. Four at one time? That was a fucking nightmare. Her section was stretched paper thin every day. The day Zane left it felt like the world was spinning out of control. She'd eked out time to work with one of her best coders, Ernest, to beta test a new firewall, one that the Bratva's son of a bitch computer genius couldn't penetrate. Ever since the Bratva's hired hell-hound of a hacker had found a way into their system, she'd been tenacious about making sure it could never happen again. Now that she knew how he'd gotten into her domain, she was able to defend against any other attacks.

Yet, Jewell remembered the moment Zane had stood, stretched, and grabbed his tablet before leaving her office. It wasn't uncommon for him to stroll about the section. Except, this time he didn't return. He didn't say goodbye, and when she'd finally returned to her apartment that night, his belongings were gone. He'd just fucking left.

Jewell lowered her toe and swiveled her chair away from her monitors. She'd found the email releasing him of his duties in her inbox... two days after her brother Jason had sent it. The fact that Zane hadn't said goodbye *didn't* bother her. Protecting her was his job. Nothing more. Good riddance. At least now she could do whatever she wanted when she wanted. She'd gone back to pretty much living in her office, showering in the gym downstairs and ordering food from the small restaurant around the corner or calling out for pizza. Pizza was her mainstay. Did it take forever to make it through the security in the building? Yeah, but hey, cold pizza rocked.

Life at Guardian had resumed its pre-Bratva ebb and flow. Critical mission information, surveillance feeds and secure communications status updates scrolled across Jewell's four, forty-inch monitors. There was always a crisis, or a mission, or a report due. She'd grown used to the stress of never ending demands. Dealing with those things without Zane to glower over her was a piece of cake.

Jewell jumped and pivoted at an almost silent ping that resonated louder with her than the sound of a five-alarm disaster. The chat room icon that had been silent for over a year blinked with a message.

> *I'm ready to play again.*

Jewell stared at the monitor hosting the Dark Web chat room she'd built. The computer was a missions shielded standalone and wasn't connected to any Guardian Systems. The chat room remained open only because Guardian hadn't caught the hacker when they took down the Bratva. She'd been ordered by her brother, Jason, the CEO of Guardian, to report any communication from the Bratva's computer savant and not to engage under any circumstances. But... this was her chance to catch the bastard that had found a way into her systems. It was her section's fault that the Bratva had the intelligence to attack her family, and she was ultimately responsible for her section. The blame rested on her shoulders. Not that anyone had said those words, but Jewell knew where the buck stopped. She pulled the keyboard onto her lap.

>**We played. You lost.**

Jewell waited and counted the blinks of the cursor to still her nerves.

>*You should play again.*

>**Not interested.**

She didn't want to fuck around with this guy. He was too damn good.

. . .

>The stakes of the game are too high to fold.

Jewell absorbed the possible meanings of the comment. The stakes are too high for who? The hacker... or her?

>I don't gamble.

Jewell grabbed one of the pencils she'd pushed into her hair and popped it into her mouth, destroying the metal band because she'd already chewed off the eraser. She pushed the keyboard back to the desk and grabbed her ergonomic keyboard that was connected to her Guardian systems. The interoffice messaging system appeared on her main monitor, and she typed in Jason's name. She'd let him know the asshole had contacted her. She tapped out a message but paused before she hit the send button. The asshole hacker had replied.

. . .

>*Smart for a cop.*

>**Smart, period**.

Asshat wasn't getting any information from her.

>*We need to meet.*

>**Hell will freeze over first**.

>*Challenge accepted.*

>**Not a challenge. Fact.**

She couldn't resist the taunt.

> *We need to meet. We could do amazing things together.*

>**Not into crazy.**

.   .   .

>*You intrigue me.*

>**I'm smarter than you.**

>*We need to meet. You are good. But I am better.*

>**Not happening.**

>*We shall see. As an olive branch to solidify our new relationship, you have five minutes until a nasty virus I uploaded six months ago activates. I could stop it if you'd give me access.*

Jewell hopped up and hit the red button at the side of her desk. A shrill warning klaxon sounded, alerting every operator in the section to immediately secure and backup all data before disabling and disconnecting all systems. She activated the countdown clock setting it to four minutes, just in case the son of a bitch had lied to her about the timing. Her fingers flew over her keyboards. She'd forced her section to practice for this very event once a week since the first breach had been detected.

Her office door flew open. Jason's massive frame filled the doorway.

"Sitrep."

"Virus, due to activate in less than," She glanced at the clock, "two minutes." She didn't stop, she was racing time to lock down all information and systems before the virus could wreak havoc.

"How did you find it?"

Jewell locked down her system before she reached behind the computer and pulled her fiber that connected her systems to the rest of the facility as well as the power cables. "It was written into script left in the system six months ago." She didn't have time for fifty questions. She barged past him and ran down the steps to help her people. Jason followed on her heels.

"Can we stop it?"

"As long as everyone follows procedure, yes. Let me finish this. I'll give you a report as soon as I can." Jewell dismissed him and started pulling cables along with the rest of her team. The klaxon sounded again giving them a one-minute warning.

"Clear in section one!"

"Clear on Two!"

"Comms are down and secured."

"Video feeds are down. One satellite feed for an overseas op in progress."

Fuck, that meant Jacob…

"What the fuck is happening?" Her brother Jacob stormed into the section, bellowing like a rampaging elephant. Jason called him over. Thank God for that. She didn't have time to pacify her family right now. They still had two sections and five information platforms to secure. Her team converged in an orchestrated dance of chaotic precision.

"All IS platforms segregated."

"Section Three is clear."

Jewell raced over to the last section. She took over and directed the operator to the back of the station. "Pull those fuckers when I tell you." She'd never typed so fast in her life. The lights in the room flickered. Fuck, fifteen seconds. She watched the system shut down and silently begged it to hurry. There!

"Pull it!"

Jewell looked up in time to see the last seconds click off the clock. The Klaxon silenced, and the lights returned to the indistinct lighting her operators favored.

"What the fuck happened." Alonzo, one of her senior operators and programmers, damn near screamed the question from across the room.

Jewell shook her head and pushed a large strand of hair behind her ear. "There is a virus that was embedded months ago. It was set to activate in five minutes." Her quiet reply carried in the sudden silence of her section. Her hands shook from the adrenaline pumping through her system.

"Jewell?" Jason's voice brought her head up. She glanced around and noticed Jacob was gone. He'd probably be trying to clean up any mess the sudden loss of intel from the satellite feed.

"How bad is the effect on Jacob's mission?" She didn't really want to know, but if people lost their lives, it would be her fault. They hadn't found the virus, and they had swept every system. Now it was a matter of segmenting systems, compartmentalizing information and mitigating any losses the virus could cause.

"They aborted without incident."

"Thank God."

"How much longer are we going to have to do this dance?" Jason leaned against one of the workstations.

The pressure of his question fell hard around her. She was dealing with a genius, she had no idea how he'd left a code for a virus that they hadn't seen.

"I don't know. At least we were able to contain it." She glanced at her team who had gathered behind her.

Jason lifted off the workstation. He surveyed the theater and her people. "You did a great job. Thank you." He turned and headed toward the door. "Fix this, Jewell," was tossed over his shoulder. God, she wished she could. Hell, she thought she had. All the hours of work. The weeks that she never left the fucking building, and still they missed a threat. How?

She flopped down onto the chair and drew a deep breath.

"Standard protocols boss?" Alonzo's quiet question prodded her into action.

"No. This time it's all eyes on every system. I want everyone to have buy-in on all sweeps. If we don't find where the virus is hiding or figure out how to stop it, we won't have an agency to work for, so it's all hands on deck. I want each section to be sanitized before we connect to anything, anywhere. We start with the mission critical equipment and work down. Understand?"

All heads went north and south. "Okay, separate into specialties. I need all my coders at the top station. We are running code, line by line. With the programs on the clean computer, we can make a comparison." Jewell looked over her shoulder and spoke to the rest of the room. "After the code is scoured we need every eye on the programs in case this shit is located in something other than the operating platforms. Nothing goes up until every one of us has cleared it. Got it?"

"But if it is a polymorphic virus we aren't going to have any contextual clues to go by. It will change its appearance with each infection." Darla plopped down on one of the station chairs as the handful of coders reached the top workstation.

"So we scan for algorithms as well as strings. Hang tight for a second." Jewell popped into her office and retrieved the clean laptop and the charging cord. She sat it down on the workstation. "My guess is we have a hybrid, a multi-partite, and a fucking nasty one."

The groan that came from several of her best

employees echoed her own internal lament, but she couldn't let them see it. "Good news is we will be getting more overtime."

Cayden snorted, "What good is money if you never have any off time to spend it."

"This shit will pass, man. We thought we had it all, but now we need to buckle down. If any of you can't hang, speak up." Alonzo's voice held no room for bitching. Jewell threw him a grateful smile. She'd go toe to toe with anyone when there was a hardware issue, but she wasn't great with the one on one interactions. Alonzo was good with people. With absolute silence following his words, they set up shop. It was going to be one hell of a long night. Jewell sighed, who was she trying to fool? They'd be lucky to get through the clean-up in... She glanced around the section she'd built and shook her head, it would take weeks to make sure they were clean.

CHAPTER 2

J ason King strode down the hallway after an hour-long video conference with the Directors of Israeli Mossad, British MI6, Italian SISMI and French DCPJ, the FBI and Homeland Security. Guardian was a 24/7/365 agency. Several operations were currently underway. The recent threat to their intelligence and communications systems had finally been cleaned up. During the chaos of a full system shut down, he'd passed a total of five operations to the CIA and his counterparts overseas. That was a hard pill to swallow, but rather than risk the security of people, resources or nations, he'd made the call. Thankfully it had only taken twelve days to purge their systems and restore operations. His sister and her team had kicked ass. She was a phenomenal force and was the reason he was still at work after the video call ended. He'd seen her piece of shit, puke-green Toyota in the parking garage when he'd returned to the office at midnight after having dinner with his wife and son.

Jason smiled as he headed to Jewell's office. His little family was the universe to him. He'd played with his son Reece and Tippy, the family border collie, in the backyard for over an hour after dinner tonight. They'd put the exhausted little boy to bed, and then Jason had spent some quality time with his wife. He would have loved to stay in bed with Faith. Unfortunately, the monthly video conference on the various facets of the Bratva's clean-up forced him to leave after she'd fallen asleep.

He entered Jewell's section of the facility and stopped to let his eyes adjust to the lower level lighting. The people who worked in his sister's section had individual work stations that had separate lighting, ergonomic desks, chairs, and keyboards. Some were using their standing desks while others sat on what looked like bouncy balls. Whatever, they were a breed unto themselves. Twenty-eight steps up to the top of the massive theater shaped room put him at Jewell's door. He placed his thumb on the keypad and entered his code. The door opened with an almost soundless click. He pushed it open and stopped dead in his tracks. *Shit.*

Take-out containers, pizza boxes, energy drinks and empty candy wrappers littered the area. The only area to escape the disaster was a large leather chair at the back of the room. Jason drew a deep breath at the significance of that tidbit of information. *Damn it.*

His sister had fallen asleep at her workstation. She was slumped onto the workstation, while curled up in the big chair she'd special ordered when she first started here. It allowed her to sit cross-legged. Jason walked over to her, intent on waking her up and forcing her to go home. He'd find garbage bags and clean the shit out of her office before he went home. It sure as hell wouldn't be the first time he'd forced her to go home.

He glanced at the four monitors and shook his head. Jewell's section was the brain of the organization, and his sister monitored everything. He flicked the screens off. A fifth computer screen caught his attention. He shifted his gaze. As his hand reached to turn off the screen, he read what was showing. *Holy fuck.* He grabbed the mouse and scrolled up and up... and up. Fuck. He read down the thread. Of all the stupid, hairbrained... The words that appeared at the bottom of the thread stopped his internal rant. He started at the beginning and re-read the words before he quietly stepped out of her office. Jason walked out of her secure area and made a call. Fuck, just when he thought things were getting back to normal. The phone rang once before it was answered.

"Reynolds."

"This is Archangel. Are you local?"

"Affirmative, sir."

"I need you to come in." Jason thanked his lucky stars that the man wasn't on an assignment.

"Where?" Reynolds asked.

"C3." Jason gave him the acronym for Jewell's section. It stood for Control, Computation, and Communications. The section did far more than those functions, but the designation had stuck.

"On my way."

Jason re-secured the phone to its cradle. He'd wait for Reynolds to show up before he woke his sister. When he did, shit was going to hit the fan.

Zane dropped his phone on his chest and scrubbed his face with his hands. Receiving a call from the CEO of Guardian Security had well and truly woken his ass up. The question was why was he being recalled and specifically why was he being asked to report to C3? No, he wouldn't speculate. There was no sense in wasting time wondering what the hell was going on. Archangel would let him know soon enough. Zane threw back the covers. Duty called.

CHAPTER 3

Zane stared at the screen and lifted away after he'd read it—three times. A small snore from Jewell earned the woman a sideways glance. Her hair fell in a shroud over the desk where she had fallen asleep. Her long lashes lay against her pale cheeks. The woman never went outside. Jason King pointed to the door, and Zane followed. They left the office and moved away from the door.

"Do you read that the same way I do?" Jason's concern permeated the question.

"I..." Zane rubbed the back of his neck. "Yes, the hacker is a threat, not only to the company but to Jewell. He has obviously fixated on her. She needs to be under a protective detail, but I'm not the man for the job."

"You are the only one who I'd trust to watch her. The others don't have your… patience or your unique qualifications." Jason took a couple steps toward a vacant workstation. "She's a handful."

"Sir, with all due respect, your sister is a hot mess, not to mention she fucking hates me." Zane wasn't going to sugar coat it. "Not that her opinion of me matters, but for me to protect her, she'll have to agree to it.

"I agree, she is a mess, but she's my sister, and I don't give a shit if she hates you. You are back with her. 24/7. I'll increase your pay accordingly. I know you put in more hours than you logged the last time you were with her."

"My objection wasn't about money. You have the entire agency at your disposal. I'm sure you could put a team or two on her." Zane didn't want the assignment. His reasons weren't all professional. A team could watch her. At least then he'd be able to forget the fall of hair against her neck or the blush that matched her pale rose-hued lips.

Fuck, he wasn't the person to watch over her. His first day with her was one he'd never forget. He'd sat in an uncomfortable as fuck chair and watched her work for fourteen hours. She bounced between her people's station and her office, logging at least five miles and countless flights of steps. Zane had a huge breakfast before he'd been pulled in and briefed that he'd been assigned as protective detail for Archangel's sister, but after the entire day had wasted away, he was hungry.

When he placed a salad and a bottle of water in front of her, she'd jumped, almost as if she'd forgotten he was there. The way she concentrated on her work, he had little doubt that she *had* forgotten. Confusion and then happiness raced across her face. It was only a split second, but he'd seen it. It buffered the snide remark that flew out of her mouth.

Jason interrupted his thoughts, "I could assign a team, but I'm not going to do it. You know her, know her routines, and in some mystical, magical way, you lasted. She likes you, or you'd be gone."

Liked him? Right, as if. "She asked you to fire me no less than twenty times, and that was while I was present. I can only imagine how many times she demanded I be removed during your closed door conferences."

"The topic never came up. Look, if you won't do this, I'll find someone else. I won't force you."

Zane stared at his boss. He weighed what he

saw on that screen against dealing with his attraction to a woman who, in his opinion, would rather see him staked out on a fire ant hill than in her office. He figured she'd drizzle his ass in honey just to make it fun for the ants.

Zane opened his mouth to speak, but Jason interrupted him, "Just ask yourself one question. What if something happens to her? If she slips away from whomever I assign? If that computer fuck actually comes after her? Could you live with that?"

Well fuck. "No, no I couldn't."

"So you'll take her on?"

Zane drew a deep breath and nodded. "Yes, but I have two conditions." Since he'd become a Personal Security Officer, he'd done his damnedest to remain as passive and compliant to directives as possible. He'd even congratulated himself for letting Jewell King talk to him like a two-year-old without reverting to his old ways. But enough was enough. He was done trying to fit in. Jason King's eyebrow raised and his eyes bored a hole through Zane.

"I'm listening." His boss ground out the words.

Zane put both hands in his pockets and drew a deep breath. "One, I'm only here until the minute this guy is caught or until we know he will no longer be a threat."

"I can live with that condition." Jason acquiesced.

"Second, I want complete autonomy."

"Define complete autonomy." Jason threw the words back at him immediately.

"If I see she needs to leave, to eat, to sleep, or to relax, I can pull her ass out of that box. I'll be granted support of other PSOs or teams if I need them." He pointed to her office at the top of the stairs. "She can bitch, but she needs to know I'll report any deviation directly to you and she needs to know my background." All the shit that bothered the fuck out of him during his assignment bubbled up and spewed out of his mouth, "She eats nothing but crap, drinks nothing but energy drinks or coffee and gets little to no sleep for days on end. The way she works? She's going to die of a heart attack at the ripe old age of thirty-three if she doesn't start taking care of herself. You won't have to wait for the hacker to come after her."

He finished his rant and realized he'd raised his voice. Every person in the section was either looking directly at them or pretending not to. Zane crossed his arms over his chest. He'd been working damn hard to change, to become what normal people assumed he should be, but with each passing day, the task was getting harder. The calm outside veneer was becoming harder to maintain.

Finally, his boss nodded and spoke, "Done. I'll talk to Jacob and Jared. But I have conditions, too."

Zane's eyes hardened as he gazed at his employer. The steel edge to the man's voice meant the terms were nonnegotiable. He waited to see what stipulations would be placed on him this time. There was no way he'd stay if he were unable to comply.

"If you see that we as an organization are putting too much on her plate, you will let me know. I'll admit that I let her run her show. I don't monitor her schedule, nor do I micromanage her section. If she needs more people, we will get them. If she needs an assistant, it is done. Anything. I couldn't live with the fact that my company causes her any harm, even by omission. Obviously, you're concerned enough to make demands. That took brass balls, by the way. Second, you will not tell her about your past. Period."

"I won't unless she asks, but I won't lie. She's an

amazing person. A stone cold bitch at times, but amazing nonetheless."

"I can live with that, and she really isn't a bitch."

"You don't work for her." Zane had. The woman could cut a person to shreds with her words. She didn't do it often unless your name was Zane, but when she did, it was a figurative blood-bath. The saving grace was except him, the people she lit into were either incompetent or negligent. She tolerated neither, and that was a well-known fact.

"True. Let's go wake up sleeping beauty and get some answers."

Zane fell into step behind Jason. The sinking feeling in his gut had nothing to do with the fact that Jewell couldn't stand him. Rather, it had everything to do with the fact that he'd fallen for the impossible computer diva. In his line of work, he couldn't form attachments. Zane tossed that thought to the side. He could form attachments, make a life or have friends. It was difficult to remember he no longer performed *those* duties. He was no longer an assassin. He was a caretaker, a babysitter and the ability to actually save lives kept him on this side of sanity. Barely. If he'd tried to remain on the other side of the black door, he'd be dead by now.

Regardless of what he was, or had become when he walked out of this office over two months ago, he'd left knowing the feelings he had for her would never be returned. Absolutely nothing had changed. Zane walked back into her world tonight knowing that fact. Little did that matter. Seeing her exhausted and asleep at her station had gutted him. Everyone, including her brothers, had their hand out expecting the impossible from her, and the woman would kill herself rather than disappoint any of them. When he was assigned as her security detail, he'd done what he could to mitigate the stress of her world, but with no authority to make her listen to him, it was too little to make a difference. It only irritated her and, maybe in the beginning, he had continued to do it for that reason. That is until he noticed no one else was taking care of her, not even herself. This time it would be different.

CHAPTER 4

"Jewell."

Her name registered at the same time as the dull ache in her back. She lifted from her computer console and blinked repeatedly, trying to get her eyes to focus. That's when she noticed her screens were blank.

"Shit!" She grabbed at her keyboard and padded around her desk for her mouse only to hit it and send it flying in the opposite direction. She dropped her legs to the ground to reach for the damn thing until the sensation of a million tiny pins and needles ran through her legs. "Ouch, fuck!"

"Jewell, relax. I turned off your monitors."

Jason's voice pierced the muddled fog of confusion that draped itself around her.

"Why? Why would you do...?" Jewell turned to face her brother. Her words dried up. Dark brown eyes stared back at her. *No.* "No. Whatever *you're* doing here, the answer is no." Jewell wiped the sleep out of her eyes and turned her back on the duo. She swiped at her face cussing to herself and hit the power buttons for her monitors. She blinked when her office was flooded with light. "For fuck's sake, turn those off!" She squinted at the brilliant intrusion to her sanctuary.

"No. What's this?"

Jewell snapped her head around at her brother ready to hand him his head on a platter until she saw what he was looking at. "That?"

"Yes, this. I believe you were ordered to report any activity and not to engage."

Jewell glared at her brother. She had been going to tell him about the contact as soon as she figured out the asshole's end game.

"There is nothing to report. He's fishing."

"No, *he* has threatened *you*." Zane's deep, gravelly voice chimed in. He always sounded like he'd had one too many drinks and smoked one too many cigars. As if. The man was a health freak.

The likelihood of him having fun and doing something wild, like drinking too much or smoking a cigar, was next to zilch. Same odds as her doing either of those things, but for decidedly different reasons.

"Why are you even here?" Jewell held up a hand when Zane opened his mouth to speak. She didn't want to hear anything from him. "Just... don't; I don't care because you're not staying." Shit, she did not need this.

"He is here because you've been threatened," Jason repeated.

"When?" She looked at her brother and pointed at the screen that he seemed obsessed with. "He hasn't threatened anything."

Jason scrolled the page down.

"'*I'm coming for you. You can't stop me. This time, I will win.*' That sounds like a threat to me."

"*Ahh... nooo...* that sounds like a hacker who is going to try to beat my systems and shut me down, but if you look, he's already admitted that he can't get in any longer. Plus with all the new safeguards we've implemented, nobody could get into our systems. I guarantee it." Jewell scrolled up and pointed to the hacker's comment about stopping the virus.

"Which leads to the next question. Why didn't you tell me he alerted you to the virus?" Jason raised his eyebrow and waited.

"I did!" Jewell traced the things that happened that day in her mind. She had to have told him when she hit the alarm... didn't she?

"You didn't."

"Well, I will when I finish my report on it. *Why is he here?*"

Zane scrolled the screen down farther. Jewell leaned into the monitor. She hadn't seen these comments, they must have come in after she'd fallen asleep.

"Okay, so that's a little creepy." Actually, the words were terrifying, but she wasn't going to admit that with Zane in the room.

"A little creepy?"

>I have found a way to make you pay. You will die for what you have done to my reputation.

The timestamp on that was twenty-one hundred hours. Jewell looked at her last activity on her other monitors. She'd probably fallen asleep about a half hour before that came in. Two hours later the hacker had sent another message.

>I look forward to hearing you beg before you die.

"What is he making you pay for, Jewell?" Jason's

words brought her attention back to the men in the room.

She shrugged as if the threats hadn't fazed her when, in fact, they scared the shit out of her. She clenched her hands into fists to stop them from shaking. "Word around the Dark Net as of about a week ago is Vista has lost several big jobs. I'm assuming what was left of the Bratva has spread the word that his work is subpar." She'd seen more than one post insinuating that Vista couldn't deliver what he was paid to do, and Vista's comments in their chat room had turned darker about the same time. She silently wished the men weren't in the room so she could burrow into the Dark Net and find out what happened to send the hacker into a tailspin.

"Who the hell is Vista?" Jason's growled words didn't bode well. She probably hadn't told him she'd discovered the hacker's handle. Not that it really mattered what the guy was called because he was a freaking real life ghost. There was nothing on him anywhere. She'd used every program to try to find anything on the man, but she still came up with nothing.

"Vista is asshat's handle. I found out maybe... three or four days ago, but then we had that blow up in the Middle East, and then the team member with medical emergency in Afghanistan and after that Jared had two Level 1 backgrounds, and I'm the only one who can complete that level—"

"Do you see what I mean?" Zane interrupted her explanation. Jewell sent him a look that could freeze hell over. He had no right to interrupt. *Why in the hell was he here?*

"Yeah." Jason motioned to Zane. "Give us a minute?" Zane gave one curt nod of his head, did an about face and left.

"*Why* is he here?" She shook. Vista's threat wrapped around her almost as tightly as her fear. She reached toward her mini fridge. Jason took the energy drink out of her hand as she withdrew it.

"Hey, that's mine. There's plenty in here, all you had to do was ask." She reached back for the cooler.

"Jewell, stop. When was the last time you went home and slept more than three hours?"

She frowned at him when he put the drink back into the fridge. "I don't know? And why does that matter? I'm doing my job. Granted, the report on Vista is late, but I've handled everything else." She pushed her chair back and stood to look out the one-way mirror of her office windows to the pit where her people worked. Yvette was working, so it was... shit..."Jason, why are you here in the middle of the night?"

"I could ask the same question of you."

"I don't have a family at home." She didn't actually have a life outside this office, except gaming, but hey, whatever. She plopped back down in her chair.

"Jewell, Zane opened my eyes to the impossible amount of pressure we are putting you under, and that is during normal operations. This Vista threat is real. You've jeopardized his way of making a living. Hell, you've beaten him in a very public way. You, like it or not, are a target. I'm going to pull Tori in, and we'll use her connections to see if they can help find this bastard. I'll call in favors from the four corners of the earth and leverage anything Gabriel has to offer to make an ID on this bastard. No one threatens my family without the entire might of this company raining down on them. The Bratva thought they could threaten us. They couldn't. This fucker isn't going to get away with it either. Zane is your full-time protection."

"No!" She leaned back in her chair and ran her hands through her bangs, pulling them down over her face. She didn't want this. No, no, no. She'd let

Zane stay before and had even been *nice* to him sometimes and then *he* left her, without a word. She…. she'd grown used to him and damn it, she'd even started to depend on him, and he'd left. "Anyone else. I don't care who. Fuck it, Jason, I'll stay here 24/7. Revoke my ability to exit the building. Vista can't reach me here."

"No. In fact, the reason I want Zane to watch over you is so you can leave. Damn it, of course, I want you to leave the fucking building."

"Why are you doing this?"

"Because I love you. We've neglected and used you for far too long. You're going to get additional help. You will train your most trusted people to do the functions that only you are doing now. If God forbid, you died tomorrow, they'd need to know how to fill your shoes. You will also work eight hours a day—"

"No one works eight hours a day!" Jewell launched from her chair.

"Granted. You can work ten hours, and you will take two days off a week." Jason stood and towered over her. That didn't faze her, she was used to her brothers trying to intimidate her.

Her body shook but this time not in fear. Anger, or exhaustion or both, fueled this reaction.

Bullshit coated the situation, and she hated the smell of the entire thing. "Fine, I agree to all that, but to not him!" She threw her arm behind her, pointing out the window to where she knew Zane was standing.

"Sorry, nonnegotiable." Jason crossed his arms over his chest.

Jewell stepped back and crossed her arms over her chest, mimicking his stance. "Fine, I quit."

"No you don't, and even if you did, he'd still be assigned as your security detail because that hacker is a legitimate threat. I will not lose my sister to a fucking maniacal geek, and the best way I can protect you is that man standing out there."

"Why is he the only option? You have a thousand people working for you!"

"Only one of them knows you better than anyone else, and like it or not, it is *that* man. He is uniquely qualified to take care of you. This is not open for debate. As your boss, I am ordering you to comply. As your brother, I'm begging you to listen to sense and stop being a hard headed tool about this. I'm not stupid enough to think you didn't look into him the second he showed up in your section. You know he's damn good at what he does, and I know he will take care of you better than anyone else in this organization. You will do as he says when he says to do it. He has my full backing. Period, end of discussion."

Jewell turned away. She felt tears sting the back of her eyes and she sure as hell didn't want Jason to see them. She was exhausted. She was scared. The threat was hard to process especially when she added a helping of blond hair, brown eyed Zane. She had looked into his background, but it had been coded, and she'd respected the agency's need to keep his past hidden. She tried damn hard not to speculate what he'd been doing for the company. Having him back in her life was a recipe for disaster because for some reason, he made her insane enough to depend on him.

"Fine." She barely whispered the word, but Jason heard her. His large hands circled her upper arms, and he dropped a kiss on her hair. "I love you, Button. Do your work, listen to Zane, and everything will work out."

Jewell swiped at a stray tear that pushed over her lashes and trekked down her cheek. Damn Jason for using her childhood nickname. Her father had once said she was as cute as a button and her brothers had called her Button ever since. He dropped his hands, and she heard him walk across the room. "Do me a favor and clean this disaster up?" Jewell laughed at the comment despite how overwhelmed she felt. She turned to watch her brother talk to Zane through her window. The conversation lasted several minutes and ended with a handshake. She'd give anything to have had a microphone in the room. Jewell grabbed her tablet and wrote that thought down. Not a bad idea. She could monitor the pit and hear them if they needed her. She dropped into her chair and opened a program. If she designed it, so it was voice activated, the recordings data storage could be minimized. Of course, she'd need to disclose the microphone to her people, but hey if she wanted to she could hack into their computers, not like any of them could hide anything from her anyway.

"Are you ready to go home?"

Jewell jumped, slinging her stylus into the air. "Holy fuck!" She grabbed at her chest. Her heart pounded against her ribcage.

"I'm sorry. You were in a zone, but it looked like you'd finished what you were working on." Zane's gravelly voice was altogether too calm. He'd taken off his suit jacket. His broad shoulders were splendidly magnified by the tailor made shirt.

Jewell looked past him to four huge black garbage bags. She'd totally zoned out and hadn't heard him picking up her office. "I don't need you to clean up after me."

"Obviously someone needs to."

If he'd had an ounce of smugness in his voice, she'd have torn him a new one, but of course, he didn't. No, not Zane. God forbid he take any offense. "Listen, I don't want you here."

"I know." He shrugged into his suit jacket and pulled the cuffs of his shirt down.

"Then why in the name of... *anything,* are you here?" Frustration edged her question, making it sound harsh, even to her own ears.

"I'm here to make sure this hacker doesn't kill you." Zane grabbed three of the bags and turned to her. "Please grab the last bag."

"He's a hacker, not a murderer." Yeah, the threats she'd received tonight did scare her, but the man was just a computer terrorist. "Scaring people is what he gets off on."

"I have a question, and I'd appreciate an honest answer." Zane sat the garbage bags down and put his hands in his pockets.

"Shoot."

"Has that hacker ever, even once, threatened something that he did not act on?"

Jewell blinked at the simplicity of the question. She ticked off the things the man had done, the jobs credited to him on the Dark Net, the way he infiltrated her systems, the viruses that were embedded, the backdoors he'd left himself that she'd found and barricaded. No, he'd always followed through. The hard reality of her current circumstances hit, hard and strong. Jewell lifted her eyes to Zane and shook her head slowly, because speaking right now was impossible. Fear choked any words.

"I'm not your enemy, Jewell. I am here to do the job that was asked of me. Now, are you ready to go home?" He picked up the garbage bags and waited.

Jewell's hands trembled when she closed out her programs, signed out and turned off her monitors. Her actions were rote and mindless, which was a good thing because right now thinking about anything other than the threat Vista issued wasn't going to happen.

CHAPTER 5

Zane opened Jewell's bedroom door and peeked in. She hadn't moved since he'd last checked on her. He shut the door and glanced at his watch, it was just past nine. They'd made it back to her apartment by four thirty. He'd waited while she showered and made sure she went to sleep, which took maybe thirty seconds once her head hit the pillow.

He picked up his cell phone and called the Guardian switchboard asking to be connected to Archangel. He waited less than ten seconds before Jason answered.

"Problems already?" The humor in the man's voice was nice to hear.

"No. She's sleeping. I need to go back to my

apartment and grab some things. Can you send someone over here to watch her until I get back? She shouldn't wake up for a couple days, but I can't guarantee that."

"I can do one better than that. I have Jared and Nicolas in my office now, and since they decided to be a pain in my ass, I'll send them over to babysit while you get what you need." Great, he just wanted someone to stand by the door, not his section's chief executive officer and chief operating officer.

"Are you sure? I just need someone to watch things until I get back. I've already made sure the alarms and cameras are in place, and I've added some redundancy in case this freak can countermand the closed system. Once my operational authority is granted and posted, I won't need to contact you for resources."

"I've already dictated the authority. It should be posted by noon. Jared will be there in about a half hour. His morning meetings were canceled, and you'll soon learn that we Kings take care of each other. I've talked to my brothers, and I agree with your assessment of the pressure Jewell is under. We have decided to take a personal interest in what she is doing, so you'll have each of us checking in and pulling her out of the section. I have every faith that Jacob and Jared can protect her so you can have some down time."

Zane ran his hand through his hair as he paced in front of the kitchen island. "Roger, that, sir." He didn't want or need down time. Jewell would be better served by having someone with her twenty-four-seven. Someone who knew the woman and would ensure she didn't do something stupid.

Zane set the phone down after they'd signed off and headed to the kitchen to take inventory. He rolled his eyes at the case of energy drinks in her refrigerator. He pulled out a plastic gallon of milk that was half full. The expiration date was over two months ago. He shook it. Yep, chunks. Zane pulled out a black trash bag and started pitching. The milk, eggs, sandwich meat that was green and quite possibly crawling away from him, everything went into the garbage bag. If he remembered correctly, most of the stuff in the refrigerator, he'd purchased for her before he'd left. She'd obviously been living at her office because there was no garbage here other than a few empty energy drinks. Speaking of which, Zane turned and pulled out the energy drinks from her fridge and deposited them into another garbage bag. He tied the bags up and put them by the door. He'd take them out when Jared arrived. He'd also stop on the way back and stock up on food that wasn't trying to make an escape.

At a soft knock on the door, Zane glanced at camera feed he'd installed. Jared King stood outside the apartment. Zane unholstered his weapon and held it at his side as he unlatched the security chain and turned the deadbolt. He opened the door and let his superior in. He waited until he'd locked the door before he thumbed the safety on his automatic and put it away.

"Zane." Jared glanced at three huge garbage bags and looked at him in question.

"Spoiled food, energy drinks, and garbage." Zane kept his voice low. He didn't want anything to wake his charge. Besides protection, the woman needed sleep, real food, and a decent work and exercise schedule. But he wasn't expecting miracles.

"Well, shit." Jared pulled off his jacket and tossed it over the back of one of the overstuffed chairs Jewell never used. "We had no idea. I mean I knew she pushed herself hard, but we downloaded her access card activity. She's basically been living at the office."

"Yes, sir." Zane knew only too well how hard the woman worked. While she was safe in the building from the threat that hacker posed, the stress of the job would kill the woman before the hacker could ever reach her.

"Thank you for opening our eyes to that fact. We are in your debt, not only for that but for agreeing to take over her security. Jason told me about your conditions. You, my friend, have elephant-sized brass balls."

Zane cleared his throat and nodded. "She doesn't want me here. I had to have the authority to do it."

"Oh, don't get me wrong, I understand, and I agree. I'm actually impressed. Go do what you need to do." Jared looked toward the kitchen. "Please tell me she has coffee?"

"Ah… no, actually I was going to stop on the way back and pick up some food and staples." Zane grabbed the three bags of garbage as he spoke.

"Figures. Okay, no problem. I'm sure I can con someone into bringing me a gallon or two. Take your time. My next meeting isn't until one." Jared grabbed the television remote and turned it on, muting the volume immediately.

Zane nodded and let himself out. He deposited

the trash and headed across town to his run-down one bedroom apartment to collect what he needed. The place was only a base of operations for him. He had nothing personal here. Everything that meant anything to him was in storage back in Colorado, under an alias; one of several he used to protect his assets.

It took minutes to gather and pack his clothing and limited grooming items. He grabbed a paper bag and took his perishable food from the refrigerator. His neighbor was a sweet, old woman on a fixed income. She'd invited him over for dinner the night he'd moved in and had adopted him the moment he'd agreed.

He stepped across the hall and knocked. He saw her approach the door through her peephole and waited while she moved the small step stool over so she could step up and see out. He waited for her to move the stool and unhook two chains and a deadbolt.

"Zane. Oh, are you leaving again? You only just got back." Mrs. Henshaw opened her door, allowing him in. He'd purposefully stocked up on the essentials even knowing that he'd be reassigned within a couple days. It was his way of making sure Mrs. Henshaw had enough. Her pride wouldn't allow her to accept any help. Her children were scattered around the world and rarely called to check up on her. But she was so proud of all their accomplishments. Zane had heard about each child and grandchild many times.

"Yes ma'am, my boss called me in last night, or rather this morning. Would you mind keeping an eye on things again?" He sat the bag down and started unloading his food.

"You know I don't mind. I still have your number. She pointed to a small cork board with his current name and cell phone number posted on a piece of floral paper.

Zane smiled and winked at the frail woman. "And yet you don't call me to flirt."

Mrs. Henshaw's face turned a pretty shade of pink as she swatted at him. "Oh, you! I'm sure you have a host of lovely ladies falling for you."

Mrs. Henshaw's eyes lit up when he pulled an expensive vanilla bean creamer out of the bag. He took his coffee black, but ever since she told him the creamer was a treat she had to give up because it cost too much, he'd bought two large containers each time he was home. He'd even remembered to pull the foil off one and tip a small portion out, so she'd believed he'd bought it for himself.

"No ma'am, I'm saving my heart for you and your oatmeal cookies." Zane handed her the groceries to put in her refrigerator.

"Oh, you are shameless. If you let me know when you'll be home next, I'll bake you a batch."

"I'd love that. Listen, this time I'll be in the city. I have to stay with the person I'm helping so I would appreciate you watching the apartment. But, if you need anything, just give me a call."

"You are such a good boy. Not everyone can be a home care specialist. I know when my Harvey fell and broke his hip I was beside myself until we got some part time help. You know my children arranged that? I told you how good they were to us when Harvey took ill?" The home healthcare cover story Zane had given Mrs. Henshaw wasn't far from the truth, at least somewhat resembled what he did... now.

"Yes ma'am, you did." Zane leaned back against the counter and watched as she looked up questioningly at him. She'd forgotten. She frowned before she waved a hand in dismissal of the thought that was bothering her.

"Yes, I'm sure I did. Well, you go and get about your business. I'll watch out for your place. But you make sure you call me a couple days before you come home and I'll cook us dinner and oatmeal cookies for dessert." Her tiny hand patted his forearm. He smiled at her with genuine fondness.

Zane damn near dropped two bags before he made it to the apartment, but he'd managed to bring up his clothes and the groceries in one trip. He sat the load down and pulled out the key to the apartment only to hear laughter from inside. His hand stopped short of keying the door and listened to another peel of laughter. The melodic sound was beautiful and rare. He opened the door to find Jewell and Nicolas DeMarco sitting on the couch, laughing at something on his phone.

Nicolas looked over and nodded at Zane. "Hey, you need help?" The man was up and moving across the floor before Zane could respond. He called over his shoulder, "Get off your lazy butt woman, you have groceries to put away." Nicolas turned back to Zane and winked.

Jewell groaned but got up to help. She was wearing a pair of yoga pants and an oversized t-shirt. Her hair was pulled back in a ponytail. Zane was pleased to notice the black circles under her eyes had reduced dramatically, although she still looked exhausted.

"Mr. King had to leave?" Zane battled the anger that welled up inside him. Jason had said Jacob and Jared would relieve him. While Nicolas was one of his superiors, the man had a reputation and he, for one, did not like the man around Jewell.

"I brought over coffee and said I'd stay so Jared could go have an early lunch with his husband." Nicolas tossed the comment over his shoulder.

Zane could understand that, but having Nicolas here still set his nerves on edge. Zane waited until the groceries were stacked along the countertop before he took his bag into the same room he'd used the last time he worked as Jewell's PSO. He took the time to unpack and stow his clothes and opened the door to take his shampoo and toothpaste into the hall bathroom. He did an about face to grab his toothbrush and body wash, but the conversation that drifted into his room stopped him in his tracks.

"So you'll go out to dinner with me?" Zane jaw tightened at the tone his boss was using. The guy was a player, by anyone's standards. Why in the hell would he be targeting Jewell? That was a sticky situation no matter how you sliced it. She was Nicolas' boss's - and his co-worker's - sister.

"I'm not interested in being one of the slew of women who fills your little black books, Nicolas. I'm not interested in you in that way." Jewell batted him down, and Zane mentally gave the woman a fist pump.

"I can assure you, you wouldn't just be a name in a book to me. Come on, go out to dinner with me. You have to eat, right?" God, again with the seductive voice. Zane gritted his teeth and waited. Jewell wasn't a push over, surely she saw through whatever bullshit the man was casting.

"Just dinner?" Zane closed his eyes and leaned against the wall at the innocence in her voice. No, Jewell, it wouldn't be just dinner. Nicolas was legendary at Guardian for his body count, only he didn't count kills, he counted women he bedded. Shit, Nicolas had to pick up on her vulnerability. Fuck, she wasn't someone Nicolas should be hitting on.

"I promise, just dinner. I'll pick you up here at eight. Zane can have the evening off, and you and I can get to know each other a little bit better. Everybody wins." Zane's eyes popped open, and he turned his head toward the living room. He sneered and silently mimicked, *everybody wins.* Juvenile, but fuck it.

"Nicolas, don't get me wrong, I like you, I mean, you're handsome and fun, but why the sudden interest?" Zane slapped his forehead. *Great, just fucking great, Nicolas is handsome and fun, while he is a forced intrusion into her life.*

He drew up short, pausing his mental diatribe to catch whatever his boss was saying. "...for a while now. I just never found the opportunity to ask you. So, Friday night? We can hit up one of your brother's restaurants, or I could make you dinner. I'm a killer in the kitchen."

Oh, I just bet you are. Zane rolled his eyes.

"I'd prefer going to yours. I've never liked to dress up and pretend to be socially acceptable."

Zane damn nearly growled out loud at Nicolas' laughing reply, "I've never been socially acceptable, so we are even. I hate to run, but I have a meeting, and your brother will throw a fit if I'm late."

Zane cracked his neck and made a production of rattling the handle of his bedroom door and walking across the hall to his bathroom. He heard the apartment door open and close and waited until he heard Jewell throw the deadbolt before he exited the bathroom.

"So, it's just us again." Jewell flopped into the couch and stared at him.

Zane nodded and headed to the kitchen. "Have you eaten lunch?" He started to pull out the makings for a salad and a carton of eggs for an omelet. His words were more clipped than he'd wanted.

"No, I just woke up about twenty minutes before you came back. Did something happen while you were out?" Jewell walked over to the kitchen and sat on one of the bar stools.

Zane cast her a glance. Her brow was drawn together, and her eyes traveled over him as if assessing him. He shook his head and started breaking eggs into a bowl. "No. Why?" He purposefully kept his attention diverted from her.

"Okay, look, I get that you don't want to be here any more than I do—but..."

Zane interrupted her without turning to look at her. "Who told you I didn't want to be here?"

"Nicolas."

Zane put down the whisk and straightened from his task. He turned around and met her gaze with a straightforward, honest stare. "My concerns about taking this case were based on the fact that you despise me." He saw a look of surprise spread across her face before he turned his attention back to making lunch.

"I don't." The comment was small and low, but he heard it. Zane chuckled and shook his head. He grabbed a skillet and turned the flame on to warm the pan while he divided some mixed microgreens into bowls. He grabbed a tomato, knife and cutting board and deposited it in front of her before he dropped a pat of butter into the skillet.

"What? You don't believe me? I don't hate you."

He glanced over and winced internally. The woman was cutting way too close to her fingertips. He took the knife and the tomato away from her poised his hand, so his fingertips were tucked back, guarded by his knuckles. "Like this, otherwise you won't have fingers."

"That would make typing hard." She chuckled at her own joke and frowned in concentration, duplicating his hold on the fruit.

Zane dropped the eggs into the skillet and swirled it, lifting the edges to float the liquid under the set eggs. "Cheese?"

"Yes, please and I don't hate you."

"The day before your brother released me from my duties, you called me by two different names, asked your brother to fire me and told me to...

what was it again? Oh, right, it was to sit down, shut up and color."

"Yeah, about that, I'm sorry. I was stressed, the damn firewall was giving me fits, and you kept bringing up the stupid meeting that I didn't have time to go to anyway." Zane added cheese to the eggs and folded the mixture over the top. He took the skillet off the flame and let the heat of the hot eggs melt the cheese.

He leaned against the counter and talked to his boot. "I was trying to tell you the upcoming meeting with Jason was about me being reassigned. But, I did what you directed. I sat down, shut up, and colored until I received my notification that I was no longer required."

"You didn't say goodbye." Jewell handed him the cutting board an assortment of irregular cut tomatoes.

He slid them off into their salad bowls as he spoke, "I'm a fairly intelligent man, Ms. King. I understand the context of 'shut up.'"

Zane slid the massive omelet onto his plate and cut it in two, giving her the smaller portion. "Ranch or Blue Cheese dressing?" He pulled the door open and glanced back at her, freezing when he saw her tears.

"Look, I'm sorry for the way I treated you. I know I'm a bitch. I don't hate you. If I'm honest, I kinda got used to you. I only asked Jason to fire you because it was what everyone expected me to do. I didn't mean it that time." Jewell gave him a half smile and snuffled before she wiped the tears from her cheeks.

Zane chuckled and grabbed the blue cheese dressing because it was her favorite. "That time?"

"Yeah, well… you grew on me." She drizzled some dressing over her greens as she spoke. "You also said you wanted to be reassigned the second Vista was caught." She peeked up at him from under her eyelashes.

Zane took a forkful of eggs and nodded as he chewed. He reached for the dressing when she'd finished. "I did. Again, refer back to the point about you hating me." Zane winked at her and stabbed a forkful of greens.

"Zane?" His eyes immediately popped up to where she sat. She'd never said his name before, at least not in his presence. The simple gesture got his attention quickly. "I'm pretty freaked out about what Vista said in the chat room. When I woke up today, I did some checking on the Dark Net. He's been blacklisted."

Zane ate his salad while he processed the information. He put his fork down and leaned back on his barstool. "I need more information, or maybe it's perspective. I know a computer hacker can cause mayhem, spread viruses, and break systems, but what exactly are hackers?"

Jewell moved her salad around and shrugged. "Hackers are just like people. There are the ones who only use their abilities for good. They are the 'ethical hackers.' They are hired by government agencies, large corporations and other entities that require someone to watch out for their interests."

"So you are an ethical hacker?" Zane leaned forward. In the months that they'd inhabited the same space, they'd never had an honest discussion.

She wagged her head and rolled her eyes before a shy smile spread across her face. "Well, yes and no. What I do is based on the needs of the agency. I have the authorization to mine for the information I need to find, but… is it ethical? Sometimes. Is it illegal? Could be."

"Could be?" Zane smiled at the blush that spread up the woman's neck and over her cheeks.

"Okay, so I bend the limits of the law, and occasionally I walk all over them, but it is never for personal gain. So I guess on a continuum from ethical to criminal I'm in the middle but leaning toward the ethical side." She speared a tomato and looked at it.

"Personal gain is the dividing line then?"

"Again, yes and no. Hackers get bad publicity because of idiots that try to do stupid shit that is way over their heads. They get caught because the ethical hackers are watching for them. The ethical hackers are the people who do things like keep the Department of Defense's systems from crashing and safeguard banking institutions."

"So where does Vista fall in all this?" Zane ate the last piece of his omelet as he waited for her answer.

Jewell sat her fork down and leaned her chin into her hand that she'd propped up on the countertop. "Vista is the antithesis of ethical. He causes damage because he can, and I believe he enjoys it. Since we eradicated the viruses he planted, and there were five, not one, he's launched a barrage of attacks against our primary firewall. So far he hasn't found a way in, but I have three of my best evaluating his methodology and building counter-measures."

"How do you know it was him?"

"I don't, but since he is the only one who has

been actively trying to break through our safeguards, it was a safe assumption."

"What happens if he gets past your firewall? Can he take Guardian down again?" Zane pushed her plate toward her. She scrunched her nose at the food but picked up her fork. "Not this time. My team and I have built…" She glanced over his shoulder focusing on the backsplash over the kitchen sink and pulled her bottom lip into her mouth. She did that when she was deep in thought. Zane wanted to reach out and pull her lip from the hold her teeth had on it. Finally, Jewell continued, "Well, it is kind of like an entrapment area immediately behind the firewall, and then we've built a new obstacle that acts as a second firewall but is, in fact, this wicked ass, self-replicating program that will attach itself to any system that breaches it. It's an irradiated nuclear version of one of the viruses he embedded as a latent program, which was pure genius and like nothing I'd ever seen before. Anyway, we morphed the basic code and grew something new. We call it Godzilla. If he makes it through the firewall, gets past the entrapment area and finds Godzilla? His systems will be fried."

Her brain was marvelous. Zane wondered how many people truly understood how brilliant she was. He pushed the thought to the side and asked, "On a scale of 1-10 where do the two of you stand as far as capabilities?"

Jewell stood and took her plate to the sink. She'd eaten nothing. "We're tens. We are pretty evenly matched. Darren Kowalski giving him access codes and intelligence on us put me at a disadvantage. Who could have imagined one of our own turning on us? The psychological exam on that guy was way wrong."

Zane agreed. Every last member of Guardian was hand selected and passed through batteries of psychological exams. It was why he was currently a Personal Security Officer instead of… He pulled himself out of his spiraling thoughts. "I guess my question then is, what does he know about you?" Zane rinsed his plate and scraped her uneaten meal into the disposal. He wouldn't force her to eat healthily, but he would limit her options, so she had little choice.

"I don't know. He was able to find out about Gabriel's wife, and that was tied up and put into a vault so far underground it should have been impossible to find. So it is safe to assume he knows everything."

A red-hot thread of 'oh shit' wound down his spine. "Do your brothers know that?"

Jewell shrugged as if it didn't matter. Zane wasn't having any of that. "No, seriously, this guy could know where you live?"

"It is a possibility. Like I said, he found Anna and the Bratva tried to take her out at the same time as they tried to kill Jason, Gabriel, Faith, and Reece. But he doesn't have any muscle anymore. He is by himself. He's been blacklisted. Anything he could do to me now would be via a computer and believe me, I'm shielded against this guy. He can't touch my money, this apartment isn't connected to me and isn't traceable to Guardian. Even if he did figure out I lived here what could he do?"

"The man was humiliated by you, and he has threatened your life. Don't discount the human factor in this equation." Zane had seen what a person was capable of doing when they wanted vengeance. He'd been the tool that Guardian used to track down and stop the people who stepped across the line between murder, corruption and even genocide.

Jewell turned to him and blinked as if he'd spoken a foreign language. "I don't know how to do that. I'm good with computers. People? Not so much." There wasn't any pride or smugness in the comment, just simple fact.

"I know, but you're in luck. I'm good with people." Zane smiled at her through the lie and handed her an apple. She chuckled and bit into the fruit. "Good thing, otherwise I'd probably be living at my office."

"You *were* living at your office." Zane spun her around and pointed her toward her room. "Get ready, we'll go in at two and work until ten tonight. You can check on your day and night shift that way. Besides, I need to talk to your brother."

Jewell spun around and cocked her head at him, "About what?"

Zane put both hands on her shoulders. Her grey-green eyes blinked up at him. He drew a deep breath that was clouded with her clean, warm scent. This was the first time he'd been this close to her without her lashing out at him and the moment didn't slip by unnoticed. "This guy has the motive to hurt you. He's already threatened you. We need to ensure he doesn't acquire the means or have the opportunity to do what he said he'd do."

Jewell lowered her eyes. She shivered under his hands. Without thinking, he pulled her into his chest. "I will protect you. I promise." Zane felt her relax into him for several long seconds before she pulled away and nodded, still looking at the floor. She turned away from him and pointed toward the bedroom. "I'm... yeah... getting ready." Zane waited until her bedroom door was shut before he let the smile he was holding in spread across his face.

Nicolas might have a date with Jewell, but Zane lived with her, and he'd learned long ago that fighting dirty was the only way to fight.

CHAPTER 6

J ewell sat in her chair and stared unseeingly at her computer screens. She pretended the situation that was compromising her concentration wasn't actually the thing that was distracting her. When Zane held her in his heavy, strong arms earlier today, she'd felt safe, granted, but it was the other sensations that she'd been trying to analyze.

One, she most assuredly wanted to feel that way again, and she'd admit she wanted more than a friendly hug from the man. Jewell was nothing if not honest. Well, at least she was honest with herself—most of the time. Two, she'd acknowledge she had wanted to wrap her arms around his neck and ask him to kiss her. Jewell squinted at the screen directly in front of her focused on her thoughts, not what was scrolling past. Three, she found him sexually attractive; wait, that was more like an addition to point one. Whatever. She'd accept that. But sex wasn't something she usually sought out. The times she'd engaged in the act it had been... meh. Hot, sweaty, uncomfortable and mostly unsatisfying. Her sister, Jade, told her it was because she hadn't been with the right man, but her options were—limited. Or they had been. Four, the fact that Nicolas had asked her out confused her, but he was amusing and harmless. Zane? Zane was... what was he? Too calm for his own good. A freaking health nut, which she was decidedly not. He worked out and ate well. She didn't. He seldom talked, she had been told she couldn't keep her mouth shut. Which was true. He didn't even know the basics of her job. She had to explain the different shades of hackers to him. She tapped her finger against her lips. She'd given his file a cursory look when he'd first showed up. He was moved from a section on Jacob's side of the house to Jared's, which meant he'd dealt with issues overseas. The redacted and masked material gave her a pretty good idea of what he'd been doing, but she couldn't be certain. He was basically her total opposite. *But that was a good thing, right? Opposites attract and all that shit?*

Shit... what point number was she on? She'd lost track of the issues. Jewell opened a note on her PC and started typing her thoughts. The soft buzz and click of her office door alerted her to Zane's presence. She pretended not to notice when Zane resumed his station just inside her peripheral vision. He'd left her alone to have his meeting with Jason. *That* was an anomaly. When he was guarding her before he'd stuck to her like a smothering coat of industrial strength glue. The inconsistency today baffled her. She used her bare foot to push her chair around to focus on him.

"What can I help you with?" Zane didn't look up from his tablet. What in the world did he read while she worked? His device wasn't connected to the internet, it couldn't be in her secured area. Whatever it was, it had to be good. He was always reading. Didn't he get bored? She bet he was a mystery or thriller reader. Maybe he...

"Jewell? Did you need something?"

His voice stopped her thoughts. She back-tracked her thoughts. Did she need something... oh! "When you had your meeting with Jason, you didn't make me go with you, and you didn't have someone else babysit me. Why?"

"I believe you've internalized the seriousness of the threat against you. I don't think you would risk your life to prove a point to me. This time. Besides, now that we are actually talking to each other instead of you dictating the way things will be, I trust you to do what you say you will do."

"I wasn't that bad." She wasn't, was she?

"Before, you'd leave the second my back was turned." Zane's calm voice irked her, although she didn't have a clue why.

"I wouldn't!"

"The Coffee Pot," He tossed the words to her.

Jewell stopped and blinked, remembering the first week he'd been assigned to her. "Oh, that's bullshit. I didn't leave you on purpose. I forgot you were supposed to be my shadow."

"Fine, I'll give you that one. What about the picnic at your brother Jason's house?" His eyebrow rose, and he cocked his head as he waited for her response.

Her lip curled up slightly. *Oh. Yeah, that was funny.* She had ditched him then. He'd been distracted, and she'd made it all the way to her apartment before he'd found her. But the man still didn't lose his calm, cool demeanor. He was insufferable that way.

"Let's not forget about dinner with your staff. The mass distraction was a good attempt, but I'd learned your modus operandi by then."

Jewell placed her hands on her knees and drew a long breath. "They were supposed to distract you long enough so I could go to the Gaming Den. Nothing nefarious would have happened around a bunch of geeks."

"You don't know that. Besides, one of the world's biggest geeks is now a legitimate threat. " He pointed to the screen where Vista's threat sat for everyone to see. She narrowed her eyes at him because anything she said now would confirm the man was right. Not that Zane being right was a bad thing. Well, not anymore. Jewell spun back to her monitors. She kinda liked being on the same side as the guy.

"Jason said I have to take some time off." She glanced over her shoulder at him, and he nodded, not lifting his eyes from the tablet. "I want to go to the Gaming Den."

Zane lifted his gaze to her. "I'll check the blueprints, see what we need to do to make it safe."

"I promise, no tricks. I just want to go and lose

myself in a game. It is one of the only ways I can relax." She picked a pencil out of her hair and stuck the eraser end into her mouth.

"I will do my best, but I *will* be there with you."

"Cool. Can we go Friday night?" There was an Onyx Death tournament starting at five. If she got there by four, maybe she could pair up with someone halfway decent and totally rule the platform.

"The Onyx Death MMORPG tournament?"

"Yeah… wait… how did you know?" Jewell twisted in her chair. "You play Massively Multiplayer Online Role Playing Games? Black Onyx?"

He laughed and turned off his tablet. "I do."

"Shut the fuck up! You do not!" She jumped out of her chair and clapped her hands. "Tell me you're good."

Zane leaned back and looked at his fingernails, huffed on them and brushed them against his suit jacket. "Level two hundred seventy-five, golden robe."

"Oh my God! No way!" She laughed and spun around. Zane's gravelly laughter washed over her. She stopped spinning and hopped over to him, too happy to simply walk. "You have got to be my partner, we will kick ass!"

"I don't know. Are you any good?"

Jewell smacked his arm. "I'm better than good. Level three-twenty, Platinum caster!"

"All right, I'll be your partner, but I'll be distracted, that means I'll need some backup. I better start that process now." He stood up, bringing him within a fraction of an inch of her. Jewell couldn't help herself, she reached up and kissed him on the cheek. He smiled and winked at her again as he headed out of her office. The delicious smell of his aftershave wasn't lost on her, but right here, right now, she was happy for the first time in... Jewell considered that thought, she couldn't recall the last time she was excited about going out.

Jewell slapped her head and spoke out loud, "Oh shit. I'm going out of Friday, with Nicolas *and* with Zane." She dropped her head back and groaned. What would Jade do? Jewell snorted, she'd do both men, but that wasn't an option for Jewell. She plopped back into her seat. Simple answer, cancel one of the activities. She'd feel like a heel if she canceled on Nicolas, but she really wanted to play in that tournament.

She pulled up an interoffice memo and typed in Nicolas' name and dashed off a quick note:

Nicolas, I have to cancel our dinner on Friday. I forgot I had a prior commitment. Will have to reschedule at a later time. ~ Jewell.

There, that was finished. She opened her fridge and reached for an energy drink. He hand swiped thin air. Jewell bent down only to find her stash had been cleared out. There was bottled water, orange juice, cranberry juice and fresh apples. Two cases of Dragon's Blood gone. Jewell groaned and slammed the door shut. She stood up and headed to the break room. If she didn't get caffeine soon, she'd have a bitch of a headache. Coffee, in mass quantities. God help the fool that got in her way.

CHAPTER 7

Zane sat down with the section's scheduler and the district manager. Pulling resources two days before an event was more than enough notice, especially when the primary was Archangel's sister.

"Where is she going?" Kannon Starling asked as he pulled his tablet toward him.

"The Gaming Den." Kannon nodded as he typed. The man's fingers flew across the keyboard before he hit the return key just a little too hard. "Okay, I've sent a request for the blueprints of the area and also any monitoring devices we can have her section tap into while she is in the area."

"We have enough assets between assignments that we can cover the outing without pulling people in from their mandatory down time." The section's scheduler, Willa, had been there as long as anyone could remember and she was a whiz with making sure her people had down time while covering every operation in the D.C. area. She glanced over at Zane and made a tsking sound before she pointed at him. "Unlike you. You were on mandatory break. You got what, five days?"

Zane shook his head. "Three days and almost three nights."

Willa groaned or rather growled, and sat back in her chair. "Did you happen to mention to Mr. King that you were on MB?"

"That topic didn't come up, and quite honestly I wasn't going to mention it."

Kannon turned on the video screen on the wall. He laughed, pulling both Zane and Willa's attention toward him. He shrugged, "About the only thing you didn't mention to him that night if the scuttlebutt is correct."

Willa chuckled and added, "True."

"Seriously?" He could only imagine how the story of that night had morphed as it filtered through the different sections.

"Yep. Heard you demanded a raise for working with his sister." Kannon couldn't keep his shoulders from moving despite his best effort to suppress his laughter.

"And a transfer to the West Coast," Willa added.

"Plus three weeks extra vacation time." Kannon's words were nearly indistinguishable between his rolls of laughter. He slapped his leg and drew a long breath before he started laughing again and held up his arms in a massive circle. "Balls the size of Texas!"

Willa pursed her lips at the comment and wrinkled her nose. "The ladies down in HR said none of those requests came through, so I don't believe it. But, from what I've heard, you did get in the bosses personal space, and you were rather loud when you did it. Although I don't doubt you did make some demands, the exact demands you made have become speculative and rather legendary." She nodded her head toward Kannon who was still laughing as if he'd escaped a mental institution.

Zane shook his head and nodded toward the screen. "Are we doing this or are we going to sit here all night while you amuse yourself?"

Kannon threw him a middle finger salute and punched up a file, but the man was still laughing. The blueprints for the Gaming Den showed the facility was two stories tall, had five mini theaters and three lounges, restrooms on both levels and an office and supply area at the back. Four entrances and six additional fire escape doors with plate glass windows at the front of the building but no other windows except in the bathrooms and the office areas. The gamers liked it dark, and the lack of windows accommodated the desires of the business' customers.

"Can you pull up the street view?" Zane asked over his shoulder as he studied the layout of the facility. The screen split, and a front and rear view of the club in addition to a map overlay appeared.

"We can put a man here and here," Zane motioned to the front and rear of the club. "I'll need one person inside with us. I'm going to be distracted, so I need someone on our six."

Kannon crossed his arms and looked at the visuals on the screen. He shook his head. "No, I want two men inside with you. One on your six and one floating. The primary is too damn important to this organization, not to mention her brothers would skin us alive if something went wrong. So that's four. Willa, do we have any teams available?"

"Yes, we have Romeo and Echo teams back. Romeo has just started debriefing, so they are out.

Echo is on standby for an operation, but the seventy-two-hour alert hasn't been given to them so they can be used."

Zane acknowledged the questioning look Kannon gave him. "I know Quinn." He'd been in the same area as one of Echo team's operations. They needed his unique skillset to silence a fucking monster. His handlers had sanctioned the hit, and Zane had done his job, loudly and with prejudice, just as the team had requested. The resulting chaos had allowed the team to get in and get out without being detected. He and Quinn had exchanged a look across a densely populated room full of panicked, screaming people. So, maybe he didn't know Quinn, but it was about as close as Zane ever got to knowing another operative. At least as close as he'd ever gotten until he cross-trained into the personal security officer career field.

"Good, then its set. What time Friday?" Kannon was typing up the ops orders as Willa was working the schedule. "She'll want to be there in time to sign up. Brief at three, deploy at three-thirty. Primary on site no earlier than four fifteen."

"Duration?" Kannon was calling out the blanks on the form.

"TBD. If she's winning, it could be all night." Zane sure as hell hoped she'd win, the woman needed some down time.

"Roger that. Known hostiles in the area?" Kannon asked.

"The threat on the primary is a computer genius. Unknown identity."

Kannon sat back and blinked as he looked at Zane. "You think it's a good thing to put her in a building full of computer geniuses?"

Zane stroked his chin with his thumb and fore-finger. He considered the question carefully before he answered. "We can't let this guy steal her life. From what I've discovered, the last time she's gone anywhere other than her office and her apartment was when we flew to Thailand to support the Bratva mission. She worked the entire trip there and back, plus all hours in between. If the lady wants to go play in a video game tournament, Guardian can sure as hell protect her while she's doing it. She's given enough to us, I think it is time to start repaying that debt."

Kannon blinked a couple times before he nodded. "Yeah, since you put it that way, I concur. You let me know anytime she wants to get out and about. We'll make it happen, right Willa?"

He looked over at his scheduler who was nodding in agreement. "We've got your back, Zane."

"I'm glad to hear it." Nicolas' voice rang out from behind Zane. He stood and turned around.

"Did you need to see me?" Zane's professional cloak slipped over him as did Kannon and Willa's. Nicolas was the Chief Operating Officer and technically their boss even though there were several layers of management between them.

"No, no… I was just curious as to what you were planning. I noticed on Jewell's calendar Friday is coded as out of office, and I know she has plans, so what exactly are you organizing?" Nicolas sat down and looked at Kannon, who was the ranking individual in the room.

"Ms. King is going to the Gaming Den Friday night," Zane spoke for Kannon.

"No, she isn't." Nicolas' brows drew together. Confusion flashed across his face.

"Sir, she is. She asked me to arrange the details. Ms. King seemed very excited about the opportunity to be involved in a tournament." Zane wasn't going to add anything about being her gaming partner. He wasn't insane, nor did he want his boss to consider him a rival, but if he saw a glimmer of a chance that Jewell could be interested in him, he'd take it and run with it.

"She said Friday night? You're sure?"

"Yes, sir. There is a Black Onyx tournament. She's an avid gamer." Zane answered Nicolas' question truthfully.

"She's a… what? She plays computer games?"

"Yes, sir. MMORPG." Zane ripped off the acronym that he didn't know existed before he met Jewell.

"Say what?" Nicolas looked at him like he had three heads.

"Massively multiplayer online role-playing games, sir. They're huge in the online gaming world."

Nicolas' eyes narrowed as he studied Zane. "Do you play these games?"

Zane shrugged his shoulders, "Yes sir, but I'm nowhere as good as she is. She's elite." He didn't add that he'd read everything on the game and spent just about every free hour he had building his character and learning how to compete with electronic foes. That would make him… Hell, he didn't even want to know what that would make him. *Enamored.* His mind whispered. He gave a mental shrug. He couldn't deny he wanted the woman. She was damn near perfect. Until you factored in the fact that she'd didn't want him around. He gave himself a mental fist bump because she'd admitted today she didn't hate him. He'd consider that a win.

"All right then. I'm assuming you have the resources you need?" Nicolas' question was once again directed at Kannon.

"Yes sir, we are utilizing Echo team from the overseas division since the avenues of approach and egress and the need for inside support would require a minimum of four personnel. They are on stand-by and not on alert as of this time." Kannon was damn good at his job.

Nicolas nodded and stood. "All right. I'll let you get on with your business." He sauntered out the door, and Kannon swung his head toward Zane. Zane gave him a slight shake of his head.

"Willa, would you go make sure Echo team gets their orders? I need to talk to Zane about his last mission."

Willa snorted, "Bullshit. His last mission was overseas and nowhere near your area of responsibility. But, I can take a hint." She gathered her tablet and stood. The woman glanced at Zane before she leveled a glare at Kannon. "It is a damn good thing you aren't in the field. Take a lesson or twenty from this one." She motioned toward Zane.

Zane winked at the woman. She blushed and left the room.

"So, what the fuck was that? Did Nicolas just try to piss on your leg? Please tell me he has no clue you are in love with this woman."

Zane shot a shocked look at Kannon. "I'm not in love with her."

"Well, you're in fucking heat or rutting then. Hell, Spock, we can call it Pon Farr, I don't care what the label is. Whatever, you can't deny you have it bad for this woman."

Zane looked at one of the few people who had known him for years. He and Kannon met while they were on their first tours of duty. Kannon was a Captain, Zane was enlisted. He shrugged and admitted, "Well I learned today she doesn't hate me, which is a plus, but you and I both know having feelings for her is dangerous. Relationships can fuck with rational thinking, and it could affect my decisions."

"Zane, your life has sucked at an atomic level for years. You deserve the right to have a life. If this woman is who you want to have that life with, I'll do everything in my power to make it happen.

If you need me, professionally or as a friend, I'm here for you. But a word of warning. Don't run against that man. He'll dissect you and use you for bait. He's powerful, and he's connected. If he finds out you are competition, you could be reassigned to Thule, Greenland."

The reference to the Air Force's northernmost base brought a smile to his face. He and Kannon had been stranded along with their respective squads at the Air Base for a week. They discovered even at remote assignments, the Air Force lived far better than the Marine Corps. Hell, they'd stopped into the mess tent, or dining facility, as the Air Force called it, and been served steak, baked potatoes and had a chocolate buffet for dessert. Allegedly it was the monthly birthday celebration, but the next night the chow was just as fucking good.

"At least I'd eat well." Zane stood and clapped his friend on the shoulder. "I'll ask if I need help. I have no idea where this assignment will lead, but I can guarantee you I will be careful."

Kannon stood and followed him out of the room. "You're a liar. If I know anything about you, I know you will sacrifice yourself to accomplish your mission. It's what you do."

"It's what we all do," Zane said over his shoulder.

"No. It's what we are trained to do, but not everyone embraces the tenets."

"Like Ski?" Zane paused at the junction of the corridor. The traitor Kowalski was a sore subject for all of them.

"Ski and others. Just promise me that if push comes to shove you will try to take care of yourself."

"If I can. But she will always come first." Zane headed down the hallway that would take him back to C3 and his primary. He glanced at his watch. It was dinner time. Ten bucks said the woman had an extra cheese, meat-lovers pizza on her workstation. He pulled out his phone and dialed the deli down the block. Ordering two salads took seconds. He'd make sure the woman had decent food. Hell, who was he fooling? He couldn't eat the shit Jewell ate and function. His order was self-preservation.

CHAPTER 8

J ewell waited inside the car as Zane had
directed. She saw the Guardian vehicle
across the street. They weren't trying to
cover their presence. Jewell understood protective
details and Zane was making a statement.

A yawn snuck up on her. She reached into her
purse and pulled out an energy drink. She popped
the top and tipped it back. *Ahh... the nectar of the
gods.* Chronic fatigue was a by-product of her job.
The work never stopped. Her section had grown
by almost thirty people in the last four years. She'd
been able to hire some of the best in the world to
work with Guardian, but with the expansion of the
business under Jason's leadership, she needed at
least fifteen more to fill the gaps, and she needed

them like yesterday. The vetting process for any applicant took over six months, but the mandatory scrub was essential considering the new hires would have access to most of Guardian's systems.

Jewell lifted the can and downed three large gulps of caffeinated heaven. The line grew outside the Gaming Den as she waited for Zane. The energy drink finished, she put the empty can back in her purse. She needed the boost to stay awake all night. She'd worked from five this morning until three this afternoon and the rigors of the day still streamed through her mind. Rarely were the demands of her day muted. She snorted at the thought. She almost never went home. Her clothes were sent to the laundry and delivered back to Guardian. She ate at her desk, showered in the gym and almost never went to the apartment. The quiet was too loud there. Anyone who hadn't lived alone wouldn't understand that sentiment, but she did. Her brothers and sisters were amazing people, but she'd never equal their caliber of accomplishments. She didn't know how to deal with people. Her dad had told her once if she brought food to a meeting it would always go better. She'd followed that advice. It was impossible to quantify the reality of the prose, but her father had been correct. It worked well to make a few friends within the Brownies when she was six, and even now she'd found favor with her brothers, and other senior players in Guardian, when she brought their favorite treats. But that was the only trick she had when working with people. They were so unpredictable. She knew how computers would react because the programming told her what it would do. People were more difficult to understand. Except for Zane. He said what he meant and meant what he said. He'd never lost his temper around her, and even when he confronted her about Vista in her office three days ago, he didn't yell or shout. Zane was a constant. The programmer in her appreciated consistency.

She watched three cars drive by the Range Rover she was sitting in. They stopped closer to the front of the club letting people out. The line was now out the door and was weaving around the block. Maybe she should have called ahead. The Gaming Den was one of ten clubs in the US that was hosting the tournament. The MMORPG community had grown a hundred fold in the last four years. That was in part due to websites like *Twitch* that allowed gamers to stream live and get paid to play. Jewell caught Zane's profile as he exited the club. He leaned over and talked to the huge man that was keeping the club goers outside. Zane's build rivaled the bulk of the hired muscle. The man nodded and shook Zane's hand. The Guardian operative who'd been waiting in the shadows near the Range Rover acknowledged Zane as he approached and then vanished into the dark. Zane tapped on her tinted window. Jewell opened the door, and he escorted her into the club without stopping, much to the dismay of the people waiting in line.

Jewell let her eyes adjust to the darkened interior. She glanced at the status board that glowed at the back of the entryway. She nodded toward the sign-up table and Zane followed.

A pimple-faced young man glanced up at her and then did a double take. His mouth dropped open, and he stared at her. Jewell got it, she wasn't the typical gamer.

"Hey, dude, chill out." The man's partner at the table elbowed him bringing the man out of his stupor.

"Oh, sorry. Did you want to sign up for the tournament?" Pimple face's voice cracked at the end of his question. Jewell smiled at him and motioned toward Zane. "Yes, we're a team."

"Okay, put your names and information plus your handles here and your levels here. Entrance fees are $250.00 per person."

Jewell reached into her jacket and pulled out five crisp one hundred dollar bills. She put the money down and picked up the clipboard. She wrote her gaming handle down and gave the sign-up form to Zane who scribbled his information and handed it back. Zane picked up the money and pushed the bills back in her pocket. He peeled off five hundred dollars from a roll of bills in his hand. "You picked the place, so I pay the tab."

Jewell frowned at the money on the table. She didn't understand why Zane would do that. She wanted to play in the tournament, she'd asked Zane. Shouldn't she be responsible for the cost of admission?

She opened her mouth to ask that question when the man next to the teenager spoke to her. "You're in theater three, station five of six. There are elimination rounds in each theater. Once the theater winners are determined there will be a four-team, single elimination bracket. Matches are pulled out of a hat. The winner is the team that remains in power after the final battle is called."

Jewell nodded her understanding. At least the kid's partner had his spiel down.

Zane's large hand found its way to her back as he guided her through the crush of people toward the theater they were assigned. "Do you want anything before we hook up our controllers?" Zane patted the bulge in his leather jacket. Over the course of his protection detail, Zane rarely dressed down. Slacks and button down shirts were the norm unless he was working out. Tonight he had on a pair of dark wash jeans, a black polo, and a black leather jacket.

Her recent acceptance of her attraction to the man was probably to blame for the shiver that ran down her spine when he slipped his arm around her waist and maneuvered her through the crowd. His subtle aftershave skittered across her senses. His strong arm pulled her close to his body when a group of people spilled out of the spectator area of the theater. She felt the hard press of his chest and thighs against hers. It may have been wishful thinking, but she thought Zane may have kept her against him longer than necessary, but there was no way she was going to complain. The man did things to her that no one else had ever done.

"You didn't answer my question." Zane's voice

rumbled near her ear as he loosened his hold. Jewell blinked up at him. *He'd asked a question?* "Do you want any snacks or drinks before we set up?"

"Oh, no. I read they provide all that for the players as a part of the registration fee."

Zane stepped away and nodded toward the participant's area. "Then, your tournament awaits, milady."

Zane signed into his account and joined Jewell's character, Scorn, with his Character Harbinger. He scanned the theater noting the exits and then started his assessment of the people in the player area. He knew Quinn's people would be watching the spectators. The characters' names started flashing up on the middle screen along with the skill levels. When Jewell and Zane's characters flashed up the crowd's cheer elevated. They were elite and had the competition beat. It was only a matter of time before they progressed to the winner's bracket.

Time passed with each win. He watched the gaming geek beside him blossom. Her laughter and smiles were well worth the time, energy and money it took to protect her tonight. She deserved to have a fun evening. They won easily and headed out of the smaller room to the main theater where the championship would be held. Zane made sure the Echo Team members entered the area before they did. He escorted Jewell to the ladies room to give them time to set up in the theater and sweep the audience. He didn't believe the hacker would be here tonight, nor did he think the man would be so bold as to attack Jewell in public, but he wasn't betting her life on it.

The tournament finalists were corralled before they could enter the theater. The event organizer explained it was to make a grand entrance. Zane examined the other three teams of players.

"Hey, I'm Prospect. This is Backdoor." The man who spoke dressed in all black, his hair, lips, eyeliner and fingernails all matched his clothing. His partner dressed like a skateboarder including the backward facing hat.

Jewell smiled and extended her hand. "I'm Scorn, and this is Harbinger." She motioned toward Zane.

"Oh man, you two were kicking ass over in Theater Three. We heard about it after we finished in One." That came from a waif thin man who had a total of at least twenty piercings placed in his ears, eyebrows, nose and lip. "I'm Spiral, and this is Tool."

"That's okay, you eliminated the dregs just like we did. You and your boyfriend better bring your A game, because I plan on killing you both." Zane turned to look at the man who spoke. His cocky attitude grated against Zane's nerves on just about every level. Jewell laughed and wrapped her arm around Zane's waist. "Don't worry, we will."

The cocky guy and his partner turned and headed into the main theater. Prospect shook his head. "Don't mind Sweeper. He's had a bad week."

"Really? How's that?" Zane put his arm around Jewell and escorted her forward, following the other two teams.

"Rumor has it the dude fucked up bad at work and his employers fired him," Prospect spoke over his shoulder.

Zane and Jewell exchanged looks. "Shame. Do you know where he worked?" Jewell asked the question before Zane could.

Spiral turned back to look at them. "He works from home. He's a great programmer if you believe his own press." The others laughed at the joke. Zane didn't. Simple coincidences made his skin crawl. Vista had access to Guardian's systems. Could he have found out about Jewell's gaming preferences? Zane shook his head. That would be a long shot. He was probably grasping at straws, but he'd check Sweeper out anyway.

Jewell stopped before they entered the theater. She turned to him with a brilliant smile on her face. "Thank you."

"For what?"

"For this. I know I wasn't the easiest person to work for. I hated having my life dictated by my brothers. But you still came back even after I treated you poorly. You set this up tonight. For all of that and for being a kick-ass player, thank you." Jewell raised up on her toes and pressed a soft kiss on his lips. It was over in a split second, and she was heading toward their consoles before his brain registered what had happened.

Quinn walked past him and bumped his shoulder. "Nice." The comment brought Zane out of his stupor. Damn it, the merest taste of the woman made his dick hard and broke his fucking brain. Zane glared at Quinn's back and headed after Jewell. He had a tournament to win.

CHAPTER 9

"We are the Champions! This deserves a celebration!" Jewell lifted the trophy onto the kitchen island. The piece of onyx-colored plastic had the tournament name and date on it along with an etched plate containing their handles. They didn't even face the dickwad with the attitude in the finals. Prospect and Backdoor sent them packing in the first elimination round. The last battle had been epic, but Jewell had an ace up her sleeve, or rather a weapon that no one else had uncovered. Zane had battled Backdoor, and they'd both lost too much power to continue without regenerating. Prospect was on the offensive and had Jewell in a corner until she unleashed some bad ass deliverance called the Chalice of Doom. It wiped out Prospect as if he was a first level newb.

"It does call for a celebration, but it is almost four in the morning. Unless you want to go out and find a twenty-four-hour diner we should postpone celebrating our awesomeness until tonight." Zane set the apartment alarm once they were inside and did a walk-through of the apartment, clearing it even though the old-school countermeasures he'd put in place hadn't been disturbed.

Jewell trailed after him. "What if we celebrate now and then go out to dinner tonight?"

Zane stopped and looked over his shoulder at her. She cocked her head at him, waiting for a response. "I'd ask what type of celebration you're talking about."

Jewell walked up to his back and leaned her head against his shoulder. "I think you know."

Every muscle in Zane's body tightened at once. *Holy fuck was she coming on to him?* He slowly turned around and lifted her head so he could look in her eyes.

"Exactly what are you saying?"

"I'm saying that we are both consenting adults."

He watched her gaze move from his eyes to his lips and back up again.

"I'm not going to lie to you. The thought of celebrating with you has crossed my mind. More than once and before tonight." Zane studied her face as his words registered. Her brow scrunched together.

She stepped back a fraction. "I sense a but coming."

Zane ran his hands through her thick black hair. It was as soft as he'd imagined. He cupped her cheek and studied her. "But, I don't just want a single night of celebration. I won't deny that I've had feelings for you for months. I know what I want, but I don't think you do."

Jewell stepped away from him. "I'm damn well past the age of consent. I know what I want, and I want it with you." She launched from serene to snide, pissed off and prickly in about a nanosecond.

"But only for the night?" Zane sat down on a barstool. He was breaking a cardinal rule of protective security details. *Do not* fall for the client, but this wasn't just another detail. He'd gladly find another job if he got fired for wanting more with her. He had enough money to last three lifetimes.

Jewell stepped closer, so his knees braced on either side of her legs. She drew a deep breath and released it before she answered, "I honestly don't know. I am intrigued by you. You made yourself matter to me when I didn't think anyone could. Besides, you of all people should know, I'm not good with the one on one interaction thing. As far as a relationship? I'll be honest, I don't know if I'm relationship material." She was looking at where his knee touched her right leg by the time she'd finished talking.

Zane put his hands on her hips and waited until she peered up at him. "You are better with people than you think. Are you strict and do you expect your people to work as hard as you do? Yes. But each and every one of those people in your section respects the hell out of you."

Jewell shrugged and looked up at the ceiling, avoiding his gaze. He knew talk of relationship or anything personal was probably weirding her out. He searched his mind for a way to put what he wanted her to understand in her language. "Let's try an experiment."

Her eyes popped to his. "An experiment?"

"Yep. Tell me how you build a program."

"A program?" Jewell parroted his words.

"Yes. When you built Godzilla, how did you do it?"

"Well, we used some of the coding that Vista had embedded in our system. It was really unique and intriguing. Then we determined what we wanted it to do and built layers of code that defined the parameters of the program's desired outcome. We did checks on it throughout the process and strengthened the weak lines, abandoned the things that were complicating the outcome or changed them to meet our purpose. Then we ran tests to work out the bugs. Why?"

Zane pulled her a little closer. "Consider this, what's between us, as a program. Right now it is unique and intriguing. We need to determine what we want, and then we will build layers of experiences—"

"Like coding?" Jewell interrupted.

"Yes, but outside of your office the world calls it dating." She smacked his arm and laughed at his taunt. "We figure out what we both like and we build on it, strengthen it." Zane waited as Jewell processed the information. He'd learned the woman mentally examined damn near every word in a conversation before she responded.

"So we would be doing a buildup and test on

the relationship." She nodded her head and smiled at him. "But I have a question." She leaned into him and cautiously lifted her hands to his chest. The light, soft touch sent what remaining blood he had in his body south and stiffened his already hard cock. "When do we get to celebrate?"

Jewell moved forward slowly, holding his eyes with hers. The desire that thrummed through his veins exploded when her lips touched his. Zane snaked his hand up her back, under her hair, and trapped her against his chest. He tilted her head and took over the kiss, licking at her lips, and growled his approval when she opened her mouth for him. Fuck, the taste of her lit him up. She was cool, pure water and his thirst became unquenchable with a just single sip. Her arms wrapped around his neck, pulling him closer. He crushed her body into his and stood up. One hand grabbed her perfect ass, lifting her. Jewell literally climbed his body. He cupped her ass with both hands lifting her higher. Her sexy legs wrapped around his waist and he walked on autopilot to his bedroom. He kicked the door open. The bedroom door slammed against the wall and whipped back, catching him on the arm. He hiked her up his body again and pushed the door out of the way with his elbow.

Zane dropped her onto his bed. Her hair spread in a halo around her. Her breasts heaved, and her face was flushed with desire. Jewell King personified his image of beauty. He lowered over her, supporting himself on his elbows. "Are you sure?" If he needed to stop, it would have to be now. As soon as he started undressing this woman, he'd be lost.

Jewell reached for the hem of his shirt and started lifting it. "In order to run a proper test, you need to actually use all of the functions of the program." He lost sight of her smile for a moment when he helped her pull the shirt over his head.

"Oh, Zane, it's beautiful." Her hand caressed the massive tattoo of a tiger that he'd gotten done after he'd made the transition to PSO duties. "Does it have a special meaning?" Her hand traced the snarling mouth as she asked.

"It does, and I'll tell you, but not right now." He lifted her blouse from her waist. She wriggled to help him remove it. Her flawless ivory white skin swelled in the cups of a leopard print bra. "Hello, kitty." He heard her laughter peel into the room as he lowered with a growl. He licked the fine edge of lace that hovered over her breasts. Her hands weaved through his hair and tried to pull him closer. He traced the bra with his tongue, up to the strap and followed it to her shoulder. The snaps at the back of her bra were a moment's work. He sat up straddling her and sent the bra flying somewhere behind him.

"So beautiful." Her face flushed as his eyes and fingertips discovered her flawless skin. He lowered and allowed his mouth to worship the skin he'd admired for months. Her gasp when he found her rose colored nipple and sucked it into his mouth acted like a lightning rod straight to his cock. He released and kissed over to the other while his fingertips stimulated the hard nub that he'd deserted. Jewell's back arched up, a muffled curse filled the air, and both of her hands held his head to her breast.

His smiled against her skin but refused to be stopped. He let his lips follow his fingers lower to the top of her jeans. His fingers popped the button and lowered the zipper as his tongue followed the freshly exposed skin.

"Zane." Her hands caressed his shoulders, back, and neck. He reached under her and grabbed the back of her jeans, pulling them down her thighs and off. He smiled at the newly exposed thong that matched the bra she'd been wearing. It took less than five seconds to remove the small triangle of leopard print material that was precariously held by two tiny straps of black lace. He simply pulled the lace and ripped it off her body.

He damn near died, or he did die, because somehow he found himself in heaven. He maneuvered lower, resting her legs over his shoulders. He kissed up the inside of one leg and then switched to the other. Her body trembled, and her hands were tangled in his hair. God, he fucking loved it. He spread her open and blew on her hot skin. The mewling noises she'd been making ceased, and she stiffened.

"I've got you, beautiful." Zane wrapped his arms around her legs and splayed his hands over her abdomen, keeping her hips from pressing up. He'd dreamed of having her under him since the day months ago when she walked out of her bedroom wearing nothing but tiny boy shorts and an oversized t-shirt. That was the day his PSO duties became more than guarding a brat computer genius. Zane smiled to himself, lowered and did his best to drive her insane.

"Fuck! Zane... Zane... you... I..." Jewell's body tightened, and Zane doubled his efforts. "Yes, God, yes!" Jewell screamed as she climaxed. Zane held her down, and his mouth rode her through her climax. Only when the trembling flesh under him relaxed did he lift and lose his jeans and boxer briefs. His hard as rock dick slapped his stomach.

"I need to grab a condom." At this point, he could stroke off and come just from the way she was looking at him, but he'd waited for too long to waste the chance to make love to her. He grabbed his cock and gave it a long slow pull.

"I don't have anything you can catch, but yeah... we need to be responsible." Jewell reached her hand out toward his cock and wrapped her fingers around the head.

"Responsible? I can't even remember my name right now and if you keep doing that we won't need the condom." She trailed a finger under his dick, sending a whole body shiver through him. "Evil." She laughed at his reprimand. Fuck, he loved that sound. Zane leaned over, found his wallet in his pants and pulled out a condom.

"I'm not evil, just... needy, and I thought I just screamed your name?" Jewell teased as he lowered between her legs, and waited for her to adjust to accommodate his body. He dipped his head and pressed almost there kisses against her lips making her chase the contact. She bit his lip to keep him from escaping. He trapped her head between his hands and devoured her mouth as he entered her. The woman was everything he'd imagined and so much more. She wrapped her arms and legs around him. He withdrew and slowly pushed forward. The wonderful push-pull of her soft heat melted any capacity to think.

"Harder. Please, Zane. I want… harder." Jewell's whispered plea was his command. He lifted away from her and snapped his hips forward. Her eyes popped open, and a soft cry came from her. "Yes, like that. Just like that." Zane committed the angle to memory and let go. His hips drove into her with a force that slammed the headboard into the wall. The pool of white-hot heat at the base of his spine was demanding release. Zane knew she was close, too. Her head tossed from side to side and her back arched. Her legs wrapped around him and she squeezed him closer. As if that could happen. Zane's vision whited out at the same time he heard her scream his name again. He wrapped her up and pulled her close as his body shuddered against the climax he'd waited almost a year to achieve.

Zane's cognitive reasoning blinked back on long enough to lift off of the panting woman under him. He kissed her shoulder and then the side of her neck.

Her hand flayed around in the air and then landed on his bicep. "Fuck, *that* was what Jade was talking about."

Zane lifted up further. Who? "What?"

"That was fucking amazing." Jewell still panted, making the words sound more than a little breathless.

Zane moved closer to her side and then hauled her against him. She settled her head on his shoulder but immediately popped it back up. "Is this okay? I mean the snuggling?"

Zane put his hand behind her head and pulled her in for a kiss. He wanted to fucking gut the man that treated her badly and made her feel she needed to ask. "If you tell anyone, I'll deny it, but I'm a ten on the snuggle scale." Her smile split her face, and her melodic laughter rained down around him.

"I don't think anyone would believe a big guy like you was a snuggler." She settled down against him and sighed. "I like it, though."

Zane kissed her hair and enjoyed her soft

warmth against him. His phone beeped, pulling his eyes toward the floor and the area he thought his jeans might be. The notification sounded again.

"If you don't go get it, I will. I can't not check a text." Jewell moved against him in a feline-esque stretch. Her back arched under his hand. His cock flexed with interest.

Zane sat up dislodging her as he moved. She grabbed a pillow and snuggled into it. He found his pants and patted the front pocket to find nothing but his keys. There was a dark shape on the lighter hardwood. He reached for it, barely reaching it with his fingertips.

Jewell pounced on him, tickling him along his exposed ribs. Zane curled up and grabbed her, but gravity and their combined weight toppled them both to the ground. Jewell's surprised gasp and then carefree laughter made the hard landing worth it. Zane grabbed, spun, and then straddled her and started tickling her.

She squealed, cursed, laughed, and screamed as his fingers found every ticklish spot on her body. He tortured her feet, knees, ribs and underarms, intent on winning her submission.

"Stop! You win!" Her gasped words came

between what he could only describe as a hybrid between a laugh and a cry.

Zane rolled on the floor and managed a scoop maneuver that landed her on top of him. "What did I win?" His arms tightened against her, keeping her on his chest.

"I would say me, but you've already had me." Jewell rested her chin on her hands, which were folded on his chest. Her hair fell down over his biceps and tickled the skin of his arms.

"I have, but I can guarantee I want more. So much more." He pushed her hair out of her face so he could see those grey-green eyes.

"That is something I'm not used to." She scrunched her nose at him and continued, "Not many of the men I've been involved with have wanted... ummm... seconds?" The confusion in her voice stabbed at his heart. She had no idea what a wonderful person she was and those men who'd used her and then tossed her aside? Zane wanted to track down each one...

The phone chirped again. They both tilted their heads toward where it sat on the floor. Jewell reached for it as it lit up again. The small smile that was on her face disappeared as she read the display.

"What? What is it?" Zane grabbed the phone from her and opened it. There were two lines of text, from a blocked number.

So easy to track. You don't stand a chance of winning. Guardian will fall. You will die.

Jewell sat up straddling Zane. She suddenly felt exposed and cold. Her arms wrapped around her seconds before Zane sat up and pulled her into his arms. He maneuvered them both up back onto the bed. His warmth seeped into her, reanimating her frozen mind. Facts and probable causalities flashed through her mind. Did Vista somehow known Zane was watching her?

"How did he tie me to you and how did he get my telephone number?"

Jewell shook her head. "I don't know." The variables of the situation tumbled through her mind as she answered his question, "Telephone numbers are easy to obtain. You'd be surprised how easy it is to penetrate the outdated and useless firewalls that surround most businesses." Jewell rubbed her arms as she thought, "He could have found emails or operation orders while he was inside the system stating you were my protective detail. Cross matching your name with phone company records would take twenty minutes, max. But that doesn't make sense. Why would he send you that message? That threat would be aimed at me, wouldn't it?"

Zane's hand continued to stroke down her hair, the repetitive motion soothed the fear that welled up inside her.

"Yeah, there is a disconnect somewhere. But, there is another possibility. He could have been at the Gaming Den tonight." The gravelly sound of Zane's voice rumbled against her ear that was pressed against his chest.

"It is a possibility, but nobody knew we were going to be there. We didn't sign up in advance. We used our handles, not our names and we paid cash. There is nothing there to lead him to me."

"Unless he knows what you look like and is watching you, not just your electronic trail." Zane rolled to his side moving her to share a pillow with her. "The asshole tonight, Sweeper, he threatened you, and he'd recently lost his job."

Jewell shook her head. Zane was grasping for straws. "He was talking shit about the game and was a jerk. That doesn't mean he is an elite hacker that wants me dead. Besides, he was taken out in the first elimination round. If he were Vista, he would have been better at the game. We watched, there was no way that man was Vista. He didn't have the intelligence to anticipate his opponent's moves." Jewell summarily dismissed the idea, it really didn't have merit.

"I'm not so sure. Can you find out the names of the competitors tonight?"

"From their handles? I could if I was desperate. I'd have to hack into the game's servers and follow the hacker's name through the system to the accounting software. I know the company who puts this game out uses damn good security programs so it would take a hot minute, but I could find out who is paying the bills for the handle."

Zane's brow creased. "So it is possible that Vista was in attendance tonight and tracked me down through the method you just described."

"Possible." Jewell acknowledged.

"Then what is preventing him from getting your information?" Zane's brow furrowed.

"I don't have credit cards. I pay all my on-line accounts with a debit gift card that I purchase, in cash, at the beginning of the month and never from the same place. I know what hackers can do, and I know how to prevent it from happening. I have no electronic footprint other than at the office, and that is the only façade that Vista can see."

"Your cell phone?"

Jewell chuckled at his comment. "I check out one of the phones from security if I need one, but I'm always at the office. My mom even calls me there, so I don't have a need for a cell." A sudden thought broke through. "Please tell me you've disabled the GPS on your phone?"

Zane chuckled, "Guardian 101. I'm untraceable."

Jewell smiled and shook her head, little did he know. "Not true. It is harder, but your signal can still be triangulated.

Zane lifted and mimicked her position as he settled on his elbow. "So what you're telling me is this guy knows where I am right now?"

Jewell nodded. "I would."

"All right. Then we are getting the fuck out of Dodge." Zane lifted out of bed. Jewell admired the muscles of his body as he moved. She felt herself blush as her eyes fell on his soft cock. He was impressive even when flaccid. She'd only seen a handful of men naked, but

Zane was the best looking man she'd ever been with.

He caught her looking at him and snapped his fingers, popping her fantastical thoughts like a bubble. "Clothes, pack enough for a week. We are relocating." Zane held out his hand toward her.

Jewell sat up and extended her hand. The warm, calloused grip pulled her to her feet and into his naked body. "Turn the phone off and take out the battery. I'll buy a pay as you go. Your brothers will need the number so they can reach us when we aren't in the facility."

"Do you think he's watching the office?" Jewell asked as she crossed the hall to her room.

"Actually, I'm hoping he is." Zane padded out to the hall. "That phone is going to be passed around to agents when they leave, so he never knows where it will end up. If he wants to play games, we are going to mess with his mind in ways he never imagined. Let's get packed and to the office. I have a safe place for us to stay, it is rented under an alias, and I pay the rent with cash. But in the meantime I want you to think of ways we can fuck with this guy. We are also going to get a court order for every tape the gaming den has and do a facial recognition run on every damn one of the people there last night and then we are going to run their backgrounds."

Jewell stopped taking shirts out of her closet. Her staff was maxed out with Guardian's current operations. All that labor for what? A hacker that hadn't done anything except some cyber terrorism? No. She couldn't justify the man hours. "I don't have the people to run hunches, and it could take forever."

Zane stalked across her bedroom floor, stopping a fraction of an inch from her. "You are the most important operation going on at Guardian. I know your brothers would agree with me." He cupped the back of her neck with his big hand and pulled her the scant inch that separated them. His heat surrounded her like a calming balm. His lips swept across hers in a feather light touch. Jewell shivered at the sensation. His breath fanned across her lips as he whispered, "You are important to me, and I will stop at nothing to make sure this son of a bitch is caught before he tries to hurt you." He lowered for another kiss and Jewell allowed herself to melt into his strength.

He pulled away and pointed toward the closet. "Finish packing, we need to get into the facility. I have to brief your brothers on my plan." His broad muscled back caught her attention and held it until her eyes dropped to his gorgeous ass and legs. When he was out of sight, she shook her head. She didn't know exactly how to classify the feelings and sensations Zane roused in her. Yes, she'd been attracted to other men, she was human after all. Had she done any more than talk smack with the women in her family? Sometimes. There was the guy she crushed on hard in college. Eugene Fotterheim. Looking back, he was a dick, but she'd have done anything for him, and she let him take her V-card. The memory was one of nightmares. He barely kissed her before he was on her. There was nothing remotely good about that experience. Jewell shook off a shudder of disgust. She moved to the dresser and removed clothing she'd need. Her mind flittered to other occasions where the sex had followed a handful of dates. It was lackluster, at best, and the men had one goal. It wasn't a relationship. Not that she would complain, that wasn't her goal either. She huffed a self-deprecating chuckle out. It would have been nice if she'd gotten off during the encounters. No, she went home afterward and used her magic vibrating rabbit to finish the evening. Lord, she could pick them.

She heard Zane move into the living room. Maybe, just maybe, this time she'd stumbled upon a winner. Her heart fluttered just a bit at that thought. Yes, he was assigned to her security, but to her, he was so much more. She closed her eyes. If she was honest, he had been for a long time now.

CHAPTER 10

Zane waited on the long leather couch outside Jason King's office.

"Are you sure I can't get you any coffee?" Jason's secretary, Sonya, asked from across the room.

"Positive. I've already had two cups this morning."

"Only two cups? How do you function?"

The wicked grin that spread across her face brought an honest smile from him. "According to Jewell, I'm a health nut."

Sonya propped her head on her palm and looked at him. "And are you? A health nut?"

Zane shrugged. "I don't think so. I enjoy a greasy hamburger or plate of nachos like the next guy, but I don't eat them all the time, and I limit my caffeine intake. But I guess that is her definition of a health nut."

Sonya smiled and started to speak. She stopped and considered him before she got up and tottered over to him in heels that would trip up a tightrope walker. She sat down across from him and smoothed the hem of her skirt. "I am way out of bounds here, and you can tell me to mind my own business, but I'm going to say it anyway." She took a deep breath and nodded as if affirming her intentions. "Jewell is difficult to get to know. She doesn't have a lot of interest in figuring out what people mean when they play the stupid little games that people play."

Zane waited. The woman would eventually get to a point—he hoped. Sonya pinned him with her stare. "She doesn't deserve what is happening, and it's high time someone took control of what is going on around her. I love her brothers, they are family to my husband and me in so many ways, but they are lug-heads when it comes to that woman. She needs a knight in shining armor. If you can't be that for her, have Jason give you another assignment before you hurt her." Sonya folded her hands primly across her lap and tilted her chin in defiance.

Zane let a slow smile spread. "I assure you, she is very important to me. I'm not a knight, and if I were, my armor would be rusted and dented. But I care for that woman," Zane glanced at the shut doors to Jason's office and continued, "probably more than is acceptable in certain arenas. I understand what you're saying, and I agree with all of it."

Sonya didn't blink but lifted her eyebrow. "Then fight for her. Her brothers mean well, but they want to run her life; they don't understand their well-meaning decisions made without her input will do nothing except crush her. Remember that when the shit hits the fan, and it will hit hard and often with them." She nodded her head toward Jason's office.

"Thank you..." The door she'd just motioned to opened. Nicolas walked out while talking to Jason. Zane's metaphoric chest puffed out. He felt the pride in knowing Jewell would never go out with Nicolas, that she was his, and that they were working on a relationship. Could he bore him? Absolutely, but Guardian paid men who worked his specialty very well. He didn't need this job; hell, he didn't need to work another day as long as he lived, but he'd go stir crazy without something to occupy his time.

A flicker of movement pulled his eye to the office beyond the men who were still discussing a case. *Fury.* The corner of Zane's mouth twitched. He hadn't seen his brother in arms in ages. Word on the street was the man was dead. Hell, that was Zane's truth too. His identity Bengal had been 'retired' after he failed not one, but two psych evals. His 'No Go' wasn't a surprise. He'd been aware of his mental battle, and his mind had been beating the ever living fuck out of him for at least three missions. He knew it was only a matter of time before he couldn't be used as the last chance weapon anymore. Defending a primary as a PSO wasn't a problem. But, he could no longer track down and kill people, even if his handlers in the organization and his nation had sanctioned the hits. It was time for him to release that life. Fury leaned against the door frame. His eyes just as blank as Zane knew his were. They would never acknowledge knowing each other. They'd never admit to the blood they could see on each other's hands. They would never speak of the hell they'd both lived through.

Nicolas walked by with a glance and half-hearted wave. Jason beckoned him in. Fury had disappeared inside the office.

"Sonya, will you call and find out where Jacob is?"

She nodded and headed over to her desk at a surprising speed for the heels she wore. Zane stood and headed toward the office just as Jacob King slammed the double glass doors open. "Hello, honey! I'm home!"

Sonya pivoted on one razor thin heel and looked at Jason. "I found your brother."

"Was I lost?" Jacob asked in the same bantering tone. He laughed at his own joke and cuffed Zane on the back heading toward Jason's office.

Zane shook his head and followed them through the door. "Close the door behind you, would you?" Jason asked over his shoulder. Zane pivoted and shut the doors before he turned. He swallowed once. It was the only tell he'd give. Staring at him was not only Fury, who by deduction of his obvious appearance was a King, but Jason, Jacob and Jared King.

"You wanted us all together, you've got the floor. What's happened since yesterday when we spoke?" Jason unbuttoned his suit jacket and sat down in the conversation group. He motioned

KRIS MICHAELS

toward a chair. Zane spoke as he moved across the room. "Last night, per Jewell's request, we attended an MMORPG at the Gaming Den."

Jared looked up from a folder in his lap. "Wait, she did what with who?"

Jacob laughed and added, "Yeah, my thoughts exactly."

Zane unbuttoned his suit jacket and sat down. He took them step by step through her request to go play in the tournament and the security measures taken to ensure her safety.

A smirk crossed Jared's face. "You mean to tell me she canceled a date with Nicolas to go play computer games with you?" His laughter rang out before he clapped his hands and rubbed them together. "Oh, the shit that man is going to be fed. By me. With a spoon."

Jason shook his head and lifted one of his size 14 boats to nudge his brother. "Shut up and let him tell us why we are here."

Zane steepled his fingers together. "This morning I received a text message." He pulled a printout of the text and handed it to Jason. Since no cell phones were authorized in this section of the building, he'd printed it out. Jason's eyes snapped to him as he handed the document to Fury.

"How did he know you were watching her?" Fury's voice brought back a flood of memories. Zane turned his head and looked directly into the ex-assassin's eyes. He saw the same vacant expression every time he looked in the mirror.

"There are two theories, mine and Jewell's. I think this bastard was at the club and got ahold of our handles. Jewell was able to articulate in no uncertain terms how she'd use the information to backtrack the handle to the accounting software which would identify the owner of the handle. From there, according to her, it would be simple to hack the telephone company and get telephone numbers registered under the same alias."

"Alias?" Jared's question chimed across the room.

"Yes." Zane would go no further.

Jason cleared his throat as if to say something, but Jacob turned to his brother and interrupted whatever Jason was going to say. "Drop any further questioning." The growl of the command broke no objection, especially coming from Jacob King; his lighthearted banter was almost legendary.

"Ah, fuck me, Jacob you can't be serious." Jared groaned. He scrubbed his face and this time when he looked at Zane his eyes held a judgment that he'd grown used to, but it still didn't make the condemnation any more acceptable. Jared placed the folder on his lap onto the table. "What is Jewell's theory?"

"She thinks when he was rattling around in Guardian's guts that he found emails or mission ops assigning me. She doesn't believe he was at the club last night and is set firmly against using facial recognition to identify each and every person in attendance. I told her we needed to do it and then run background checks on everyone. If we could identify him, he'd no longer be a ghost." Zane's eyes darted between the brothers.

Jason stood up and walked over to the phone on his desk. "Sonya, get with HR and find out where we stand on those new hire applications for C3, please?" He sat the phone back down on the table.

"I agree with you that we need to identify this guy and if there is one chance in a million, we'll take it. Jacob, can you spare Tori to help? If she can work with her counterparts in the CIA, we can split the workload. They owe us, and I'll call the Director to personally remind him of that fact."

"I can let her go if I can pull her six hours before one of my missions goes live. I've briefed you on the op. I need her to run the satellite images in the area. This one is touch and go, so I need my best people on it before we put boots on the ground."

"Granted. Jared, I'll need some personnel to go through the backgrounds as soon as they are spit out of C3."

"You got it." Jared acknowledge.

"I'm taking her to the ranch," Joseph spoke freezing everyone.

"You are not," Zane spoke clearly and distinctly.

Fury, or Joseph as he'd learned the man's true name was, slowly turned his head to make eye contact with Zane. "Who is going to stop me?"

Zane used the same cold, distant tone. "I will. She will stay here unless she wants to leave with you."

"Excuse me, but seriously dude, just who in the hell do you think you are?" Jared stood as he spoke.

"I am the man who has shadowed your sister twenty-four hours a day for almost a year. I know her better than any of you. If you think for a moment she's going to allow you to ship her away to keep her safe, you are dead wrong." Zane hadn't moved a muscle, but he'd identified every weapon within his reach. He didn't want a physical altercation with her brothers, but he was prepared. Fuck, he was always prepared.

"For God's sake Jared, sit down," Jason muttered, sending his brother a glare that would blister paint. Jared gripped his hands into fists several times before he sat down.

"Why?" Jared asked.

"Why what?" Zane responded.

"Why won't she go if it's for her own safety," Jared asked.

"Because that woman is as selfless as they come. She's worked herself damn near to death with the barrage of requests that are processed through her office on a daily basis. Her operators never complain, but they are stretched so damn thin you can see through them. She picks up all the slack so her people can go home after twelve-hour shifts. She's wearing the responsibility of that computer genius getting into her system like a sweater. Have any of you told her that she wasn't to blame?" Zane felt ice run through his veins. He was shaming four of the most powerful men in the world, and he gave zero fucks about hurting their feelings.

He saw the looks passed between the brothers. "I'll take the silence to mean no one has. Were you aware that she's taking all the blame for the attacks? Gabriel, Anna, you - Jason, Faith, Reece, you - Jared, Christian, Jasmine and Chad? She has a list of the dates printed out and posted on her console. It took me awhile to figure out what they were, but once I did, I asked her about it. Of course at the time she wasn't speaking to me because of you," he waved his hand at the brothers, "you'd rammed security down her throat without explaining why it was required or caring that she didn't need to be watched at work in a secure facility like a six-year-old. So she started acting like a child, and that is why the other PSOs didn't last." Zane finally ran out of steam. He'd been quiet too fucking long, and he'd used this meeting to vent. They could fire him if they wanted, but he'd be damned if he'd leave Jewell's side.

"How long have you been in love with our sister?" Fury's voice floated across the embarrassed silence.

Zane turned toward his former brother in arms. "Does it matter?"

Jason stood. "Zane, could you give us some time? Go ahead and go back to C3. I'll call you up after we've had a chance to figure out what we are going to do."

Zane stood and looked the big guy in the eyes. "You don't get it, do you? She needs to be involved in that discussion. She is way more than your sister." He turned on his heel and left the office. Zane's composure fell over him like a familiar cloak as he pulled the door shut quietly behind him. He smiled and winked at Sonya on his way out.

"Zane. Hold up." Joseph's voice froze him before he reached the double glass doors that segregated the CEO's office from the rest of the executive wing. He contemplated his one-time counterpart as the man stalked across the room. When Fury nodded toward the conference room to the right, Zane followed his lead.

Joseph closed the door and hit the button that frosted the windows. "How long have you been out?" He took a seat in one of the massive leather chairs.

Zane sat opposite the man. "I got a 'No Go' two years ago. Crossed over to PSO duties."

"Why?"

Zane knew the question was why he was washed out of the program, not why he moved into Personal Security. "I lost myself." Zane shrugged and added, "I realized I didn't want to live like that any longer, and *that* would have eventually gotten me killed."

Fury nodded. "You still go to psych sessions?"

Zane narrowed his eyes and leaned forward, placing his elbows on his knees. "Let's cut through the bullshit."

A slight tug on the corner of Fury's lip was the only reaction he got, and Zane damn well knew the man let him see it. "Hurt my sister, and I'll kill you."

"Why would I hurt her when she has four brothers that have a corner on that market? And you could try." Zane's eyebrow rose in challenge. He knew his skills, and he was younger than Fury. It might give him an edge, but he wouldn't bank on it. Hell, both of them had taken inventory of every weapon available to them as soon as they'd entered the conference room.

"They didn't know." He motioned with his head toward Jason's office indicating his brothers.

"They do now."

Joseph's head dipped once. "They're going to pull you."

"Why? I'm no different than you."

"I'm a stain on the family's fabric, they can't do anything about me. You? You they can wash away. They don't understand us even though they say they do. Nobody does. We make them aware of monsters. The brothers protect Button because she's different. They'll reassign you."

Zane noted the pet name Fury used. He leaned back and locked his stare with the assassin across from him. "They'll try."

"It isn't easy. Being... normal."

"I know." Zane had mastered the even keel and quiet appearance, but what was inside his façade would never disappear. He was an assassin, he was an expert in killing. He knew he'd take out anyone to keep Jewell safe. If they tried to pull him away from her when there was a threat against her... The quiet, deadly rage that he hadn't felt in almost two years bubbled under his skin.

Fury stood and extended his hand. Zane copied his actions and gripped the assassin's hand. "She deserves better."

"Fuck you. I know she does." Zane did know that, but he wouldn't step aside. He couldn't, not after he'd watched over her for months. He'd seen her at her worst and watched her at her best when she did the impossible. Those impossible feats, in turn, brought new and harder demands upon her. He'd held her in his arms, and he'd be damned if he'd leave now. The only way he'd walk away was if Jewell asked him to leave.

Fury's lip twitched before he nodded and left the room. Zane followed him out. The exchange reinforced his already granite-hard resolve. Worst case scenario, he'd be fired. He didn't give a flying fuck. He'd watch over her from the shadows or in plain sight. He'd kill the hacker if he made a move on Zane's woman.

CHAPTER 11

J ewell glanced up from her monitors to catch a sight she didn't often see. Four of her brothers filtered through the doors to her section and started up the stairs toward her office. Jewell checked the time and swept her eyes to Zane's empty seat. He'd popped back after his meeting with Jason. He'd left about five minutes ago to wait for their lunch delivery at the security area of the building. She had no doubt it would be something healthy.

She could have opened her office door with the buzzer she had under her workstation, but she wasn't feeling too inclined to be receptive to the bundles of testosterone heading her way. Something was up, and whatever it was, she had a feeling she wouldn't like it.

Jason worked the cipher lock and opened the door. Jewell sat back and crossed her arms over her chest as her brothers filtered in.

"To what do I owe this pleasure?" She looked at her oldest brother, Joseph. "Hi. When did you get in?"

"Hey, Button. This morning." Joseph leaned against the back wall and crossed his arms over his chest before he looked at Jason.

"Okaaay... why are y'all here?" She figured it was something big if they were all here presenting a united front... although she didn't think they had Joseph's buy-in from his body language.

"We've discussed the situation about this Vista character." Jason unbuttoned his jacket and sat in Zane's chair, which irritated her.

"Really? Good to hear it." Jewell turned toward her monitors and took a quick assessment of the missions and programs running. She grabbed her mouse and sent an IM to the operators of the mission in Debriefing Room One. The satellite they were using was precariously close to losing coverage. She watched the camera view switch to another orbiting satellite and turned back to whatever was happening behind her.

"We think it is best if you go home with Joseph until we find him and take him out."

Jewell took three huge mental steps backward. Instinctively she knew this wasn't all they were here to say. She lifted an eyebrow and met each of her sibling's gazes before she directed her gaze at Jason.

"And if you are at the ranch, you won't need Zane to be your PSO. He'll be reassigned." *Ahh... all right so her brothers were playing God... again.*

Jason opened his mouth to continue, but Jewell held up a finger and turned toward her computer console. She clicked on a word document and hit print. The laser printer under her station spit out the letter. She stood, grabbed a pen out of the cup holder, dated and signed it.

In one motion she opened her drawer, grabbed her purse and handed the letter to her 'boss.' "Laters, dudes." Jewell headed straight for her door.

"What the fuck is this?" Jason's question was the spark that lit her fuse, and it was one short motherfucker.

Jewell spun and glared at her brothers. "*That* is my resignation. Effective immediately. It would appear I'm not competent enough to make decisions for myself, my section or this organization. According to the Alpha Male brain trust currently dictating what they feel is the correct course of actions, I'm too damn delicate to handle my section while the big bad Bratva hacker is out there tormenting me with threats, *and absolutely nothing else*. Well, fuck y'all very much. Evidently, I'm not the person you need running this Top Secret, international, multi-million dollar section! I'm sure you'll find someone else who will work twenty hours a day seven days a week with absolutely no input or say in anything, but it will no longer be *me*."

She spun around and slammed into a broad chest. Familiar arms enfolded her in immediate comfort, but she wouldn't melt into him in front of her brothers. She pushed back and noticed Zane's glare at the men behind her. He was just as pissed as she was. Well... good... maybe... hell, she couldn't think. Damn her brothers and their high-handed, bullshit approach to fucking everything.

"Well, that went as well as Zane said it would."

Joseph's comment spun Jewell's head around toward Zane. "You *knew* about this?"

Zane dropped his gaze down to hers. "No. I

told them they shouldn't make decisions for your section, or for you, without consulting you."

"Well at least someone has sense." Jewell grabbed Zane's hand. "Come on, we are fucking out of here."

"Zane works for me, not you, Jewell." Jason had his glasses off and was pinching the bridge of his nose. "Would you please sit down and let us explain why we feel it's best if you go to the ranch."

Jewell felt a hysterical laugh bubble up and bounce out before she could stop it. "Ahh... that would be *no*. If this situation involved overseas operations, domestic cases or a coded hit, yeah, I'd listen to you all day, every day. But Vista is just like me. I understand him. I know what makes him tick. I know how to counter each jab he has thrown or will throw. Cyberspace is my specialty, not yours."

"And what if he physically comes after you?" Jacob finally spoke.

"Then Zane will protect me. That is why you assigned him to me, right? Or do you suddenly doubt his qualifications? I pulled up his records. I'm not stupid; at least I'm not if you believe my fucking *Mensa* membership. I saw the similarities in his file and Joseph's."

"So you know he's a killer?" Jared flipped the question out there.

"Oh yes, *please*, let's fucking go there. How many men have you killed in the line of duty?" She glared at Jared. "How about you or you?" She pointed to Jacob and then to Jason. "You know what? I refuse to deal with any of you any longer." She turned around and tugged Zane's hand, heading toward the door.

"I'm not accepting your resignation."

"I don't give a flying fuck, Jason! I'm not letting you treat me like a six-year-old girl who is afraid of the dark. Thirty minutes ago I ran the largest white-hat cyber crimes and information organization in the world. My qualifications are beyond impressive, yet because I'm your sister, you mandate that I run home to mom and hide while you big boys find the bad guy and make my world safe. Do I look like I need a fucking hero to slay my dragons?"

She tugged Zane after her and pulled the office door open. They'd made it four steps before the klaxon alarm erupted through the silence of the work center. Jewell glanced at the main screen. "Damn it!" She bounced her stare between the screen and her office.

"What's going on?" Zane asked at the same time as Jason launched out of her office. "Someone activated Godzilla." She turned toward her brothers. "If I were still working for you I'd be able to trace who was fucking with our system and maybe follow the hack back to where it originated, but... you know... little girl." Jewell braced herself against every instinct screaming at her to fly to her keyboard. She headed down the stairs.

"Son of a bitch! Fine. You win this time. Zane, you're still being reassigned." Jason moved to make way for Jewell to go back to her office.

Jewell looked from the screen to Jason and shook her head. "No. He stays for as long as I say he stays."

"Jewell, I can't trap him! If you don't get on this, we will lose any chance of tracing this guy." Alonzo yelled from his workstation.

Jason nodded. "Go."

"That wasn't an agreement." Jewell stood fast, she knew she had at least two minutes to activate the embedded code that would allow her to trace Vista and it was better if she did it later rather than sooner. The bastard should be too involved with what Godzilla was doing to his computer systems to notice the trace. Maybe.

Jason's face turned a dark red, but he ground out, "Fine, he stays." Jewell vaulted up the stairs and flung her purse down as she slammed into her chair and slid into place behind her systems.

Zane stood with Jewell's brothers and watched the huge screen at the front of the theater as lines and lines of gibberish scrolled at an incredible rate.

"What the fuck is Godzilla?" Jacob asked.

"A firewall," Jason replied.

"Actually, it is a new program that Jewell and her people created using the hacker's own code. They made an entrapment area behind the primary firewall and forced the hacker to leave or go through Godzilla. If he tried to go through, the program would attach itself to his system while it systematically laid ruin to his computer. While he's fighting the attack, the code embeds itself, and that somehow allows Jewell to identify the system being used and the location."

Zane turned away from the screen to have all four sets of eyes on him. "What? I asked, and she explained it."

"You realize it wasn't personal. We felt the

stress of the situation could be detrimental to her. Getting her to the ranch would allow her to decompress," Jared spoke quietly.

Zane looked back at the screen. "Bullshit. I've seen the way this organization uses her. Don't paint this as you trying to relieve her stress. You don't approve of me. You've all read my file by now. You know I had two 'No Gos,' and you don't want me around your sister. Of course, I wasn't a threat until you found out I had feelings for her." He glanced up at the mirrored windows of Jewell's office. He knew she was working like a mad woman right now and didn't need him or her brothers in the way.

"Can you blame us?" Jacob's eyes were focused on the nonsense streaming on the screen when he spoke.

"Nope." Zane popped the 'p' in the word. "But I'm not going anywhere because she's wrong about one thing. This guy is a serious threat. He's lost something that every hacker in the world aspires to have. He's lost his society's respect. She's beaten him on a massive stage with the entire Dark Net and all the White Hats watching. He'll try to make good on his threats. He's in a corner." His explanation was emotionless because if he let his anger and, yes, trepidation out, he'd let loose a monster he didn't know if he could control anymore. The hacker was a ghost and could be anyone they passed on the street.

He felt Jason turn toward him but didn't move. Zane realized he'd basically done the same thing to his CEO. The stage was smaller, but he'd defied the man in front of his brothers.

"Mr. Reynolds, you are one bold son of a bitch." Jason's words dripped with ice.

"Yes, sir." Zane acknowledged the fact.

"Jared, get your people ready to move on this son of a bitch. If he's local, I want him as soon as Jewell grabs his location. Jacob, if he is overseas I want locations of our assets and availability. Get Tori to reach out to her contacts in the CIA and put them on standby. I'd rather share the collar than lose the bastard because we don't have feet on the ground."

"Roger that," Jacob responded as Jared nodded and headed down the stairs. Jacob followed on his heels.

Joseph stepped down and stood next to Zane and his brother. He crossed his arms over his chest and watched the screen. Zane waited and watched. Alonzo's head popped up, and he turned to look up at Jewell's office. Slowly every person in the section stood. The code flew across the screen. One man's hands slowly crept up and locked over his head almost like he was trying to take cover.

The coding on the screen broke. Every eye in the theater turned toward Jewell's office. The gibberish fired across the screen again, and a massive cheer broke out. "She did it! Son of a bitch! She did it!"

A single line sat stationary on the screen. Zane recognized the pattern. It was a latitude and longitude. She'd found the son of a bitch.

Rage thrummed under Zane's polished exterior. He wanted nothing more than to hunt down the son of a bitch.

Jewell opened the door to her office and walked down the stairs to the shouted congratulations and whoops of joy. "I sent the lat-longs to Jared. He's in Alexandria."

Zane watched Jason turn toward her. "You and your section did a great job. Congratulations."

He started to head down the stairs but pulled up short when Joseph gave a short, sharp whistle. "I don't much give a flying fuck if you are the CEO of this company," His words were low, so no one but the four of them heard his words. "She is the best at what she does, and her section wasn't who did this. Get over yourself little brother. She is just as invaluable to this organization as you are."

Jason stepped back and looked his brother dead in the eye. "*She* is invaluable, period. So are you, Jacob, Jared, and every other sibling that works for *me*. You don't lose sleep at night because you made a call to put or keep your own blood in harm's way, so get the fuck off my back, *Joey*." Jason glared at all of them before he walked out of the theater.

"Well… damn. He kinda scared me there." Jewell leaned into Zane as she spoke.

Joseph turned and took a deep breath before cracked his neck. He rolled his shoulders and drew another deep breath. "Take care of her or deal with me." The man's fists clenched and unclenched. "Excuse me while I go remind my brother that nobody but my wife calls me that name."

Zane turned to Jewell as Joseph exited. "What name?"

"Joey."

Zane let that one go. Obviously, there was something there, but he wasn't involved, so he was out. Jewell headed down the stairs and called to him over her shoulder. "Come on, I want to see Jared nail this guy."

CHAPTER 12

J ewell ran the operations control unit as Jared's men surrounded the house. The cameras attached to the personal protective gear gave a muted and bouncing view of the target.

"We have movement." The words cracked over the open channel. Every eye watched the monitors.

"Foxtrot One are you ready?" Jared's words echoed slightly in the com room.

"Roger that, sir."

Jared glanced at Jason who nodded. "Foxtrot One, you have a green light."

Zane leaned forward, bringing him against her chair. His breath mingled with hers as they watched, enraptured by what was happening on the monitors. The camera pictures blinked and

144

shifted radically. One camera showed the sky, the other the ground and a bloody hand. At the same moment, a glass-shattering blast echoed across the small room's speakers. Jewell sat forward. All her equipment was functioning. There was nothing for her to do but listen to the shouts from Jared and the team leader.

"Status!" Jared yelled as if he needed to scream to be heard over the blast.

"Explosion! Foxtrot Two, check on Four, he was on the southwest corner."

"Control we need an ambulance and fire, stat!"

Jewell nodded to Jared when his head whipped around. She was almost done with the notifications before he'd looked her way.

"Control. Send the medical examiner. Foxtrot Four."

Jewell swiveled her head toward the screen. The personal camera captured the vivid, hellish details of the man's demise. Jewell covered her mouth to prevent her breakfast from coming back up. She grabbed Zane with the other hand. He stood and pulled her away from the console. One of her people slid into her seat.

Oh, God. That man is dead because of me.

"No, he isn't. He's dead because the hacker

either booby-trapped his base of operations or he set us up. He is the reason the man is dead, not you." Zane pulled her into his arms. Jewell didn't realize she'd spoken the words aloud.

"No, there was no way he could have known. He didn't have time. He'd need at least ... " she looked at the monitor's digital display. No, nobody was that good.

"ETA on fire?" Jared's harsh bark echoed through the room.

"Four minutes, sir."

"Zane, get her out of here." Jared's words were soft compared to the barking orders he'd been issuing earlier.

Zane's arms tightened around her. *Damn it, no!* There was no way she'd give her brothers ammo to plunk her into the shrinking violet category again.

"No, I'm good. I... I just needed a moment." She glanced at her operator and nodded toward the side. He slid to the next chair over, and Jewell stepped out of Zane's loosened hold. She sat down and put on her headset. "Fire and Rescue are on the scene." Her words rang with clarity and authority across the small space. She glanced at her brother who was staring at her. She lifted an eyebrow at him. He blinked and turned toward the screen. "Get Archangel here. He needs to be briefed."

Jewell hit the keyboard and sent the interoffice 911message. Her brother would be here within minutes. Jewell focused on the work at hand. Zane's presence was near and comforting, but never overbearing or smothering. Jason responded to the message. Her brother aged before her eyes when Jared told him of Guardian's loss. The weight of his office became a tangible weight, pushing down with a force she couldn't compre-hend. Jason took the downed officer's name. She watched him close his eyes and bow his head. The tears that she'd kept at bay broke over her lower lids. She could only imagine the pressure Jason was under. Her regret for the grandstanding she'd done not an hour ago dropped over her like a cloak of lead.

Jewell lifted from her position and walked over to Jason. She lifted her hand and rubbed his huge, muscled arm. He glanced up at her. "I'm sorry Jace. I didn't know he'd kill himself. I'm sorry about everything. Your man, this morning." Air pushed from her lungs when Jason pulled her into his chest.

He held her tight against him and whispered,

"None of this is your fault. We only wanted to protect you."

"I know, but I'm a big girl now, Bubba." Their words were whispered in the cocoon of his embrace.

"You are. You know that man cares about you, right?"

She pulled away and looked up into her brother's eyes. "Yeah, I do. Can I tell you a secret?"

Jason gave her a half smile. "Anything."

"I kinda like him, too." She glanced over at Zane, who was talking with Jared. "And he hasn't run away screaming yet."

Jason laughed, the rumbling sound landed around her like a gentle rain on parched ground, welcome and needed. "He's an assassin. If he had, I'd be concerned."

Jewell shrugged. "Nobody said I was easy to deal with."

Jason pulled her in for another hug. "He'll stay with you until we have confirmation this fuckwad is dead."

Jewell nodded. She didn't want to think what would happen between her and Zane if there wasn't a need for him to be here, involved in her life. They hadn't talked about... hell, anything.

Her gut dropped. It wasn't like they'd declared their undying love. Hell, she really didn't know how deep her emotions were for the man. He'd made one hell of an impact in her world, and he'd admitted to wanting her for months, but what did that actually mean? Jewell recalled the way he compared their relationship to developing a new program. He seemed to be willing to try to build on whatever was between them. Fuck, she hated that she was so bad at all the relationship crap that everyone else seemed to do effortlessly. She thought of her brothers and Jasmine. They'd all found their spouses and managed to fall in love. She, Jade and Justin still looked for that magic. And if you asked her, the way they fell in love was just like magic. One minute they were single, the next she was invited to a wedding. How did they manage to attract, date and then fall in love with someone without the drama and angst that Jewell felt boiling inside her? Lucky fuckers.

"What are you thinking about, Button?"

Jewell blinked at her brother's words. Shit, she'd zoned again. "Work. Always work." Lying was easier than trying to explain how completely insecure she felt about her emotions and feelings.

Besides, her brothers really didn't want to hear about her.

"Yeah, I need to go. McCaully's wife is local. I need to go make the notification." Jason kissed her forehead and turned abruptly toward the door.

"I'm sorry." She whispered the words under her breath as she watched him leave.

Jared's barked commands brought her attention back to the events of the last hour. Zane lifted his chin, beckoning her over to him. Jewell glanced at the computer station to ensure her employee had everything under control before she moved to his side.

Zane's eyes canvased the room before he spoke, "I need you to put all of this out of your mind for a moment. Is there any possibility Vista wasn't at that location?"

She whipped her head around and looked at the fire department working to put out the blaze on the screen. The cogs of her mind whirled, searching the events that had transpired. "I don't know. I do know for a fact the attack on Godzilla originated from that address. He is the only one we have dealt with that has the skill level and systems to get inside that firewall and fight off Godzilla's attack. Could it have been someone else? Yes, but the probability of that is ridiculously slim."

"But there is a chance?" Zane pinned her with a direct stare. Jewell pulled her bottom lip between her teeth and chewed on it for a few seconds while she thought. She finally nodded. "Of course there is a one in a million chance, but I tracked the hack. There wasn't a remote tunnel or connection to this location. I made sure this was the origination point." She pointed to the screen showing the now smoldering structure that had once been a house.

Zane straightened and drew in a deep breath. "But you have no way of knowing if the person at that keyboard was Vista."

A thought struck her. "Yes, I can. I need to get back to my office. I want to review the data on the original attack. Every person has a, well for lack of a better way of describing it, a finesse when they hack. It is damn near impossible to detect, but if that were Vista, I'd know it." Jewell glanced one last time at the computer console and the operator who was talking with Jared. She wasn't needed here, and she had a forensic analysis to complete.

CHAPTER 13

The illuminated hands of Zane's watch peeked out from under his jacket. He glanced down and realized he'd left Guardian headquarters six hours ago. Jewell had promised him she'd stay within the confines of the facility, and he wanted to trust her, but the distinct memory of months of her flagrant disregard for her own safety taunted him with their clarity. He'd alerted security to contact him if she attempted to leave the facility. He would trust but verify. Zane crouched down in the lengthening shadows of a vacant home across the street from the house that had exploded earlier today. He'd been here, hiding in plain sight as the medical examiner loaded two dead bodies into the meat wagon and left. One was

Guardian, the other was supposed to be Vista. He watched the neighbors and onlookers as the firemen rewound hoses and stowed their gear. The last remaining police car vacated the area after the two-man unit had wound crime scene tape around the burnt out shell. Zane watched as the local news wrapped the remote broadcast and interview of several neighbors. He'd observed the fire investigator and his assistant as they carefully examined what remained of the domicile. Patience was a virtue in his business. Hell, it was his only virtue. He observed the darkening corners of the neighborhood. Lights were coming on in the small homes along the street, and he could smell wood smoke from a grill. The infrequent laughter of children and almost constant barking of dogs had stilled as night started to settle.

Zane lifted from his sheltered darkness and let blood once again flow to his lower extremities. He didn't know what he was waiting or looking for, but one thing was certain, every nerve in his body was telling him the entire event this afternoon was too clean. *Here you go, Guardian, your hacker is dead. All tied up in a nice bow. Now go back to business as usual.* No, his experience told him this afternoon had been a smokescreen or a setup. The bastard had to have known Jewell would track him. He probably didn't know about Godzilla or the fight he'd have to wage to get out of her systems, but Zane would bet his last dollar the bastard had wanted to be discovered and tracked. There wasn't any other reason for the man to attack Guardian again. He wasn't being paid by the Bratva any longer. Unless his pride forced him to make such a glaring error. Zane discounted that idea. The guy was a strategist. This... Zane took in the house and the damage... this wasn't a mistake. This was a planned event.

A late model vehicle drove down the street and crept by slowly. Zane watched it as it pulled into a driveway, reversed and drove back down the street, slowing as it passed the burnt out abode. The car pulled into a driveway three houses down, and the occupants went to the front door. The tone of friendly greetings carried by the wind wiped the car and its erratic behavior from his mind.

Zane felt the presence before he heard a foot-fall. He waited, silent and still, but primed for action.

Fury's form emerged from the darkness. The

shadows of the house for sale that Zane had been using as cover also kept Fury from sight.

Zane glanced at the man but immediately returned his attention to the house across the street before he asked, "Bored?"

"Family dinner at Jacob's tonight."

"And?"

"Jewell needs to be there." A car started up two houses down. Both men pushed farther back into the shadows. Zane kept his eyes fixed on the house. Joseph added, "I'll take her."

Zane nodded once before he motioned to the house with his chin. "This shit's all wrong."

"Your gut or was something found?"

"My gut."

Fury stood with him for several long minutes. He extended his hand and gave Zane a card with a telephone number on it. "Trust your instincts. I'll stay with her until you get back."

Zane didn't respond. There wasn't any need; Fury was no longer beside him. He pocketed the card. In his former line of business, the card would have been the golden ticket. Fury offering his assistance at any time. Zane had given his card out four times and had received four cards in return.

This made the fifth. Who said assassins weren't a social group? He chuckled at the thought.

Zane waited until dark covered the area. The streetlights cast small pools of light down the residential street. Visitors left, and lights were extinguished. He moved across the street. During the last three hours, he'd shifted through the events of the day. He knew the medical examiner wouldn't have any autopsy results until tomorrow at the earliest. Even the power of Guardian couldn't speed up the painstakingly slow process of uncovering any evidence the charred remains could provide. Dental records would be the best bet, but to match dental records, they needed to know Vista's identity. They didn't have a clue who the bastard was, so dental records were next to useless. He'd hope for a miracle on the ID, but his gut told him the person they hauled out of that house wasn't Vista. The investigative element of Guardian had gone door to door and questioned neighbors. Zane had watched them as they worked. He'd request the documentation in the morning.

Tonight was about watching, waiting and thinking. Zane had been batting around what he knew about the hacker, which wasn't much. He was making assumptions based on his experiences. The fucker could be a seasoned killer, but he doubted it. The hacker was comfortable away from the events that he forced to happen. He hid behind a keyboard and directed the dance, he didn't get out on the dancefloor himself. The psychology of a first-time killer, one who wasn't a psychopath, was to feel remorse at taking a life. If his hunch was right, the hacker had killed someone today and was dealing with those emotions. Revisiting the crime scene would be stupid and risky. Vista didn't take unnecessary risks. Zane made his way across the street and melted into the shadows of a hedgerow. He wasn't an investigator, he was an assassin. What he needed was background. Background that Jewell couldn't provide.

Zane held still in the darkness and mentally stripped of the layers of civility he'd painted on himself since he received his 'No Go.' He reached deep inside himself and yanked the beast that he'd tried to eliminate into the forefront. For Jewell, he'd become the shadow again. He'd let go of his humanity and slip into the mindset he'd struggled to keep at bay. He needed only the smallest scent to track his prey, and he knew where to go to get it. Zane pulled his phone from his pocket and shielded the glow as he tapped out a text and hit send. Only one person had the information he was looking for. Darren Kowalski. The fucker that had sold out Guardian to the Bratva. Rumor was the traitor was currently in solitary confinement where he would wait until a mountain of evidence compiled against him had been combed through and presented to prosecutors. Zane needed time alone with that son of a bitch.

CHAPTER 14

Jewell sat gingerly on her couch, her head was pounding, and her eyes were scratchy and tired. Her mind's eyes still saw code scrolling across a black screen. Not even the distraction of her family and five rambunctious nephews at dinner tonight could break the mental calisthenics she'd been doing. She was positive the man she'd been working against this afternoon was Vista. Everything pointed to him. She couldn't find a single keystroke that wasn't consistent with the man's past attacks. She pulled her hair out of the haphazard bun it was in and groaned in appreciation when a bag of cookies and a soda appeared in front of her.

"You spoil me." She opened the bag and offered

her brother, Joseph, a cookie. He took one and sat down across from her. "When is Zane going to be back?"

Joseph picked up the remote and shrugged. He powered up the television, muted it and reached for another cookie. "When he figures it out."

"Figures out what, exactly?" She waited for him to fish out another double stuffed and then popped one into her mouth.

Joseph leaned forward and examined the cookie like it was a priceless coin. Finally, he lifted his eyes and spoke, "People like Zane and I aren't normal. We play at normal but never quite get it right. He's got feelings for you. He needs to protect you the only way he knows. He'll go after Vista. He's learning that he can't leave his past behind him. It will always be a part of him. The question is, are you going to be able to live with who he really is, under the veneer."

Joseph popped the cookie into his mouth and leaned back, turning his head toward the television. Jewell separated her cookie and scraped the frosting out of the middle with her teeth while she considered her brother's words. In theory, the answer to that question was yes, she wouldn't have a problem with the man's past, but she wasn't going to bypass Joseph's concerns and comments with a glib answer. Jewell turned his words over in her mind and searched her preconceived beliefs and values. She bounced the dynamics of her life against what she believed his past experiences would be like.

Jewell glanced down at the cookie tray beside her. She'd eaten half a line of cookies and finished her soda while she was thinking. She swiveled her head toward her brother. He flicked his eyes from the TV to her. She handed him the tray of cookies as she spoke, "The man I know is a good man. At least the portion of him that he has let me see is. He is calm, quiet and unflappable. For months I've purposefully shown him my worst side and yet he's still here. He claims to care for me, and I believe he does. I won't deny that he has become important to me. I'd like to believe he can show me his worst and I'd stick with him. I think I would, but until that happens, until I see him for who he truly is, I can't answer your concern with certainty."

Joseph took the cookies and stood, heading to the small kitchen. "It won't be easy, Button."

Jewell stood and stretched. "Nothing is easy. I'm going to shower, take some aspirin and go to bed. You crashing on the couch or in Zane's room?"

Joseph looked at her and raised an eyebrow. "You assume I'm going to sleep?"

Jewell dropped her arms and shook her head. "Sorry, forgot you didn't function like the rest of us humans." She walked over and leaned up on her tiptoes to kiss his cheek. "Night."

Jewell felt the mattress move and jolted awake.

"Shhh... it's just me." Zane's gravelly whisper surrounded her as did his body. Jewell turned toward him and snuggled up under his chin, folding her arms across her chest to press as close to him as she could. His arms wrapped around her. She laid a soft kiss on the hollow of his throat. His chest hairs tickled her chin and cheek. The full moon filled the room with a soft silver glow. She reached up and traced one of the ears of the massive tiger that found life on his chest.

"Did you find what you were looking for?"

"No. But I will." Zane drew a hand down the length of her hair.

"And what will you do when you find him?"

Obviously, Zane didn't believe the dead body at the crime scene was Vista. She knew that Zane was still searching for the hacker, but he was using a different path to get to him than she would use.

"I'll kill him." The matter of fact way he spoke sent a chill down her spine. His repetitive stroking of her hair stopped at her shiver. "I won't allow him to harm you."

Jewell nodded, although tucked up against him her head only moved a fraction of an inch. "I know. But what if I have another option? I was thinking in the shower tonight. If we assume Vista is still alive, like you believe, the easiest way to catch this guy is to set a trap for him."

Zane pulled away and looked down at her. His eyes narrowed in concentration. "Using what as bait, information or a system at Guardian?"

"No, think bigger picture. You and I both know I'm the logical bait in this scenario. I'm the one he wants dead. He blames me for his failures."

"There is no way in hell either your brothers or I would use you." The gravel of his voice turned into a possessive growl. She probably should have felt marginalized by the caveman tactic, but oddly enough, the protectiveness didn't feel stifling.

Jewell lifted up on her elbow and put a finger

over his lips, stilling the next series of words that no doubt would remind her that she wasn't an operative. Hell, she *knew* that. Nobody needed to remind her of the fact. "No, I would not be the sacrificial lamb, but what if we were to flaunt his failures in his face? Publicize the fact that Guardian has thwarted Vista in a public forum. If we make him mad enough, he might make a mistake, which would allow us to catch him."

Zane held her gaze. His breaths came in short regular intervals, and those were the only two reasons she knew he wasn't a freaking statue. He didn't move for several long moments. Finally, he leaned forward and brushed his lips against hers. "I have one avenue that I need to try first. If it doesn't pan out, we—as in you and I, will develop a plan on how to entice this man out of the woodwork and we will present it *together* to your brothers."

Jewell couldn't help the smile that spread across her face. "You actually like the idea?"

Zane pushed her back onto the mattress and slid his leg through hers. She wrapped her arms around his neck. "I like more than your idea." He dropped his lips to her neck and... Oh, God, his tongue slid down her neck to her collarbone. He swirled his tongue and nipped her skin before he soothed the sting with a kiss. He positioned his body over hers and slid between her legs when she moved to allow him access.

Her hands traveled down his back to the base of his spine. It dipped under her hands as his hips thrust sliding his hard cock against her clit and labia. Jewell gasped at the sensation of his hot shaft pressing, releasing and pressing again. She tilted her hips, wanting more pressure.

Zane's hands and fingers moved down her body followed by his lips, tongue, and teeth. Her mind and body were teased with an array of sensations, never the same one twice. A lick, caress, nip, kiss, or light pinch followed by low groans of need and huge hands that cradled and held her and then effortlessly lifted and moved her. His hand finally made it to her sex. She lifted up and bucked against his hand as his thick, long fingers found their way into her. She threw her head back and clutched both of his biceps when his tongue swiped against her clit. Her strangled breath should have been a scream of delight, but her muddled brain couldn't conceptualize how to function.

Zane rose up to his knees and reached toward the nightstand. Jewell put a hand on his arm and stopped him. "Wait, I want to…" Her courage failed, and her words disappeared.

Zane dropped down on all fours, hovering over her. "What do you want?" He lifted a hand and pushed her hair out of her face. "Tell me." He whispered and lowered down to brush featherlight kisses against her lips.

"Can I…" Jewell slowly reached down and touched his cock. It leaped in her hand, and she watched his reaction when a full body shiver followed. His eyes were closed. His lips parted, and his breath was coming in ragged pulls of air. "Can I taste you?"

Zane's eyes popped open at her question. He nodded and dropped to her side, moving to lay on his back. Jewell straddled him as he had her. She dipped down and kissed his abs just above his navel. His smell became stronger as she worked her way lower. Her chin bumped the head of his cock on the next kiss, the wetness spreading on her skin. Jewell lifted and examined his shaft. He was thick, long and uncut. She reached out and grabbed him, bringing the head of his cock to her lips. She slid her hand down his hardness and pulled the foreskin back. A drop of glistening precome ran down his shaft. Jewell leaned forward and lapped the clear fluid from his body. Zane's body vibrated, and his thigh shook under her hand. Jewell pumped the hand circling his shaft up and down as she sucked his cockhead into her mouth. Zane's hands flew to her hair, and he gripped two handfuls, not stopping or guiding her, just... holding her as she explored his body.

There was no way she would be able to swallow the man. Instead, she worked his cock with her hand while she sucked what she could fit into her mouth. She popped off him and looked up. His body was covered in a fine sheen of sweat, his eyes were closed, and his hands still gripped her hair. He opened his eyes and tugged her up his body. She went willingly. He ravaged her mouth until she had to pull away or pass out from a lack of oxygen.

He reached for the condom and opened the package. He handed the thin latex disk to her. "Put it on me and then mount me." A wave of desire pulsed through her at his demand. It wouldn't take much to get her off. The sensations between her legs had grown to an ache like none she'd ever had before. Jewell trembled as she slid the condom down his rigid shaft. She positioned herself and reached back to angle his cock toward her sex.

"That's right babe. Slide down me. I want to be deep inside you."

Holy fuck, Jewell loved his dirty talk. She moaned as his body split hers open. "That's right. I want your hot little body. I want to feel you tight around me. Fuck, yes." Zane pushed up as she moved down. Jewell grabbed his shoulders and sat on him. She moved her hips forward and back, singeing the nerve endings of her sex with the most intense sensations. She gasped and rocked against him again, dragging her clit against him.

"You like that, don't you?"

Jewell could only nod. She lifted up, slid down and rocked again. "Oh, God... fuck that feels so good."

"Perfect. Just like that." Zane held her hips, guiding her up and down but not so tight as to stop the figure eight she did when she hit the bottom of his cock. She was so close. She could feel that pressure, the one that demanded just a little bit more. She lost the rhythm and groaned in frustration. "So close... please, Zane..." She barely recognized the husky whisper of her plea.

Zane grabbed her hips. "Put your hands on my shoulders." He barked the demand and Jewell complied without hesitation. Zane lifted her and then thrust up into her. An explosion of air pushed from her lungs as he seated himself deep inside her. "Fuck, yes!" Zane growled and slammed home over and over. His hips pistoned faster and deeper when he pulled his legs up. Her body drew tight, her mind gone, only primal instinct remained, and she chased her orgasm with every fiber of her being. Zane pulled her down as he thrust up and ground against her. Zane's hand snaked down and found her clit. His fingers opened her, and within seconds of his touch, she exploded. She rode out the wave of sensation and faintly registered Zane's growl as he wrapped his arms around her and pulled her into his chest. She panted against him.

Jewell lay on top of Zane as they recovered. Sweat slicked their skin and cooled rapidly, but none of that mattered. What mattered was the man under her. The way he'd always treated her with respect, even when she might not have deserved his respect. The way he listened to her and didn't dismiss her ideas. The fact that she missed him when he wasn't with her and enjoyed his company. She traced circles on his shoulder until he rolled her off of him, kissed her sweetly and took care of the condom. When he returned to the bed and wrapped her up in his arms again, she sunk into him. "Why a tiger.? She could see the darker outlines of the animal. The artist who tattooed the animal was phenomenally talented.

"When I worked in the other section, my code name... I got it as a tribute to the lives I saved." Zane's chin rested on the top of her head so she couldn't see his eyes, but she could hear the emotion in his words.

"Is it hard?" She arched her back so she could look at him.

"What?"

"Joseph said it was hard playing normal. I've never been normal. I don't get along well with most people. I have always felt like you were unflappable, at least you always have been around me. Is it hard being this version of you?"

Zane pulled her back into his chest. His hand played with the ends of her hair. She waited for his answer, but none came. That was fair, she always took the time to think about difficult questions. Sometimes they couldn't be answered. She adjusted her position in his arms and felt her eyes drifting shut.

"I like this version of me because it has you in it. This version is mandated to save lives instead of taking them. Is it hard? Yes. I struggle to keep who

I was from surfacing." Zane rolled onto his side, so he was facing her on the pillow. "I'm a weapon, one that is defective."

"You're not defective." Jewell reached up to bring her palm to his cheek.

"I am. I can no longer do the mission I was trained to perform. I attend psychiatric sessions to try to understand how to adapt and how to let go. Your brothers understand my situation, and they don't want me near you, at least not in a personal sense."

Jewell lifted up onto her elbow so she could see him in the moonlight. "My brothers have a belief that they control my life. They don't."

"My past could come back to haunt us at any time." Zane pulled her down with him again.

Jewell rolled onto her back and put her head on his shoulder. "*My* past is haunting us now. How is it any different? Won't we just work together to remedy the situation like we are now?"

Zane cocked his head to look at her, and she glanced over at him when he spoke, "Is that something you'd be willing to try? Having a future with me?"

Jewell sat up in bed and twisted, so she was facing him. "Wait. What? Isn't that what we agreed to? We set this relationship up and tweak it to make things work? That's what you said. Did you change your mind?"

"No, but I needed to make sure you didn't."

Jewell turned to face him full on. She hated this. She didn't know how to tell him what she was thinking without coming off as cold or what did the people in college called her... a calculating bitch. Her people skills sucked.

Jewell glanced over at Zane. She pulled the sheet up over her breasts, because that seemed to be where Zane's eyes had wandered to and stuck. He looked up at her and winked. She flashed him a smile and then glanced down at her fingers that were twisting in her lap. "Okay, so I didn't know the full extent of your past. But I assimilated the information, and we talked about it, right? That was the premise for the program, remember? We gather the information, and we make informed decisions about the relationship based on that information. Did I misunderstand?" She searched her memory recalling their conversation. Hadn't they already determined this course of action?

Zane lifted up and scooted back to lean against the headboard. He beckoned her closer. Jewell slid up the bed and sat next to him. He dropped his arm over her shoulders and tugged her into his side.

"I'm not trying to renege on our agreement. I am however giving you all the information to make that informed decision. Being with me won't be easy."

Jewell leaned her head onto his shoulder. "Well, that makes two of us. What does that say about us?"

"That we are both determined, strong-willed people who are willing to fight for something we want?" Zane's voice rumbled around her. He maneuvered them back down onto the bed and spooned his body behind hers. The comfort and simple indulgence of being with him like this resonated deep within her. She had always felt guilty about spending time away from Guardian, but not tonight. In Zane's arms, she found contentment and peace.

CHAPTER 15

J ewell climbed the stairs to her office for the fiftieth or sixtieth time today. Three missions overseas would keep any section busy but add to that the normal day to day requirements of the domestic side of the business and her people were swamped. She glanced at Zane's empty chair and then at the clock. He'd dropped her off this morning before he'd gone to interview Darren Kowalski. Jewell checked the operational status of her systems before she folded up into her chair and pulled her keyboard toward her. There were endless tasks to accomplish, and she should be focused on them. Instead, she wondered what information Zane could obtain from the traitor. It seemed like a waste of time to her; unless Kowalski surrendered an identity for Vista, there wasn't any real way forward. From everything she'd read, the man hadn't provided any information since he'd been apprehended in the Maldives.

Jewell glanced at the Dark Net chat room she'd set up. When Zane got back, she'd need to outline her idea to him. The plan was as simple as it was obvious. Jewell would make a public proclamation that she'd single handedly defeated Vista. If the man were alive, he wouldn't be able to resist responding. Figuring out how to trap him once he surfaced, that would be the issue.

Jewell glanced at the dormant chat room again. She wasn't sure Zane was right. Something told her Vista was dead. She knew for a fact the person she tracked yesterday was Vista. Could he have left the house before Guardian's people got there? Yes. But why would he? Jewell put herself in his place. She let her imagination put her in the man's shoes. If her computer, her main computer, had just been infected with a virus like no other that she'd ever seen before, what would she do? She'd shut down, curse the stars and then replace the hard drives. She had ghosts of her hard drive. She'd replace the drive and bring her system up to the configuration that she'd last ghosted on her computer. Then she'd isolate the hard drive in a standalone system and then examine the fuck out of the virus that had attacked her. None of that would require the man to leave the house. Unless the house wasn't his? Or maybe he had his backup hard drives stored somewhere else. Jewell cast a glance over her shoulder toward the safe where her backups were located. No, that was reaching. She had nothing to substantiate that theory.

The snick of her door lock brought her out of her thoughts. A smile split her face when her sister-in-law Tori walked into her office. "Hey! How did you get away from Jacob with three missions going?"

"Two are done, and the third is wrapping up. I've learned to escape before the hot wash begins unless there is a reason I need to be present. Once they start scrubbing the mission, I'm stuck for at least three hours." Tori motioned toward Zane's chair as if asking permission to sit.

Jewell smiled and waved her hand at the chair. "Thank you for dinner last night, it was fun."

"Bullshit, you were distracted the entire evening. Hell, Joseph talked more than you did."

Jewell's laugh exploded before she slapped her hand over her mouth. "Yeah, it's this Vista issue."

Tori leaned back in the chair, slid off her heels and pulled her legs up with her. "I'm not following. Vista died yesterday."

"Zane doesn't think so. He believes it was too neatly wrapped and presented. He's with Kowalski now trying to get something from the man to track our hacker in the physical world."

Tori wrapped her hands around her legs, leaned and rested her chin on her knees. "He doesn't have a physical footprint, wouldn't it be easier to work the digital track?"

Jewell mimicked Tori's position and pulled her bottom lip into her mouth to worry it while she thought. "I've searched for a digital trail. I couldn't find one."

"Ah, but you don't have the assets the CIA has." Tori's eyebrows rose. As the liaison for the CIA, her sister-in-law had access to systems Jewell would love to explore. Guardian's tech was better, but the long history of the CIA and the human contacts they employed outmatched Guardian at least five to one.

"You think they'd play ball?" Jewell grabbed a

pencil from her hair and tapped the eraser end against her lips.

"If Jason approves it and makes a call to the director, I think they would. Every agency in America needs closure on the Bratva's human trafficking case. If we tie the trace of Vista to that closure, it should be a slam-dunk."

"Slam-dunk?" Jewell tried to hide her amusement of her sister-in-law's comment.

"What can I say? I live with five men. Five. Granted four are smaller, but I swear that each and every one of them secretes enough testosterone to sink a ship. You've seen my yard. Football, soccer, basketball, hockey, lacrosse and t-ball equipment long ago overtook the flowers and the sheer volume of crap is threatening to choke out the hedge line." Tori screwed up her face and looked cross-eyed at Jewell.

"Like you're not out there playing with them!"

"True, but if I wasn't, I'd never see them except for bath time and bedtime. Talon is reading so well, he's reading us his bedtime story now." The mom-pride oozed from her sister-in-law.

"They are amazing kids, but I may be prejudiced."

"Thank you." Tori glanced at the clock displays

behind Jewell. "And those amazing kids need me to rescue their nanny in about an hour, so do you want me to hit up Jason and try to get the CIA to help?"

"It couldn't hurt. Zane can work the physical, you can work the nonexistent digital with the spooks, and I'll work on the backup plan." Because if Jewell were forced to give odds on the success of either Zane or Tori's plan, she'd end up broke.

"Don't forget the human intelligence factor. The CIA has resources that boggle your mind on that front. What's your backup plan?" Tori unfolded from the chair and slipped her heels back on.

"Just an idea right now. Zane and I will flesh it out if we need to present it."

"Zane? I thought his name was Adrian Monk, Gil Grissom, or Shawn Spencer." Tori rattled off a list of the TV cop names Jewell had called Zane during his first stint with her. Jewell wanted to hang her head in shame. She'd been such a bitch. "When did you start calling him by his real name?" Tori's question spiked a rush of blood to Jewell's cheeks. Thank goodness the lighting in her office would cover it.

"Okay, okay... I realize I may have been a bit of a bitch to him, before."

Tori put her hand on her hip and lifted one perfectly arched eyebrow. "A bit?"

"Uhhggg... all right, I was horrible to him, but he still forgave me and..." Jewell hid her face in her hands. "...I like him. A lot. And he likes me, and I don't know what to do with that, but I think this might be more than like and my brothers hate him and are also assholes who are trying to run my life." The words ran together as they poured out of her mouth. Jewell grabbed her hair and pulled it in front of her face, mortified that she'd confided such personal secrets to another living soul.

She watched through her hair as Tori slowly sat back down. "Okay, first things first, I'm so happy for you and Zane. Second, screw the brothers. They mean well, but we've had to unscramble their well-meant macho screw-ups before, we can do it again. What matters is that you like Zane. You know if he makes you happy the brothers will eventually settle down. And if not, we can pull out the big guns."

Jewell swept her hair back from her face. "The big guns?" She had no idea what Tori was talking about.

"Yep, your mom and my dad."

The Cheshire grin that spread over Tori's face was too much. Jewell groaned and shook her head. "See, that's just it. This is so new *and* unexpected. I don't know what to do or even if what I feel is real? I mean could this just be a phase or what if he isn't the right person for me. Don't get me wrong, I want him to be the right person, but what if he isn't?"

"Okay, then let's make this real simple. If Zane were to walk out of that door and leave, never to return, would you be okay with it?"

The question hit her hard. Harder than she expected, because it wasn't just a mental shock, it was a physical reaction. Her stomach clenched and adrenaline filled her system. Jewell inventoried the responses, both mental and physical. She'd be hurt, that was a given. When Zane had left before, the hole he left in his wake was a tangible force, and that was before Jewell had gotten to know him—intimately. No, she wouldn't be okay. Jewell lifted her gaze to Tori and shook her head. "No. I don't think so."

"Then the chances are he is the right person for you. Will he be your forever love? Who knows, but if you don't take the chance and let him get close to you, you'll never know. You can't analyze your life the way you examine the data that pours through this office. Trust him to lead you through it. Take a chance, Button, or you might miss something fantastic."

Jewell picked up the pen on her workstation as Tori's words sunk in. "We've already agreed to try to make it work. I guess I'm just second guessing myself."

"We all do that. It's normal." Tori stood and placed a hand on Jewell's shoulder. "I'm here if you need to talk. You know, girl talk."

Jewell snorted. She'd listened to her sisters and mom talk about men and had tried to chime in when appropriate. Girl talk… lord above she'd always thought it was a waste of time. Maybe she needed to re-evaluate that assumption, too. "Thank you." She called out the thought just before the door shut behind Tori. The woman gave her a thumbs up sign through the mirrored glass and headed down the stairs.

Zane entered the interrogation room and sat across from one of the most notorious men

Guardian had ever apprehended. The kicker was the man used to be a brother in arms. Zane leaned back in his chair as he sized up Darren Kowalski. He was big, brown hair and brown eyes. Sharp eyes that missed nothing. His manacled hands sat folded one over the top of the other. His shoulders were relaxed, and he met Zane's gaze without hesitation.

"Who are you?" Kowalski asked as soon as Zane sat down.

"Nobody you know."

Kowalski huffed and shook his head. "No shit, that's why I asked."

"I'm known by many names. The one you might have heard is Bengal." Zane saw the flare of recognition in the man's eyes before Kowalski's cocky attitude returned in full force.

"So what, the mighty Guardian is going to kill me? Bring it on. I don't give a flying fuck." Zane leaned forward and steepled his fingers together. The information Guardian had been able to amass on Kowalski was all the leverage he needed. He'd spent the last hour going over his file, thanks to Jared King. To say Jewell's brother's gesture surprised him would be putting it mildly. But he was never one to look a gift horse in the mouth.

"You? No, not you." Ice dripped from his threat. He'd channeled his past life and yanked that bitch front and center. Zane stared at Kowalski. He didn't blink, and he didn't give any indication that he would speak again. He'd had people in this position before, granted it was usually with him pointing a suppressor at the fucker's temple, but he could do civil. Since Kowalski had started the questioning, it was best if he kept the bastard talking. If he shut down, the upcoming threat might not have the same effect.

"Really, then who?"

Zane pulled out three pictures from his inside coat pocket. He laid them down one by one and watched Kowalski grow paler and paler. Finally, the man shook his head and spit out, "Bullshit. I worked for this organization. There is no way the Kings would go after my wife or children."

Zane let the corner of his mouth curl up. "Vista has threatened their sister. It is a tit for tat scenario. You save their sister, they'll spare your family. You should know nobody threatens the Kings. It is, after all, the reason you are sitting in this room. You grew too bold and assumed they wouldn't respond."

A puzzled expression crossed Kowalski's face. "Who or what is Vista?"

"Your hacker." Zane saw the man blink in recognition. A slow shake of the man's head followed. "I don't know who he is. We contacted him via a landline. I know he is in the United States, or I assume he was. We called a US number and left a message. We told him what we wanted, and we'd receive a price via the Dark Net. We'd deposit the funds in his account, and it would happen."

Zane pulled out a pad and pen and slid them to where Kowalski's hands were shackled. "Routing number to the account, website address and telephone number." He tapped the photographs and then spoke again, "Do them a favor and forget trying to pretend you don't know them."

Kowalski wrote the information on the pad but hesitated before he handed it over. "How do I know you'll honor your word?"

Zane sneered at the man and growled, "I'm not the scum who dishonored the code. That was you."

"What has Guardian ever done for you except teach you to kill?" Kowalski demanded.

"They didn't teach me to kill, Uncle Sam did that. They gave me a purpose and a function. The missions I've completed for them have made this world a better place. What did you do?" He pointed at the two little girls in the photograph. "Your daughters were lucky. How many little boys and girls did you murder or sell into slavery? You disgust me. You're not a man. You have no honor, and when you die in prison for the crimes you committed against the thousands of children you sold, there isn't one person in this world that will mourn your loss. Your wife? She filed for divorce. Those little girls? You'll never see them again. I hope you enjoy hell because the one thing prison inmates hate worse than a pedophile is people who prey on children and sell them to those sick bastards."

Zane retrieved his pen and notebook. He stood and pocketed the information before he turned toward the door.

"Did she really file for divorce?" The question was soft, but it was asked.

Zane turned and examined Kowalski. The swagger was gone, but who knew if it was an act. "She cleaned out your accounts, filed for divorce and sole custody. She packed up and left Russia for the Mediterranean. If I find out this information is incorrect, her holiday will be shortened. Dramatically."

Zane stepped out of the interrogation room at the same time as Jared King exited the observation room. Jared extended his hand for the information Zane had acquired.

"We need to talk about a way forward." Zane didn't hand the information. He knew Jewell's section could ferret out the information he needed. If there were anything to go on, he'd get with Jason to find someone to watch Jewell while he went on the hunt. Because it was going to be a hunt and slaughter as far as he was concerned.

Jared crossed his arms over his chest and stared at Zane for several seconds before he nodded and turned on his heel. The 'come with me' was spoken over his shoulder.

Zane drew a deep breath and looked toward the ceiling. He'd been skating on the fine line between his former life and his current one. If he couldn't show her brothers he was capable of living in her world, he'd never stand a shot of gaining their blessing. Not that he needed it, but he knew Jewell seemed to crave her brothers' approval, despite the little show she put on two days ago. His feet moved forward after his boss. Zane pieced his armor back into place as they headed to the executive wing of the building. Kowalski would be taken back down to Guardian's holding facilities.

Jared waited for Zane by the elevators. "You got more from him in five minutes than my team of interrogators have in the last month." There was a small amount of respect in the tone of Jared King's voice.

Zane shrugged. "I'm sure your people didn't threaten to kill his wife and children."

"No, we can't use coercion to elicit information... not if we want it to stand up in court and in his human trafficking case, everything has to be by the numbers. We can't let that bastard off on a technicality."

"I understand completely, but this hacker bastard isn't going to court." Zane entered the elevator when the door opened.

"He needs to be apprehended. He has violated at least a dozen laws in as many countries." Jared pushed the button to reach the level where Jason King's offices resided.

"I beg to differ. He's a threat to your sister."

"He's been a threat to all of us. Yet we've managed to remain alive and, if I'm not mistaken, keeping my sister alive is your basic function; at least until this threat is neutralized." Jared leaned against the wall and watched the floors change on the display.

Zane narrowed his eyes and turned his head toward his superior. Did the man doubt his desire to take care of Jewell? "Meaning?"

"Meaning if you take out of here chasing ghosts, who will be here to protect her?" Jared's eyebrow lifted, and his chin rose in an act that reminded Zane of Jewell.

"I won't be chasing ghosts. If there is a trail to follow, I'll find him. If not, then there is a plan B."

Jared paused as the door opened. "Plan B?"

"Yeah, but you aren't going to like it any more than I do." Jared did a double take as they headed toward the executive offices.

Jared sighed, "Then we better hope we find a trail."

CHAPTER 16

Jewell's phone had been ringing nonstop for the last fifteen minutes. Someone in HR had opened an email with an attachment... and of course, they clicked on the attachment without confirming they knew the sender. The malicious little virus had been contained, but now everyone in HR was screaming at her section. As if it wasn't Clarisse Thompkins's fault they didn't have access to their systems, oh no they acted like it was her section's fault. Jewell wanted to find Clarisse and do bodily damage to the woman. People making stupid mistakes made her section's life miserable.

The phone rang again. She answered it with a keystroke and a growled, "What the fuck is it now?"

"I take it you're having a bad day?" Her brother, Jason's voice, resonated within the confines of her office walls.

"If I ever find a certain Clarisse Thompkins I'll string her up and... hell, I don't know, I'll do something drastic!"

"What did Ms. Thompkins do to upset you?" That was Jared's voice, and the bastard was laughing.

"She didn't have the brains *not* to double click on an attachment from someone she *didn't* know. So now HR's systems have been quarantined, thanks to her, and I have three of my people trying to undo what shouldn't have been done, all while the powers that be in HR are screaming at us to do it quicker. I'd rather just leave them down for two days and teach them all a lesson."

"Right, well I can understand your angst. How about I get HR to stop calling you and you come to my office. We need to discuss a few things that have come to light recently. Also, bring your tablet."

"Like I go anywhere without it?" Jewell glanced over at her snack stash. Two bags of her good chocolate should be a decent offering. She knew her brothers were bottomless pits, but they were discerning pits. "See you in a couple minutes." Jewell grabbed a sticky note and scribbled Zane a message as to where she was going. She stopped halfway through the process and looked at the paper and pen in her hand. A slow smile spread across her face. She didn't want to worry Zane. That meant she cared and the validation sunk in just like warm sunshine on a cool day. She finished the note and put it on his chair before she grabbed the candy and her tablet.

Jewell headed down the stairs but stopped by Alonzo's workstation. "I've got to go to the X-wing. I'll be back shortly." Her staff had shortened the executive wing's name years ago.

Alonzo peered over his monitor at her. "Who did you tell off in HR to get you drug up there?"

"Ha! No one! I was good... well, I wasn't bad enough that they reported me, but this is a different issue. Do me a favor? Make sure Clarisse, the little sweetheart, takes at least three different training modules before you let her system go back online?" Jewell turned to leave but spun around before she pointed at Alonzo and directed, "Make them the longest, driest computer based training modules we have. I want her to suffer."

Alonzo laughed and gave her a thumbs up. Jewell spun again and headed out the door.

She managed to eat seven pieces of chocolate before she made it to Jason's office. Jewell tossed a piece of candy at Sonya when the woman pointed to the big conference room door while she was on the telephone. Sonya snatched it out of the air. They'd perfected the maneuver over the years.

Jewell pushed the door open, and stutter stepped when she saw her brothers, Nicolas and Zane sitting around the conference room table. Zane looked up as she entered and grabbed her attention. He smiled and winked at her from across the room. The feeling of safety and comfort that always surrounded the man seemed to seep into her pores. She smiled back as she walked across the room. She pulled a chair out beside Zane and tossed a bag of chocolate to Jason. He grabbed, opened and spilled the candy on the conference room table letting everyone take a piece or twenty.

"So why am I here? I'm assuming it has something to do with Vista?" She grabbed a handful of candy out of the bag she retained and passed the bag to Zane. He handed it to Nicolas without taking any. *Naturally. Health nut.*

"Yes, I think we need to consolidate our approach to this situation." Jason unwrapped the heavy foil from around his candy. He took a bite and chewed it for a moment before he spoke again. "Zane isn't convinced Vista died in that explosion yesterday. I'm not ready to put this case away without knowing for sure. Do we have a dead body? Yes. Do we know for sure that the guy down in the city morgue is our hacker? No, we don't. I agree with Zane that it was just too neat. The initial fire investigator's report is in. The explosion was fed by the natural gas line to the house. The inspector believes there was a detonation point in the basement. There was what he believes was a homemade triggering device. Guardian has requested permission to run forensics. The autopsy on the young man found in the house hasn't turned up anything of use. He was burned beyond recognition. They weren't able to pull prints. The report from the fire department says the house was rented by a housing management company. They were unable to get ahold of anyone until about two hours ago. The house was being rented and was being occupied by a Benjamin Lufkey. Age 23."

Jewell's fingers flew across the tablet. "Turn on

the screen for me, Jace?" She didn't even look to see if he had before she accessed the wall mounted monitor. She pulled up DMV records and gasped. Everyone turned to look at her. Jewell glanced at Zane at the same time she swiped her hand across the screen and threw the image onto the seventy-inch monitor. A picture of the pock-faced young man with the squeaky voice that had registered both her and Zane the night of the competition appeared.

"Fuck me." Zane's almost silent comment echoed in the room.

"Do you know him?" Jason whipped his head toward Zane.

"Yeah, he worked the Black Onyx tournament at the Gaming Den. He was at the registration table." Jewell answered for them both.

Nicolas leaned forward, his eyes cut to Zane and then back at Jewell. "How much personal information did you put on that form?"

Zane huffed and turned his head away from Nicolas. Jewell wanted to do the same thing, but she answered, "Nothing. I know better than that. I used my alias, so did Zane. The only thing on there that could be traced back to me is my handle. But they could only follow it back to a pay as you go credit card and nothing else."

"What about you?" Nicolas's stare was pointed at Zane.

"Same as far as the credit card. The apartment I listed as my address was provided by Guardian when I transitioned. There is nothing for anyone to find there."

"No personal items of any kind?" Nicolas fired the question at him.

"What do you think?" The warning tone in Zane's voice prompted Jewell to place her hand on his forearm. His muscles bunched under her hand and then relaxed.

"I think you're both compromised." Nicolas' face reddened as he glanced from where Jewell lay a restraining hand on Zane to Jewell and then back to Zane.

"I don't agree." Jason's voice cut through the tension. Jewell didn't move her hand, and Zane didn't attempt to make her. "We have a way forward now. Zane, I know you want to take the lead, but we need our investigators on this. Nicolas, you get the teams briefed and out in the field, as in I wanted them out of the building ten minutes ago."

Nicolas nodded and picked up his tablet and stylus. He rose while delivering Jewell one more long look. She had no idea what Nicolas' issue was today. He'd never been so hostile. If anything, the man was usually the welcome comic relief. Jewell watched him turn to leave before she swung her attention toward the other men at the table. "What's his problem?" She pointed to the door that slammed shut behind Nicolas.

Jared huffed out an indignant sound. "As if you don't know."

Jewell blinked several times as she stared at her brother. She didn't know. "I don't know. I've monitored all the feeds, the reports are being processed and are on time. We don't have any backups in any of the intelligence gathering departments." Jewell stabbed her tablet with her finger and confirmed she hadn't missed a suspense that would jeopardize any cases that Nicolas or Jared was working on. "No..." Jewell gulped at a horrible thought and lifted her eyes to Jared's. "Is he mad about the HR debacle? That isn't my fault. I don't know how to make it any clearer when we do quarterly and annual training. You do not open unsolicited email attachments from unknown sources."

Jared's mouth went slack as he stared at her. "What? What did I miss?"

She glanced over at Zane who gave her a reassuring smile. "Nothing. Nicolas was upset because he figured out that you and I are seeing each other."

Jewell looked at Jason who was trying to hide a smile. Jared still looked at her like she had three heads. "Why would he be mad about that?"

Jared palmed his face. "Didn't you have a date with him on Friday night?"

Jewell nodded. "I did, but I canceled it because I wanted to play in the tournament with Zane. It wasn't like we were any more than friends. I told him I didn't want to be added to his list of conquests."

"He asked you out, Jewell, because *he* likes *you*." Jared glanced at Jason who shrugged.

Jewell swiveled her head toward Zane. "But I don't like him. I told him that. Why would I sleep with you if I like him?"

"Holy Shit!"

"Jewell!"

She spun at her brothers' simultaneous outbursts. "What?"

Zane put his hand over Jewell's. "I'll explain it

later." The low, gravelly voice didn't sound like a request to her ears, and she wasn't quite sure why, but something told her she'd messed up. Again.

Jewell grabbed a pencil out of her hair and bit off the brand new eraser. What had she missed? Why was everyone upset? She glanced at Jared who shook his head. Jace didn't seem too upset, but she was never sure with any of her brothers. Except Joseph. He was always pissed. That was just a given.

"All right, so we have a way forward with the young man who lost his life. Jewell, we will need a complete background. Zane, until we know for a fact this kid was our hacker, you'll be working with Jewell. Track the accounts, phone numbers, and email addresses. However; if you find a lead, no matter how slight, Jared's people will take over. I'm not risking her life for your satisfaction. Understand?"

Zane nodded his head, but his jaw was locked tight. Jewell could feel the pent up aggression rolling off of him. She dropped her now mangled pencil onto the conference room table. "Zane believes Vista is still alive." She blurted the statement out because she wanted to talk to the plan she and Zane should be formulating.

All three men directed their eyes toward her. "I want to set up a trap. If this guy was Vista and he is dead, then there is no harm in going through with it."

Zane sighed and leaned back into his chair. "We now have three avenues we are working to ensure we know for a fact Vista is gone. We don't need to worry about the fall back plan until we exhaust these leads." Zane looked at Jason after he finished.

"What is the plan?" Jewell swiveled her head toward her brother when he asked.

"Oh, it is simple. I announce that I defeated Vista, that I was the reason he was ousted from the Bratva. I simply state Vista was the reason the Bratva failed."

Zane added, "If he is alive, he wouldn't be able to resist coming after her. I think he is laying low now, biding his time, hoping we believe he's dead. The entire event was too contrived. If I had limited knowledge of operational tactics, it would be a ploy I'd consider. My gut says this kid," he motioned toward the screen, "was a victim or a patsy that Vista used."

"We don't run investigations on gut instincts." Jared leaned back in his chair and tossed his stylus onto the table. "But we damn sure pay attention to them when we have them. I don't like the plan, simply because it puts you in danger." Jared lifted his hands and rubbed his face before he leaned forward again. "My vote is to continue with this line of investigation. Follow the physical evidence until we find the answers we need." He turned to look at Jason. "You said you authorized Tori to go to the CIA and ask for assistance tracking Vista through their channels?"

Jason nodded. "They have a vested interest in making sure he's actually dead."

"Then I say let these avenues run. See what happens. If we need to implement Jewell's plan, we can address safeguards at that time."

Jason stood and stared at the kid on the screen. "I agree. The plan is a last-ditch effort." He turned toward Jewell. She blinked at the finger pointing toward her. "You are not authorized to do a damn thing without my express permission regarding this plan. Do you understand?"

Jewell scowled at her brother. "I'm not mentally impaired. I do understand instructions."

"And yet you disregard them." Jason rolled his shoulders and put his hands in his pockets. "Zane, if she fails to abide by my rules, you will pay the price for her disobedience."

"Hey, that's bullshit!" Jewell launched out of her chair.

"I agree, it is. But you have no regard for your own safety or, as you've proven, my directions. Anything you do outside the normal duties of your job will cost Zane. Think about that before you decide to countermand my decisions."

Zane stood and buttoned his suit jacket. "I accept your terms." He stepped away from the table and extended his hand so Jewell could precede him. She glared at her brother for several long moments before she slid in front of Zane and marched across the office.

"Take care of her, Zane." Jason's words caused her feet to falter.

"Always." Zane's comment pulled her head up and toward him. His eyes connected with hers. He bent around her to open the door. His hand brushed hers at the handle, and a thrill went through her at the contact. "I'll always protect you." Zane's words were whispered and for her ears only. Jewell swallowed hard and cast a quick look toward her brothers. They might not have heard the words, but from their expressions, they knew what he said.

CHAPTER 17

"Do you want to call out for dinner?" Jewell asked as she watched Zane clear the apartment even though the alarms had been activated while they were gone.

"I'll cook." His voice carried from her bedroom. *Of course, he'd cook.* Jewell wandered into the kitchen and pulled down a bottle of Chardonnay. She wanted a small drink tonight. The events of the last forty-eight hours spun through her mind like a movie that was stuck on repeat. She wanted to turn off the noise, just for a moment, but every time she tried she ended up processing the same information. The variables were limited. Either Vista was dead, which meant they were spinning their wheels or he wasn't, and they were wasting time. And then there was the stress-filled situation in Jason's conference room this afternoon. She'd been slammed with work as soon as she left the meeting and hadn't had a chance to think about that mess. Her gut told her she'd screwed up, but Zane promised he'd explain and she trusted him to do so.

Jewell reached into the cabinet for a corkscrew and felt his warm chest press up against her back. "I'll get that for you if you get us two glasses." Zane's lips brushed her temple as his arms encircled her.

She leaned back against him and felt his arms tighten around her. "I don't want to move."

"Mmm." His chest rumbled against her back. He turned her in his arms and pulled her against him. She tucked her head under his chin and melted into his solid body. She sighed. It felt so damn good to let him hold her up. But the worry that she'd been trying to process prevented her from relaxing completely. "What did I do wrong today?"

Zane stopped nuzzling her neck and pulled back so she could see his face. His brow was creased as if he was perplexed. Damn it, why couldn't she ever talk without confusing people? "About Nicolas."

"Oh, sweetheart, you didn't do anything wrong." He kissed her soundly then reached around her and grabbed the wine. A couple seconds later the cork popped out of the top of the bottle. "Here, you fill our wine glasses, and I'll bring out some meat, cheese, and fruit to the living room. We can talk about it out there." Zane kissed her softly before he released her and popped her on the ass with his hand. She couldn't help the laugh that bubbled up at his playful actions. Thank God she hadn't messed something up. Jewell put down his wine glass on the coffee table and kicked off her shoes before she crawled back into the corner of her sectional with hers. The soft cushions were heaven after a day of hunching over a keyboard. Jewell took a long sip of her wine and watched Zane in the kitchen. His movements were easy and natural as if he belonged here in her world. More and more she was beginning to believe he not only belonged here but was a central piece of her reality.

Zane made quick work of chopping some cheese, ham, salami and piling on grapes, apple slices and a sleeve of crackers. He put the tray between them on the couch and grabbed his wine glass.

"So?" Jewell took a bite of a piece of cheese. It paired well with the bright bite of the wine. She popped the rest into her mouth and waited for Zane to respond. He seemed to gauge his response before he spoke. Maybe he was picking up some of her traits? She gave an internal groan at the thought. Poor man, if he was picking up any of her habits, he was in poor company.

"So… it would be my assumption that Nicolas has been interested in you for some time." Zane took a drink and waited. She really appreciated the way he gave her time to process what she heard against what she wanted to say. Her mother and her sister Jade did the same thing. It was considerate and kind. While the rest of the world wanted instantaneous personal interaction, Jewell shied away from it. She wasn't the best at subtextual clues, as evidenced by Nicolas being upset.

"I know that, but I told him I wasn't interested in *him* that way."

"True, but you agreed to go to his house for dinner even after you told him you weren't interested. He may have inferred that you were playing coy."

Jewell's glass stopped halfway to her mouth. "What?"

"Sometimes one of the two people in a relationship play hard to get," Zane explained.

"I... I understand that, but I wasn't doing that. I told him point blank I wasn't interested."

"And then you agreed to go to his house for dinner."

Jewell pulled her bottom lip into her mouth and worried it while she turned her wineglass by the stem. Her eyes jumped up to his. "How did you know that?"

"What?" Zane wrapped a piece of cheese in a slice of salami as he asked.

"That I agreed to go to his house." Jewell cocked her head at him. "You weren't out here when we had that conversation. You were in your bedroom."

Zane shrugged and ate the cheese and meat wrap in one bite. "I may have overheard your conversation."

"May have?" Jewell's eyebrows rose and a smile played at the corner of her lips.

"Did." Zane acknowledged.

"If you were in Nicolas' position would you have thought that I was playing... coy?" Jewell sat down her wine glass and waited for his response.

Zane once again considered his words carefully before he spoke, "I can't honestly say. But, if you'd agreed to go out with me, I never would have let you cancel without finding out why, nor would I have assumed that there was no competition for your attention."

"You wouldn't have?"

Zane sat his glass down and reached over for her, bringing her onto his lap, so she was straddling his hips while she faced him. "No, you are far too beautiful and smart."

"You think I'm beautiful?" Jewell felt heat rise to her cheeks. She was fishing for a compliment, and she'd admit it. It made her feel so... wanted when Zane said things like that. He smiled and pushed her fall of dark hair away from her face, cupping her cheek in his hand. The warmth and slight scratch of his callouses made her nerves tingle and come alive.

"I think you're stunning and irresistible." He pulled her closer and touched his lips to hers. She softened into him for a moment before she pulled away because a thought had wedged itself between her and her desires.

"Wait... Nicolas didn't ask why I was canceling.

Does that mean he didn't think anyone else could be interested in me?"

Zane shook his head and reached up to draw a thick strand of hair through his hand. "I think Nicolas thought he was the only person who was interested in you *and* that he was the only one that had access to you. I also think he thought he had the time to get you to see he was actually very interested in you. But now he knows that someone else is more than interested."

Jewell laid down on his chest and tucked her head under his chin again. The way they fit together was heavenly. "I don't want anyone but you. Is that wrong of me to tell you? Should I pretend that I'm on the fence about that?"

Zane stroked her hair and leaned down to kiss her forehead. "No. Neither one of us likes to play games. We are both literal people."

"We are."

"Telling your brothers we are in an intimate relationship the way you did was… interesting."

"Yeah, I got that when they both yelled at me. But I don't give a shit. I don't have a say in who they sleep with, why should they care who I'm involved with?"

"Because they are overprotective brothers who are trying to guard you against a very real threat."

Jewell closed her eyes and drew a deep breath before she responded, "But that is why you were assigned to me. Just because we are together doesn't mean you are less effective at your job, or is that an assumption I've made in error?"

He chuckled. His chest lifting with each rumble under her ear. "I would say it has made me hyper-vigilant. I won't let anyone harm you."

Jewell lifted up and smiled at him. "I know you wouldn't. Would you object to me telling you that I'm not hungry?"

Zane moved his head slowly from side to side. "I'd be concerned, but I wouldn't object."

"Would you object to me telling you that I'm horny as fuck and I want you inside me?" Jewell's eyebrow rose with the question.

Zane immediately lifted from the couch while holding her legs. His move was so sudden she let out an undignified squeak and grabbed at his shoulders to keep herself upright before she started laughing. She barely heard his growled reply, "I wouldn't object. On the contrary, I insist on taking action."

Zane gripped her ass with one hand and lifted

her so she could wrap her legs around his waist. He didn't stop at his room but carried her down the hall to hers. Jewell found her way to the juncture of Zane's neck and shoulder. She pulled the collar of his shirt away and began to suck up a bruise. She wanted everyone to know that he was a taken man, even if marking him like this was a juvenile thought. Zane's chest rumbled with a deep sound. He put his hand on her head and held her to the spot as he walked. Jewell doubled her effort and was rewarded with a tightened grip. She felt him let go of her legs and found her feet beneath her.

Jewell released the suction from his neck and licked the red spot she'd created several times. She pulled away and looked up, locking her desire filled stare with his. "I want you." Her whispered words seemed to break his trance.

If asked, Jewell couldn't have articulated how they became naked, nor when Zane had settled between her legs. She'd had to have been cognizant of outside factors to have that knowledge. The only thing that registered in her mind was the feel of his lips and hands on her body. The way this insanely strong man held her as if she was fragile and precious. Jewell felt tears build behind her lashes when what was happening registered. Zane wasn't fucking her, he was making love to her. Every tender touch and kiss held that promise and so much more.

Zane's thumb wiped a trail of tears from her cheek. "Why are you crying?" His voice held an uncertainty that Jewell couldn't let linger.

"Because you make me feel special." She ran her hands up his biceps and shoulders to lock them behind his neck.

"Of course you're special. I love you." He lowered to claim her lips. Jewell responded, not caring if it was illogical to feel the depth of emotion that she felt for Zane. Two weeks ago he'd been a missing piece of her life. Something that had been taken from her and made her feel incomplete. Now? Now the man was wound through literally everything in her life. But the feeling wasn't restrictive. No, it was as freeing as it was foreign.

Zane's mouth traveled lower, down her neck and further. Jewell's brain fritzed out again. Her body took over. Zane lifted her legs as he entered her. His size and girth contacted every possible nerve ending. Her moan consisted of nothing but bliss. He withdrew and held, not filling her again.

She opened her eyes, ready to beg him not to stop. His blond hair was mussed, his dark brown irises were blown wide, so they appeared almost black. He entered her as they stared at each other. Jewell could no more pull her gaze away than she could stop the earth from rotating.

"I love you." Zane reaffirmed his profession as he lowered to kiss her. Her hands traveled down his back and rested at the dip of his waist. His hips' steady thrust matched his tongue's dominance of her mouth. Jewell pulled away slightly to breathe. They stayed like that, millimeters apart, consuming each other's air as they became one. Jewell's body tightened, she was so close. She wrapped her feet around Zane's thighs and arched her back, begging for the release her body craved. Zane shifted a leg, giving him more leverage and thrust again. Her world exploded into a canvas of white punctuated with intense red spots. She vaguely heard Zane shout her name as he climaxed.

The air in her lungs exploded outward as Zane collapsed on her. She panted with tiny shallow breaths, not wanting to disturb him. He lifted onto his elbows, and she drew a deep refreshing breath. She started to notice small things, like how much they'd both sweat, the coolness of the air conditioning hitting her skin. The slight scrape of his chest hair against her. Jewell ran her hands through his damp hair and blinked as another sensation registered.

Jewell put both hands on Zane's chest and pushed him up. His eyes popped open at the same time, and she knew he knew. "Fuck." His exclamation confirmed the look that crossed his face. It would have been funny in any other context.

"Condom?" She asked the question. She had to because she wasn't on birth control. Hell, there hadn't been any *need* for her to be on the pill.

He nodded and pulled away from her. Jewell looked down, yes he had worn one, but it had broken. Zane ripped the remainder of the latex off before he stood and walked into the bathroom.

Jewell threw an arm over her eyes. She had to think. There were options. Her mind raced through as many as she could think of, several of which she instantaneously disregarded. Personally, she could never abort, nor could she bring herself to use a morning after pill. Her beliefs were rooted in her upbringing. She didn't judge anyone for their beliefs, and she refused to let anyone judge her for hers.

"Hey." She lifted her arm and looked up at him. He'd wrapped a towel around his waist.

"Hey." She responded in kind only because she had no idea where Zane's thoughts were. If they were racing like hers...

"Come on, We should probably talk." He held out his hand to her. Jewell nodded and reached for his hand. When she stood, he pulled her close to him and rocked back and forth with her for a while. Finally, he moved away and led her into her bathroom.

The huge Jacuzzi tub was almost full. Zane tested the water temperature and then turned off the taps. He dropped his towel and got into the tub, extending a hand to her before he settled down into the warm water. Once he had her sitting down between his legs, he encouraged her to lay back on his chest. He turned the jets on and let the water bubble around them.

"What are you thinking?" He needed to understand what was going on in her mind. He had his own demons to chase, but right now they were unimportant. Jewell's wellbeing was paramount.

"I'm trying to figure out what the chances are of me becoming pregnant and of course what I will do if I am." Jewell's voice floated to him above the noise of the jets.

"We."

"What?" She turned slightly in his arms as if to hear him better.

"What *we* will do if *we* are pregnant." Zane felt her stiffen in his arms.

"You'd want to be a part of it?"

Zane knew this question would make or break everything he was trying to have with this woman. "Absolutely. It is your body, and I'll support whatever you decide, but if we created a baby, then we shouldn't make any decisions in a vacuum."

Jewell nodded. "Well, I guess we should wait to see."

"I wasn't just saying the words to hear myself speak." Zane wanted her to know that he meant it when he said he loved her.

"What?" Obviously, Jewell's mind wasn't tracking, or rather it was working overtime tracking down countless avenues of possibilities. He could only imagine how many directions her thoughts were racing now.

He pushed her away enough to turn her around

to face him. "I love you. I know you don't believe me yet. That is something that will change with time. I've been in love with you for months. I fell in love with the snarky computer genius who is overworked, underappreciated, and hell on wheels when people do stupid shit or get in her way. I love how you drive yourself until you drop, how you sacrifice for your brothers and our organization without them asking you to do it. I love the compassion I see when I'm melted into the background of your office, and you've forgotten I'm there. I watched as you took five extra shifts in one month so your people could go home when they had special events like a birthday or anniversary. Sweetheart, I love all of you, and if we are pregnant, I'd love our child, too. I see *you*, Jewell, and you are absolutely beautiful to me."

He watched as she took in the words he forced her to hear. She nodded and closed her eyes. Zane stroked her thigh under the bubbling water. He waited patiently for her to compose a response.

"I don't know if what I feel for you is love. I'd like to believe it is, but I've never been in love, so I don't know. I have nothing to compare these feelings against. When you weren't with me, there was a hole in my life, and it felt horrible. You are an amazing man, and I believe you see me. I believe you believe you love me."

Zane leaned forward and brushed his lips against hers. "I'm sorry."

"For what?"

"The condom breaking."

"That wasn't your fault. I don't blame you." Jewell spun around and leaned back on his chest. She entwined her fingers with his and raised his hand to her mouth, placing a kiss on his knuckles. "I really want to love you, too."

CHAPTER 18

Zane glanced down at the information that had been uploaded to his tablet. He was following the investigation in damn near real time thanks to Jewell. Since Wi-Fi wasn't authorized in her section, the tablet was docked and updated at the same time as the mainframes. The only time he was behind was overnight when he insisted Jewell leave.

For the last two weeks, Zane had sat on his fucking hands while others ran with the leads they had garnered. He'd always worked alone, so watching the slow-moving, and at times stalled, investigation had driven him insane. The only thing that kept him from losing his calm was the woman sitting next to him. She spun the bottle of orange juice on the high glossed conference table. Zane had been more insistent that she eat regularly and healthy. If she was pregnant, the baby needed nutrients, not junk food and caffeine. If she wasn't then he was just as pleased in making sure she remained healthy.

Jewell glanced over at him and smiled. She gave him a long slow once-over, sparking his well-sated lust. She'd rode him hard and fast this morning before they headed into work. Jewell initiated sex every morning. Who was he to deny her? She told him about a week ago she wanted to feel him throughout the day. Fuck, his inner caveman loved that comment. He chuckled at his mental image of him with a club beating his chest grunting 'my woman.' Jewell glanced over at his low laugh. He winked at her and watched the blush rise from her chest to her cheeks. She had an idea of where his thoughts had gone. Not that he'd ever share the— me man, you woman mentality with her or anyone else.

People he didn't know started entering the conference room. Zane moved, bringing his body slightly in front of Jewell instinctively. Sure, they were in Guardian headquarters, but unfamiliar people still made him itchy. The fact that they were currently sitting in the massive conference room housed on the executive level of the facility didn't matter in his mind. They were meeting here because Jason King needed to be updated on all the avenues of the investigation and, according to the memo they received this morning, there were too many players to hold the meeting in his office.

Five suits meandered in dropping into chairs toward the front of the conference room table. Zane leaned over to Jewell, "Do you know them?"

She glanced up from her tablet. Gave them a dismissive once-over and replied, "Nope." She popped the 'p' in the word and grabbed her bottle of orange juice. Zane saw her struggle to open it and took it, popped the seal on the bottle and handed it back to her.

"My, how domestic."

Nicolas' voice brought Jewell's head around as she lifted the bottle of juice to her lips. She placed a hand on Zane's arm stilling him from rising. Jewell stared at Nicolas as she took a drink. When she finished, she put the cap on the bottle and sat it on the table carefully. "Do you really want to do this here? I'm game if you are." The challenge in her voice was more than enough to bring a look of caution to Nicolas' expression. Zane didn't even try to hide his smirk. He'd have no regrets wiping the floor with his boss. The job be damned. Jewell's immediate hand on his arm stopped him short. He was glad he stopped. He sure as hell admired the feistiness his woman pushed out into the world.

Jason King entered along with Tori and Jared, bringing all conversation to a halt. "All right, this meeting is to put everyone on the same page. Nicolas, give me a run down on what your team has found."

Nicolas stood and grabbed the remote to the monitors that were installed around the conference room. "Right. The house is owned by a seventy-five-year-old woman who is currently alive and well and was found vacationing in Florida. She rented out the house to her grandnephew, Benjamin Lufkey. Young Ben was a programming language major at UC Berkeley. He graduated three years ago."

"Wait, wasn't he only twenty-three?" Tori asked.

"Yep, graduated high school at fifteen, entered UC Berkeley at sixteen, and graduated at twenty." Nicolas hit the button changing the slide. We dug through his college career and sent out a team from our west coast office to talk with anyone still remaining that he may have interacted with while he was there. From all data points, we gathered the kid was a loner. No friends that anyone remembers. His degree advisor said Benjamin spent his time on the computer, gaming or going to class. Graduated at the top of his class."

One of the men Zane didn't recognize snorted, "So a nerd and a loner."

"Hardly. Many extremely intelligent people find like-minded allies and communities online. Even if he didn't have physical support, he might have had a community online." Zane's mouth engaged before he gave his retort a second thought. He knew Jewell's team had been data mining for this guy's associates, but he was damn good at covering his trail.

Nicolas acknowledged Zane's outburst with a nod but continued his briefing, "We can't find any connection from his recent activity to Berkeley, so we started to look at what he had been doing in DC since his arrival two years ago."

"Tell us what happened to the year between California and him showing up in DC." Jared interrupted.

Nicolas hit the remote again, and Zane read the information along with everyone else. "Actually, that is my primary point to this briefing. His mother, his only source of support, was diagnosed with cancer. Her husband, Benjamin's stepfather, passed two years earlier. The insurance agency denied her benefits stating it was a pre-existing condition. The company was wrong in its exclusion of her from benefits, but they didn't acknowledge that until after she'd died. Benjamin received a hefty settlement check. Anyway, he spent that year as one of her primary caregivers."

"One?" The question echoed around the table. Nicolas nodded and flipped the briefing slide again. A Massachusetts driver's license popped on the screen. "His stepbrother, Carter Lufkey, was the other." Zane searched the young man's face and glanced at the issue date. He mentally aged the kid ten years to account for the lapse of time. There was no glimmer of recognition. He hadn't seen this guy at the tournament.

"Do you have a background on Carter?" Jason flipped over a page in his briefing file obviously looking for the information.

"Sir, the report is almost finished. We just got back from Massachusetts where Carter grew up. Basically, Carter Lufkey was a boil on the ass of society. He was a below average student in high school, again a loner." Zane listened to the same man who'd called Benjamin a nerd, at least he didn't make the same mistake with this characterization. Zane categorized the guy as a judgmental prick but listened to his report carefully. "He didn't go to college, held minimum wage jobs until he was fired. Usually for failure to show up to do his job. Three weeks ago he was arrested for breaking and entering, into his bio mom's home. A neighbor called it in when she saw someone go in the house when she knew nobody was supposed to be home. The only thing he took was some old computer equipment that he'd had stashed in the basement. Bio mom dropped the charges and Carter vanished."

Jewell grabbed ahold of Zane's arm with an alarming strength in her grip. Eyes as big as silver dollars turned and gaped him. "What?" He didn't give a shit about listening to the man who continued to drone on, not when Jewell was cutting the blood to his hand off.

She leaned over and whispered, "That connects. This could be Vista. If he was going for his ghost drives, he could be in a rebuilding phase, especially if his primary assets were destroyed in the explosion."

"Is there something we need to know?" Jason's voice cut across their whispered conversation.

Zane nodded to Jewell. She let go of his arm and turned to face the head of the table. "Yeah, okay... well, when Zane first presented the idea that Vista hadn't died in the explosion I asked myself why he wouldn't be at the house. Because I know the person I was tracing *was* Vista. You can tell by the unique repeats in the signature—"

"Jewell, please." Jason's plea cut through Jewell's rambling.

"What?" She looked blankly across the table at her older brother. Zane would bet his next paycheck she'd forgotten where she was going with her comments.

He leaned over and whispered, "Why do you think he left?"

"Oh. Right, see one of the several scenarios that ran through my mind was that our program, Godzilla, had damaged or corrupted his system to the point that he'd need to start over."

"Like what? Buy a new computer?" One of the suits across from her asked.

She shook her head and waved one hand in a dismissive flick before she took a pencil out of her hair and twizzled it in the air as she spoke. "No, see that is what someone who doesn't have even a rudimentary knowledge of computers or the need for a dynamic system may do. Five hundred dollars, new PC, boom you're fixed. But hackers have their own programs that they build. Some of them are so complex they can take years to perfect. There are things people who create the programs would never want to lose, so they ghost their systems. That way they always have a baseline to go back to. Someplace to start again. This company ghosts their systems routinely so if we are ever hacked, as we were when Vista found a way in, we can reestablish a normal operating tempo much faster than starting from scratch."

"So he went back to get his ghost drive?" Jared asked.

"It would make sense, especially since they said he broke in for old computer equipment. Did the police say what he was supposed to have stolen?" Jewell swiveled and asked the bank of suits across from her the question.

One of them flipped through his tablet before he spoke. "Two Eastern Digital Green 1T hard drives."

"Shit. Well, they're old, like circa 2012, but that is two terabytes of storage. Those could be his baseline. He'd have to build another computer."

"Why couldn't he just install those hard drives into a new store bought computer?" Jason's voice turned every head his direction.

"Because the system he'd need to build would require upgraded circuit boards, memory, audio and video cards... everything. He wouldn't come after me without being one hundred percent ready. He couldn't afford to do that, he's already been spanked by us, so he's after blood. He'll hole up until he knows his systems are perfect."

"That would line up with what my sources in the CIA are telling us," Tori interjected. "Most of the human intelligence we have been receiving has indicated that he is underground and waiting. They didn't know what he was waiting for, most assumed another client to take a chance on him. But all of them agree Vista is still a viable player. None have heard he is dead and a few have said they have friends of friends who have said he was active on the Dark Net."

"Do they know what he was doing?"

"Yeah, we got a lead from a reliable source he was looking for specialists."

"What kind of specialists?"

Tori shook her head. "We don't have reliable information. One source said hired muscle, the other said he was looking for a professional, but that source indicated Vista was looking for the professional to obtain something. Suffice to say we know he is active and up to something, but we don't know what."

Zane ground his teeth and locked his jaw in a half-assed attempt to keep his mouth shut. It didn't work. "We need to find the son of a bitch before he can hire some bastard to do whatever it is he is working on."

"We've just sent in a request to run the Angel program for the entire Northeast. If the bastard so much as catches the periphery of any public camera, we'll have him." Jared interjected.

"As good as the face recognition program is, it isn't going to be enough this time. Cameras are easy to defeat, and this guy won't make another mistake." Jewell dropped the pencil she'd been playing with to the table. "Our only option is to pull him out before he is at one hundred percent ready to face us."

"How?" Jason's question rang across the suddenly quiet room.

"Plan B."

"No, I don't agree. There are too many variables we need answered, and I'm not sold on this guy being our primary. Carter doesn't strike me as someone who could be our hacker. He's lazy and a poor student." Jason countered with the information Jared's people had brought to the table.

"Jace, I'm not so sure." Jewell directed her question to the suit with the attitude that did the initial in-brief. "Did you ask about his computer or gaming habits?"

"Yeah, he was always on the computer. His mom said that was why she finally kicked him out. He was glued to it twenty-four seven. She was afraid he was selling drugs to support his gaming habit. He had money but no job."

"I'd bet he was a poor student because he was bored to tears. Been there, done that." Jewell said the words almost to herself before she pointed her eyes to her brother. "Jason, I need to see if my team can find a digital trail on this guy. If I can't, I'd say he is a person of interest."

"Pretend I'm not a computer genius for a moment. Explain why no digital trail would mean he's a POI?" Jason leaned back in his chair as he spoke.

"Okay, so everyone who uses a computer of any

type leaves a digital trail. Usernames, passwords, electronic banking, direct deposits, electronic payments, shopping or gaming online, cell phone's data usage, social media—it all leaves a trail showing a person's digital travels. Companies across the globe are buying and selling this information to reach the customers they want to target. Hackers use the information to find ways into systems, break passwords, manipulate records, steal, or even monitor a person without their knowledge. Regardless, if you live in this century, there will be some digital trial. If Carter Lufkey has a presence, we can track it. If not, he may well be our hacker. Not too many people know how to conceal their trail."

"If he's so great, why doesn't he erase it?"

Tori laughed and pulled her tablet into her lap. "Because nothing is ever really erased online. If you know where to look, forensic computer specialists can reanimate any deleted information."

"All right, gentlemen, please continue trying to track down Carter Lufkey in the physical world. Hopefully, this guy is just the bumbling buffoon you were led to believe. If you get any information at all, no matter how insignificant you feel it might be, contact your superiors immediately. Nicolas, I want a priority report on all information related to Lufkey or this case. Make sure your teams know."

"You got it."

"Jared, Tori, Zane and Jewell, I need to see you in my office. Give me an hour to clear my calendar. Tori, get ahold of Jacob, he's not going to want to be left out."

Zane remained seated as did Nicolas and Jewell. Jared gave his business partner a look before his eyes bounced to Zane and Jewell. He cleared his throat and motioned to Zane. "Can I see you outside?"

"Do you need me to stay?" Zane asked Jewell before he acknowledged Jared's request.

"Nope." Again the woman popped her 'p.' Zane recognized the verbal clue and the attitude that flew with it. If Nicolas got stupid, Jewell would make him live to regret it. He'd leave her with his boss, but he wasn't going far. Zane's stare locked and held on his boss. Nicolas gave a small nod acknowledging the implied threat. Zane stepped behind Jewell and walked toward Jared, and the conversation he knew wasn't needed.

Jewell watched Zane's broad shoulders walk out of the conference room before she turned her gaze toward Nicolas. She'd always like him, until recently. For some reason, she wouldn't have pegged the man as a sore loser, and that was what he was acting like.

"How long have you and Zane been dating?"

Nicolas's question was direct. She liked that. She could deal with that better than trying to deduce some contextual clues that she had no idea how to decipher. "We haven't had a date. Well, maybe the tournament was a date because he paid, but I asked him when we were just working together, so I'm not sure. But it probably was. Although I'm not considering it a date. I like him."

Nicolas looked at her like she had three heads for a moment. He closed his eyes and pinched the bridge of his nose, reminding her of Jason. "So, you aren't sleeping with him?"

"Oh, no, we're sleeping together. How is that your business?"

Nicolas' mouth opened and closed several times before he asked, "But you've never dated?"

"I'm not sure I understand your reason for asking. Why would I need to date someone I've lived with for almost a year? He knows me better than anyone around here." Jewell popped the cap off the orange juice bottle and took a drink. Her stomach was sour this morning so drinking orange juice wasn't probably the best idea she'd ever had, but Zane had given it to her. She recapped the juice and waited.

"When I asked you out…"

"—I told you that I wasn't interested in being one of your conquests."

"…granted, but I was interested in telling you that I cared about you." Jewell blinked at his honest statement.

"I'm sorry. I really don't know how to respond to that. I like you, but as a friend." Jewell picked up her destroyed pencil and flipped it around in her hand while she watched a myriad of emotions cross Nicolas' face.

Finally, he gave a sad laugh. "Hell, I guess I deserved that after the multitude of women I've told the exact same thing."

Jewell stopped twirling her pencil and cocked her head. She didn't understand the correlation. "You've told women you only like them as a friend."

"Yeah, after…" Nicolas blushed as he looked

down at his tablet. "I should have told you much sooner how I felt about you."

Jewell reached across the table and put a hand over his. "Nicolas, it wouldn't have mattered. I've had feelings for Zane for a long time. I just didn't recognize what I was feeling. He's good to me."

"He's an assassin, Jewell, one that has been removed from the program for cause. He's dangerous." There was a pleading sound to Nicolas' voice although Jewell had no idea why Nicolas was pleading.

"Yes, I believe you're correct. Zane is a dangerous man, and I don't doubt for a second that he would kill anyone who tried to hurt me. But I also know that he loves me. He would never intentionally hurt me."

"Do you love him?" Nicolas's gaze lifted from the table where it had dropped during her answer.

"Again, I'm not sure any of this is your business."

"I'd like it to be my business."

"I'm sorry, Nicolas." Jewell stood and gathered her drink and computer. "I'd like to remain friends if you think that is possible, if not…"

"I'll take what you'll give me." Nicolas' words followed her as she walked to the door.

Jewell opened the door to see Zane about three feet away, arms crossed and leaning against the wall. He lifted away and held out his hand toward her. She extended her hand and fell into stride beside him.

"You okay?" Zane squeezed her hand as he asked. The warmth and reassurance radiated through her.

"I am." She squeezed his hand back.

"Is he?"

Jewell gave a small shrug of her shoulders. "He has feelings for me that I don't have for him. I didn't know what to say, so I just told him the truth."

"And that was?"

"That he didn't have a chance with me. Not for a long time now."

"You don't say?"

"Yeah. Some big ol' gorilla my brothers assigned me kinda wormed his way into my affections." She looked down to try to hide the smile that spread across her face.

"Gorilla, huh?"

"Hmmm? Yeah, massive beast. Blond hair, brown eyes. Health nut."

"Health nut? How do you survive?" He stopped

at the cipher lock to her section and placed his thumb on the keypad.

"I know, right?" She watched him enter his code and walked in as he opened the door. They climbed the stairs to her office. Once inside Zane pulled her into his arms and kissed her. She sighed into the sweet feel of his lips against hers. He pulled away and waited until she opened her eyes.

"I love you." His eyes skittered across her face like he was memorizing it.

"I know you do." She lifted to her tiptoes, grabbed his cheeks and gave him a kiss that set him back on his heels. "That is going to have to hold you until we get home. We have Plan B to flesh out, and," she looked at the digital display to her right, "thirty-eight minutes to do it in. Grab your chair."

CHAPTER 19

"I don't like this." Jacob's words greeted them as Zane opened the doors to Jason's office.

"Noted." Jason's voice fired back.

"I take it y'all are talking about Plan B." Jewell sauntered across the office.

"Yeah. It is ridiculous to put a target on yourself." Jacob sat down next to Tori. His wife put a hand on his thigh. He dropped his hand onto hers, and they locked fingers. Jewell had always wondered what it would be like to have that type of connection. Now she knew.

"I agree. That's why we've modified the plan." Zane sat down at the conference table.

"How?" Jason, Jared, and Jacob asked in unison.

"Vista doesn't know who at Guardian stopped

him. We made that leap, and the logic is faulty. We need to make him believe I am the reason he failed, not Jewell. We researched my operational orders. Because it was a family matter the only thing the transfer indicates was I was to be placed at the helm of C3."

Every eye swept from him to Jewell. "Can you do that?" Jason directed his question toward his sister.

"Yes, I can. We went through all the transcripts of the conversations I've had with him. I never made an admission. We can leave a trail, one that only Vista could find, and draw him to Zane."

"Which would also lure him out of his hole so Jewell and her team can track him while he is tracking me," Zane explained the twist to her brothers.

"So you're out there as the bait in the trap and Jewell is the one here, working to catch Vista?" Tori pointed from Zane to Jewell. "And you're okay with that?" She extended her finger to Jewell.

Jewell nodded. She and Zane had a long conversation about this plan. If it were only her to worry about she'd have demanded to be the bait to the trap, but if there was even the slightest possibility that she was pregnant, she couldn't risk it.

Neither she nor Zane was willing to jeopardize the life of their unborn child... if, in fact, she was pregnant. The pregnancy test in her purse was still unused. Quite frankly, she was too scared to know the truth. Afraid that she would be pregnant and unbelievably, that she might not be. She changed her mind about one hundred times a day on whether not she was thrilled or terrified. Anyway, Zane knew how to take care of himself, and he'd assured her that he'd be careful and that he had a couple aces in the hole. Not the 100% guarantee that she wanted, but she knew about his background. He'd survived in hostile territory performing missions so complex she couldn't conceive of the difficulty he'd encountered. If he said he would be safe, she'd have to trust him.

Jason leaned forward and pulled off his glasses. He rubbed his eyes and made a groaning sound that reminded her of memories of her dad. "I don't want to put either of you in jeopardy. Zane, you'll be followed."

"No, sir. I won't need you to do that, and this guy is smart. We know what he looked like when his DMV picture was taken, but that was when he was eighteen. He's had ten years to change his appearance. Plus, he's lost his stepbrother and put an advertisement out for a specialist on the Dark Net."

"By the way, the advertisement was pulled down. I thought maybe we could use the contact information. My guys are working on trying to get through the firewall to try to gain access to the site, but it is top tier encryption. It could take weeks, if not longer."

Zane nodded and picked up where she left off, "So it is evident that we don't know what mental state all this shit has put him in. If he can't get to me, he could react in a completely different way and attack innocent lives. One way or another, this kid is going to come after the people he thinks murdered his brother and ruined his life. I'll take every precaution, but a team would tip this guy off."

"Fuck me." Jacob's comment echoed Jewell's concerns.

"Besides, if I'm worried about a team I'm not going to be able to do what I do best."

"And that is?" Jared threw the question at Zane.

"Turn the tables and hunt."

Jacob leaned back and crossed his arms. "That just might work."

Zane blew a huff of air out of his lungs and

looked at Jason. "It's worked many, many times before."

"What happens if he tries to take you out?"

Jared's question earned the same reaction as Jacob's statement seconds before, but with a little more disdain. "I take him out."

"I won't sanction an operation without just cause." Jason looked directly at Zane and Jewell knew he was saying something not many others understood.

"You won't have to. If he comes after me, it will be self-defense."

"Until you go on the defensive."

"I won't kill him unless I have clearance or he is breaking the tenets of personal security operations."

"What are the tenets of operations?" Jewell asked, because it seemed like she was the only one not following the conversation.

"I will only use deadly force to prevent a loss of life." Zane swung his eyes to hers when he answered.

"Your life is included, right?" She looked around the table at her brothers and sister-in-law.

"He has the right to defend himself." Jason acknowledged.

"Then what is the problem?" She and Zane had worked through the plan, but they needed to refine the timing and devise the trail they would use to lead Carter to Zane.

"All right. Run me through the details." Jason leaned forward and put his glasses back on. "Let's figure out a way to get this son of a bitch and put all of this shit behind us once and for all."

CHAPTER 20

Zane leaned forward and watched Jewell's fingers fly over the keyboard. "And that would be a door that only the best will be able to find and open." She scrolled through the lines of what appeared to be gibberish before she pushed her keyboard forward and stood to arch her back. Zane stood behind her and put his hands on her shoulders, squeezing her muscles gently.

"Then we're done for the day." He caught her weight as she sagged back against him.

"Hopefully Vista is still rebuilding. If he is, he'll reacquire his background information on me, or rather you."

"That's when he'll see the breadcrumbs?"

"No, not crumbs, plural. Crumb. One piece that is slightly out of place."

"You didn't bury it too deep, did you? Zane used his thumbs to roll the delicate muscles of her neck. He was rewarded with a sensual moan that sent most of the blood in his body straight to his cock.

"I *had* to bury it. If I didn't, it would send a ton of red flags up, and he'd know it was bait."

"So now we just wait?" Zane pressed a kiss to her ear as he spoke.

"Hmmm… yeah, since we couldn't find a digital trail and Jared's people are out hunting a ghost, we have no alternative."

"Good. Then let's go."

"Where?"

"I have a place, not the one I registered on the tournament paperwork. I want to be able to make love to you and then fall asleep for at least eight hours. We both need to sleep."

"We can't do that at my apartment? Are you concerned that someone may follow us?" Jewell turned in his arms. Her gray-green eyes peeked up at him through her thick lashes.

"No. I trust you when you tell me that Vista

couldn't have identified you. Until he takes our bait, we are relatively safe. But, I've called in a few favors and made arrangements. We won't need to worry."

"But I don't understand. After the text, we packed up, but then you decided it was okay to return to my apartment when Lufkey was supposedly blown up. Why are we moving now?"

"I want a night with you in a place that I know is secure. No worries about alarm systems, no need to get up in the middle of the night to prowl around the apartment, just a night of us, alone."

Zane had arranged for their security. He'd also made a call to Joseph. Zane wasn't asking for permission, rather informing the man of his plans. Zane was calling it a professional courtesy. Besides, if what he'd heard about Fury was correct, the man needed to be at home with his wife, who was due to deliver soon, not here watching over his sister. Not that Zane had seen him, but he understood the man and knew his loyalties would be pulled in two directions.

Jewell dropped her head against his chest. "Okay, I get it. Food, sex, and sleep. That sounds amazing."

"I take it you're hungry?" Zane laughed as her

stomach rumbled at almost the same instant he asked.

"Yeah, I could eat." She snuggled under his chin and ran her hands up his chest. Zane pulled her into him and held her. The simple act filled him with such peace and contentment. For most of his adult life, he'd believed that any type of connection with another person would be impossible to obtain. The conscious act of ending that portion of his career during his psych eval had been the stepping stone to reaching normalcy. Well, at least as normal as he could achieve.

Her stomach growled again forcing him to move away. "Come on. We'll pick up something on the way. What are you in the mood for?" He asked while he retrieved his jacket and she pulled her purse out of her desk drawer.

"Prawns in red curry sauce." Her answer surprised him, he would have bet on pizza.

"Really? Not the usual?"

"No, you like Thai food, and I had pizza yesterday." She logged out of her system and turned off the monitors before she spun and smiled up at him. He couldn't resist smiling back. Seeing her happy made him feel ten feet tall and bulletproof. Two years ago he wouldn't have believed he'd be in a position to enjoy his life. Hell, he'd have bet he'd be dead by now.

"All right. There is a place about two blocks from the apartment. Let's go." Jewell headed out in front of him and called over her shoulder as she almost ran down the steps, "I want extra rice and a massive iced tea! I love Thai iced tea."

Zane shook his head and followed her down the stairs. There was no doubt, but he'd bet she loved the heavy dose of cream and sugar in the tea most.

Zane carried the takeout bags in his left hand and asked Jewell to open the apartment so he could keep his right hand free. Although he knew he had backup coming, he didn't know when Thanatos and Anubis would arrive.

Mrs. Henshaw's door opened a crack, pulling her security chain tight. "Oh, Zane!" Her voice carried across the hall. Jewell glanced over her shoulder at him, her eyebrows raised in question.

Zane cast a quick glance up and down the hall before he smiled at his neighbor. "Hi, Mrs. Henshaw. How have you been?"

The door closed and the chain could be heard as it slid through the block and then dropped against the door jamb. Jewell opened the door and handed Zane his keys back.

"Oh! You have a friend with you!" Mrs. Henshaw shuffled out of her apartment and extended her hand. "I'm Agnes Henshaw."

Jewell took the frail hand in hers. "It is so nice to meet you, Mrs. Henshaw, my name is Jewell."

"Oh, what a beautiful name." Mrs. Henshaw's face split into a wide smile. "Zane, she is absolutely beautiful. I'm so glad you have found a lady friend."

"So am I." He put a free arm around Jewell and pulled her, kissing her temple. "We were just going to have some dinner, Thai food. Would you like to join us?"

"Oh mercy, no. Even if I could tolerate such spicy food, I don't want to interfere with the evening you have planned. I just wanted to tell you that there was a man here earlier. He said his name was Thad or Thaddeus? He said to tell you that he'd arrived in town with his brother and that they'd see you later."

Thanatos. The Greek god of death and one of the few assassins that Zane had worked with in person. The man was lethal, silent and the most talented garrote killer Zane had ever seen. His brother, or rather brother in arms, Anubis, was given his code name because he was the guardian of the underworld who specialized in killing with poison but was just as deadly with his hands. Hell, tonight Zane could sleep like a rock with the apartment door wide open without any concerns.

"Ah, yes, thank you, Mrs. Henshaw. I'd forgotten to tell you they may stop by." Zane opened the door to his apartment and handed Jewell the take out bag. "Would you mind taking this into the kitchen while I escort Mrs. Henshaw back into her apartment?"

"Not at all." Jewell smiled at the older woman and winked at Zane before she ducked into the hallway, shutting the door behind her.

"She is lovely, Zane." Mrs. Henshaw took his arm when he proffered it to her.

"I think so, too." Zane walked slowly with the elderly woman before he opened her door for her and waited for her to shuffle through the door. "Do you need anything tonight? Can I run to the market for you?"

"Oh dear, no. I'm fine. But do stop by for coffee soon if you have time. I got a call from my son. He wants me to move closer to him. It is an assisted living facility, but I'd have my own apartment. I'd like you to take a look at the brochure he sent and tell me what you think."

"I'd be honored, and I'm so happy your son wants you closer." Zane lifted Mrs. Henshaw's boney, heavily veined hand to his lips and kissed it. "But I will miss flirting with you."

"Oh, you! Go put some of that sugar on the beautiful woman across the hall." A vivid blush tinted the older woman's cheeks.

"I will, but only because you keep rebuffing me." Zane started to close the door but stopped and looked over his shoulder at the old woman. "Make sure you lock up after me."

"I always do. Now go pay attention to your lady friend." Mrs. Henshaw made a slow shooing motion with her crippled, arthritic hands. Zane winked at her and pulled the door shut. He waited until he heard the deadbolt engage and the chain lock into its carrier before he crossed the hall.

He opened his door and strode down the short hall into the kitchen. He swept the tiny kitchen, living room and bedroom. The door to the bathroom stood open, but he didn't see her anywhere.

"Jewell!"

"What!" She popped up from the other side of

the bar that separated the kitchen from the dining room.

"What are you doing down there?"

"I spilled some of the sauce from the curry, and I didn't want it to stain the carpet." She held up a wet kitchen towel as evidence. "Why did you yell?"

Zane chuckled as he threw his keys on the counter top. "Because I didn't see you."

She blinked several times as if trying to compute how that would cause him to yell. "Oh, I see. I'm sorry?"

"Nothing to be sorry about." Zane pulled down the plates and handed them to Jewell along with several spoons for serving dinner.

"Did you get double vegetables?" She held a spoon over the large plastic container.

"Yep." He laughed when she scrunched her nose. He opened a container of rice and put two scoops on her plate and three on his. She ladled prawns and red curry over her rice using the majority of the sauce on hers and then ladled the rest, which included most of the vegetables, onto his plate. He watched as she picked out the few carrots that escaped into her curry and deposited them on his plate. He picked out the chunks of mushrooms and gave them to her. Jewell handed him a napkin as he handed her a set of chopsticks. He opened her straw and pushed it through the top of the plastic cover of her drink, and she gathered the paper to put back in the bag.

Jewell leaned forward and grabbed the largest prawn he had on his plate with her chopsticks. "You know, we've kinda got this down to a routine." She made a circular motion indicating the dinner dance they'd just completed. The prawn still dangled from the tip of her sticks, and a huge drop of red curry pooled toward the end of the shrimp. Zane focused on the tip of the prawn, waiting for the curry to drop to the counter. Jewell carefully drew the prawn to her mouth and stuck out her tongue, licking the tip.

Zane swallowed hard and pushed his stare from her tongue to her eyes. She lifted one arched brow and slowly sucked the prawn into her mouth before she pulled it out partially and sucked it back in.

"Oh, fuck." Zane's cock filled as he watched her mimic fellatio on the prawn.

"Mmm… later, after food." Jewell sucked the tender meat into her mouth and ate it as he continued to stare at her lips. Jewell opened her mouth and licked the sauce from her lips before she hummed in a low sexy way that conveyed she was interested in way more than the prawn. He closed his eyes and drew a deep breath.

"Aren't you hungry?" She pointed toward his plate and smiled as she picked up another prawn from hers. Zane watched her as she sucked the end of the shrimp into her mouth in a replay of her previous show.

"Woman, you are adding fuel to the fire. Teasing me like that won't go unpunished." He reached for his iced tea and drew a long pull on the straw. The small apartment was fucking hot as hell all of the sudden.

Jewell picked up another prawn and held it up while her finger caught a small drop of curry. She brought her finger to her mouth and sucked it in while looking at him in a direct dare. "You don't want to punish me." His gut clenched and he lifted slightly in his chair as he adjusted his cock in his pants.

"I don't?" Zane took a huge bite of the curry. It could have been sand for all the attention he gave the taste.

"Oh, no." Jewell transferred a portion of rice from her chopsticks to her mouth and pulled the black varnished wood out of her mouth. "I think you'd want to reward me." Zane's eyes dropped, following Jewell's gaze as it moved to his hard cock. "Eat your dinner, and I'll show you why."

Jewell fed herself another bite of rice and mushrooms. Zane forced himself to look away from her mouth. Her delicious, full, pouty lips and that tongue that he wanted wrapped around his cock were a distraction that caught and held his attention. The spicy food he consumed was bland compared to the temptress across from him. He waited for her to finish. She winked at him when she picked up the last prawn and consumed it.

As soon as she put her chopsticks down, he was around the counter and had her in his arms. She tasted of red curry and iced tea. Her arms wrapped around him as his fingers found every button and clasp, loosening all of them and pushing away the cloth that hid his prize from him. Her hands made quick work of his shirt, belt, and pants. Their clothes hit the floor in forgotten piles. He kissed down her neck to her bare shoulders. "Beautiful. So fucking beautiful."

He walked her backward the handful of steps it took to reach his bedroom where he controlled their fall onto the bed. He felt her push against him with both hands. He lifted away immediately. "Did

I hurt you?" Did he not brace far enough above her?

"No, I'm fine. Lay on your back." Jewell licked her bottom lip before she pulled it into her mouth.

"Oh fuck, yeah." Zane rolled to her side and slid up the bed, propping himself up against the headboard. If the woman was going to give him head, he was going to watch her do it.

She crawled in between his legs and licked the defining line from his abs to his groin. Her hand wrapped around his cock and slowly stroked up. He lifted her mass of black hair and pulled it away from her face so he could watch her. She glanced up at him and smiled for a split second before she lowered to his balls and started to lick and suck them. He dropped his head back against the cushioned board and reveled in the wet heat of her tongue and breath against his balls.

Zane tugged her hair up toward his cock. She gave a low chuckle and gave a final swipe to his balls, extending the stripe up the underside of his cock. She circled his head and licked at his precome with small laps of her tongue. Zane's hand tightened its grip on her hair, and she moaned around the head of his cock. His balls drew up. He was so fucking close. There was no way he'd last in her throat.

He gently tugged at her hair. "I'm close." He wasn't going to make her finish him, although, God, he'd love to finish that way, but he didn't want to be a selfish lover. Not with her, never with her.

Jewell popped off him. Her full lips were glossed with spit, and her face was flushed. "I want you to come in my mouth. I want to taste you." She lowered down onto his cock before he could put any cognitive thoughts into play. Zane arched up and lodged at the back of her throat. She gagged, and he immediately pulled back. She moaned and chased him, impaling herself on his cock. The small gagging noise happened each time she lowered and forced him into her throat. Zane's balls drew up tight, his lungs burned because for some insane reason he was holding his breath. He pushed the air from his lungs and gulped in a lungful of fresh air. Her hand cupped his balls and when she lowered this time she squeezed slightly. Zane barked out a shout and was unable to prevent himself from hipping up as he shot his load. His world expanded then folded in on itself as the only thing he could focus on was his release. It took several seconds before he realized she'd lifted to the crown of his cock and then released him. He didn't open his eyes as he grabbed her and pulled her up his body. "Fuck, that was…"

"Epic?" Jewell laughed as he opened his eyes and blinked at her.

"Epic. Yeah, epic would cover it." He pulled her down and kissed her, tasting himself on her tongue.

"Good. Now I believe the next thing on the agenda is eight hours of sleep." Jewell laid down at his side and snuggled in close to him as she pulled at the sheet that had somehow slid off the side of the bed.

Zane lifted away and helped her with the sheet before he rolled her over onto her back and made her look at him. "Give me a couple minutes, and I'll return the favor." He felt her arm lay across his chest. She kissed his jaw before she released a contented little sigh. "Would it be horrible of me to ask if you'd give me a rain check? I'm exhausted, but I guarantee I'll fuck your brains out in the morning." She yawned and found her spot tucked up against him. Her arm reached across his chest and up to his hair, snaking her fingers in the strands until they tangled there. In less than three minutes her breathing had regulated, and her body relaxed against his.

Even in post orgasm bliss, Zane couldn't relax. The plan to get Vista to target him was a long shot. And because it was, he'd implemented a backup plan without his bosses' knowledge, but he'd be damned if he'd ask permission to protect his woman. Technically Thanatos and Anubis weren't allowed to operate in the states, and he doubted if Jacob King knew his black door operatives were back in the States. After an asset had been given an assignment, for the most part, he or she was allowed to pick the time/date and method of completing the directive. He'd often followed a mark back to the States to watch for vulnerabilities. Spilling blood inside the United States without specific permission got you slapped with a psych eval and a host of other unpleasant consequences. He closed his eyes and drew a deep breath. But that was another life, and that life was over. He placed a kiss on the top of Jewell's head. She was his life now, and he'd be damned if wouldn't use every resource at his disposal to make sure she was safe.

CHAPTER 21

J ewell blinked at the bright sunshine that poured into the bedroom. She tucked the sheet around her and lifted up into a sitting position. She turned searching the apartment for Zane. It was so small she could see the kitchen, living room and bathroom from where she sat on the bed. Her sleep muted brain took in the fact that Zane wasn't in the apartment. Jewell yawned and scratched her arm before she realized she wasn't alone.

A man stood by the front door of the apartment, his arm barely visible, but there none the less. She gasped and pulled the sheet up to her neck.

"I'm not here to hurt you." A slight European accent floated along with the soft words.

"Then why are you here?" Jewell backed to the other side of the bed and pulled the sheet with her when she stood.

"Zane left this morning to get you clean clothes and breakfast. My brother is watching him to ensure he hasn't been followed. I am here with you. There was another outside of this building. I didn't get close enough to see who. I positioned myself here to ensure nobody but Zane came through that door."

"Oh." Jewell stood in the corner of the room. Adrenaline coursed through her veins making her hypervigilant. She glanced around for any possible weapon, but the room was spartanly furnished. Jewell kept one eye on the doorway as she swept the area again. Damn it, there was nothing. The man hadn't moved and hadn't looked at her. She wouldn't be able to tell anyone what he looked like, except that he was tall based on the height of his shoulder.

"Go, take a shower. Your man will be back by the time you are done."

"Who are you?" Jewell wrapped the sheet around her and glanced around for clothes. They were strewn in small piles across the living room floor.

"A friend."

"Okay… but you have to have a name."

"I do not." The voice that responded seemed hollow and lifeless. "Go, Ms. King, and take your shower. You can ask your questions of your man when you are done."

Jewell pulled her bottom lip between her teeth and did an assessment of the situation. The man hadn't attempted to harm her in any way. He knew Zane's name and her name. Even if Vista had found the information she'd left him, there was no way in hell he could have found out that much information. She pulled the sheet up from around her feet and shuffled the four feet necessary to get into the tiny bathroom. She closed the door and leaned against it. Jewell glanced at the door and then clicked the lock. Not that it would stop the man from coming after her, but she'd be stupid not to lock the damn thing; after all, that was one scary ass stranger out there.

Jewell started the shower and dropped the sheet to the ground. She waited until the water warmed and she stopped shaking before she stepped under the spray. Her mind clicked around the information she'd been given this morning. She dropped a large dollop of shampoo into her hand and lathered her hair. Her hands stilled for a moment as a simplistic thought punched through the minutia her mind was trying to process. *What do you really know about Zane?* She knew his profession, but his past before he became an asset of Guardian was a void. Jewell finished her shower and dried off. There was no way in hell she was going out of this room in her towel to try to gather her clothes. Not with a stranger in the apartment. The more she thought about that, the more it pissed her off.

Jewell took her time working Zane's comb through her hair after she'd towel dried it. As she stared at herself in the mirror over the tiny vanity, she took into account the information she did actually know about Zane. Well, that wasn't his real name. He'd admitted it was a cover name. So she didn't even know the name of the man she was sleeping with. Hell, she could extrapolate that one step farther. She might not know the name of her baby's father. Wouldn't that just make her mom's day? *Shit, her mom.* How in the hell would Jewell tell her mom she was pregnant? With words, obviously, but she could just imagine how that conversation would go. She knew her mom would support her, but she could see the look of sad disappointment in her eyes. She'd seen it so much growing up. Each time she'd misunderstand someone or didn't understand a situation and her mom would have to explain shit that seemingly everyone but her understood. Jewell loved her mom and her family with every fiber of her being, but she knew she was the odd duck in the family. She'd never fit in. With anyone. Jewell considered that statement as it rolled through her mind. It wasn't necessarily accurate. Her siblings had always been inclusive. Her sisters had been amazing, especially Jade. The woman was a hellion, but she was fiercely loyal and remarkably easy to talk to because she had no boundaries and no filters. But for the same reason, it was sometimes hard for Jewell to make Jade understand her issues or concerns. She could only imagine what Jade would say about her being pregnant. She rolled her eyes at her reflection. No, she wasn't going to go there.

Jewell flinched at a small knock on the bathroom door. She grabbed at the top of her towel and backed away from the thing as if it might bite her.

"Jewell, are you all right?"

Jewell launched toward the door and unlocked it, nearly catapulting herself onto Zane's huge body. "Hey, I've got you." He wrapped her up in his arms and held her. She pulled back the tiniest distance and peeked around him looking toward the door where the stranger had been. "He's gone."

Jewell nodded and stepped back. She looked from the door to Zane and then did what any woman who had been placed in her position would do. She smacked Zane in the arm with a balled up fist and all of her strength. "Of all the bullshit things to do! Why in the hell didn't you tell me you were leaving! Did you know I woke up with a strange man in the apartment? Do you have any idea how freaked out I was?"

"But Jewell…"

"Don't you dare 'but Jewell' me! Never again! Do you understand me? I will not wake up with a stranger tucked into a corner, talking with an accent, and saying shit about someone outside stalking us. And I sure as hell will not wake up with you *not only not* in the bed with me but *not* even in the fucking building." Jewell knew she was losing her shit. She could tell by the way Zane had stepped back and plastered the passive fucking expression on his face, just like he did when she'd gone off on him when he'd watched over her the first time.

She stomped to the bed and grabbed a pile of clothes. She stormed into the bathroom and slammed the door behind her and locked it just because she could. Her body shook as if it knew now that she was safe she could freak out. She plopped down on the edge of the bathtub and started to cry, which pissed her off and made her cry harder. She heard the door open but didn't lift her head to see him enter. *Damn assassins could obviously pick locks.*

Zane kneeled down in front of her and placed his hands on her knees. "I'm sorry sweetheart." His whispered words made her cry harder.

"I… was… so… scared." Her words tumbled out behind sobs that filled the small bathroom. Zane tugged her gently, and she moved forward into his arms.

"I know. I'm sorry." He rubbed her back, and they rocked on their knees on the damn puke pink 1970's tile of the teeny little bathroom. Jewell rested her head on his shoulder and took a shuddering breath.

"I'm sorry I hit you." She cringed at the thought of physical violence unless it was against her brothers. Growing up they usually instigated situations that drove her and her sisters to the point of an all-out brawl.

"I deserved it."

"Yeah, you did." Jewell agreed with him immediately. That earned her a small laugh.

"Come on. Get dressed, and we'll talk." He stood and extended his hand to her, helping her off the tile. She grabbed the clothes out of the sink where she'd thrown them and followed him into the bedroom.

"Why did you leave so early?" She dropped her towel and reached for her underwear. "And for future reference, the lace thongs are for evening attire, not a day of work." She hung the baby blue thong on a finger and put the other hand on her hip.

Zane's cheeks flooded with heat. "Yeah, but knowing that is under your clothes..." He lifted his eyebrows and smiled.

Jewell stepped into the tiny straps of lace and turned her back to him while she put on the matching sky blue lace bra. She looked over her shoulder and smothered a laugh. "So, the reason you left early?"

"What?" Zane's eyes snapped up to her. "Oh,

yeah, well I got a notification from Thanatos that there was someone scoping out the building. If Vista had somehow figured out who I was already I needed to draw out the person watching the building. I left, and one of my associates followed me, the other stayed here. He wasn't supposed to wake you."

Jewell pulled the dark blue silk button-down on and hooked the small material covered buttons through the loops. "Yeah, well that happened. You could have woken me and told me what was happening. That way I would have been... oh, I don't know—dressed when he showed up." Jewell pulled on a pair of black Dior slacks and tucked in her shirt.

"Granted, but you were exhausted last night. I didn't want to wake you and add more stress."

"Ha! I gotta say, you missed the mark there." Jewell grabbed her hair and started working it up into a bun. She twisted the ponytail she'd pulled her hair back into and then wound the twist around itself, tucking the end in under the tightly twisted hair to keep it from unraveling. She could put her hair up in her sleep she'd done it so many times.

"Noted. But I was able to work with my

associate to isolate the person who was staking out the building.

"Anyone to be concerned about?" Jewell looked around for her shoes.

Zane grabbed the pair she wore yesterday and handed them to her. "It was a private investigator. He is allegedly working on a cheating case. He'd been stalking the husband, and when he holed up in Apartment 4C, the man took up residency outside. I've called Jared, and he's already authenticated this guy is on the level. He has a team going over to the man's office now to make sure he is actually working the case he says he's working, but I think he's a non-player. He was sweating bullets when Ani approached him."

"Ani?" Jewell's attention caught at the female's name.

"Short for Anubis."

"As in the Egyptian god?"

"Yeah." Jewell waited for more, but Zane seemed to find his fingernails extremely interesting.

"So these guys that are helping you. You know them from your past?" Jewell headed into the little kitchen and breathed a sigh of relief. Two large to-go containers filled with coffee sat on the counter.

She opened one. Not hers. She handed the black coffee to Zane and popped the insulated top on the other. Oh, nirvana. The cream and sugar infused caffeine was exactly what she needed this morning.

Zane took a sip and nodded. He glanced at her and then back at his cup.

"What?" Jewell had been around him enough to know he wanted to say something but was hesitating.

"Your brothers don't know they are here or that they are helping." Zane took another sip of his coffee and stared into the depths of his cup as if it was going to reveal the answers of the cosmos.

"I won't say anything. If they ask me a direct question, I'll answer it, but I'm not in the practice of having idle conversations about assassins with my brothers." Jewell lifted her eyebrows several times and smiled at the look of relief on Zane's face.

"They are helping us. If Jacob or Jason knew that they were here, it would cause difficulties, for everyone."

"Right. Not an issue as far as I'm concerned. But you owe me." Jewell glanced at the digital display on the stove and then back at Zane.

"For?"

"I was supposed to have awesome morning sex." Jewell picked up her purse and tossed his keys to him.

Zane caught the keys in midair and groaned. "Yeah, believe me, I thought about that."

"Well, you get to think about it all day." She turned her back on him and slid her hand down her ass. "The thong will be waiting for you." Jewell threw back her head and laughed when she heard his pained groan.

She waited at the door for him. Lifting onto her tiptoes, she kissed him chastely on the jaw. "I'm worth the wait."

He slid his arm around her and lowered his lips to hers. "I know. That's why I'm still here. I love you." The words were a mere whisper against her lips. Jewell leaned into the kiss, sealing her lips to his. She let his words sink into her soul. She wanted to be able to tell him the same thing. She wanted desperately to be in love with this man, but she was afraid that this wonderful little bubble they were living in would implode. If she gave him her heart, where would she be when that happened?

CHAPTER 22

"You're playing with fire." Anubis sat down across from Zane at the small restaurant where he was picking up his and Jewell's lunch.

"I am. But you knew that when I briefed you on the phone. You don't have to be here." Zane pushed his water bottle to the side and leveled his stare at his… well for the lack of any other term, his friend.

"I have five people in my life that I would extend my neck for. You are one. If you hadn't been there for me in Bolivia, I wouldn't be alive."

Zane nodded. Ani had been between a rock and a hard place. He'd successfully poisoned his mark, but the poison he'd been able to use was incredibly unstable and worked too fast. The entire kitchen and wait staff for the party had been thrown into holding cells, and they were being systematically tortured and then executed. Ani was four hours into his torture session when Zane had made it into the country and to the backwater hellhole where Ani was being held. He'd fought like the beast they'd named him after. Hand to hand combat was his forte and that day he killed fifteen people to get Ani out of that place. That rescue mission had been the beginning of the end for Bengal.

"Why?" Ani's question brought him back from his thoughts.

"Why, what?"

"Why did you risk your life to save mine? It isn't worth the air you breathe." The man's eyes never stopped searching the small restaurant, as if the ghosts of his enemies would appear out of the vinyl booths that lined the walls. Thanatos had given Zane Ani's location. They were to meet and combine forces for the next mission. Thanatos had to go after their mark, but Bengal was between missions, so he went after Ani. There had been no hesitation, but a rescue wasn't expected. Assassins knew the risk, and they knew if they were caught they were dead.

"Because we all deserve a chance to live a life

other than the one you have now. I made it out. You can too."

Ani fixed his stare out the picture window and shrugged. "I'm fine here. I belong here."

"That is a decision only you can make." Zane rolled the water bottle in his hands. "But it is a decision. You can stop."

The evil laugh that floated across the table stilled Zane's hands. "What if I told you I enjoyed my work? I take great pleasure in ensuring the scum of the world no longer prey upon the weak or the innocent." Anubis' eyes locked with Zane's for an instant. It was enough. Zane understood the need, he'd been driven once upon a time.

"Then it's good. Hopefully, this little detour will be over before long." Zane watched as Thanatos walked into the establishment. He'd waited to make sure no one was being followed before he'd entered.

Zane nodded to the man as he sat down and started his brief without hesitation. "The intel that we've been given is the target in this operation has been looking for muscle. The man is a ghost and a computer hacker. I haven't met many that were experts in one field and also ours."

Both men chuckled. Assassins had many skills,

but it was unheard of for a specialist from another field to also be an assassin. "So he'll hire out his grunt work." Anubis finished their mutual thoughts.

"Jewell has left a piece of cheese for our rat. Should he discover and take the bait, I'll be his target. I'm going to leave Jewell at the facility. I've arranged it with her brothers, they are making accommodations for her so she doesn't leave."

"That's an excellent idea. A hardened facility would require more than just hired muscle to take down." Thanatos spoke in a low tone after the waiter had passed.

"I'll make myself vulnerable. The secondary address I've given you is her apartment and where I'll be commuting to and from. If he's as smart as they say, he'd find out where the person in charge of that department is staying. I need to make sure there aren't any warning flags for this guy. I'm hoping to give this guy the opportunity to grab me. Then I will pull him from his hole and give us the opportunity to take him."

"Take him?" Ani chuckled. "Well, that will be a new one for me."

"Yeah, we need him alive if possible. Jewell thinks he's got something big planned as retribution. We need to find out what was planned and allow her to plug any holes that son of a bitch has drilled into Guardian's computer systems."

A waiter approached but was waived off by Zane. The disgruntled look that was tossed his way made him chuckle. He'd tip the kid for using the back booth for his meeting.

"Not a lot to go on." Thanatos picked up a menu from the metal clip on top of the condiment holder.

"Agreed. But it is all we can do. This bastard is good. I have to be able to draw him out. If I have you two at my back, I'll let them take me to him."

"We have your back." Ani's statement was clipped. Zane glanced over at the man. "I owe you my life, so does he. We have your back."

Zane nodded. The intensity of Anubis' reply struck him. He'd wondered earlier if the man was a friend. There was no doubt in his mind now.

"Shit."

Zane's head snapped toward the door. A smirk spread across his face. Fury slipped into the booth next to Zane.

"So, these two are your backup plan." Fury grabbed Zane's water bottle, cracked the seal and downed half of it in one gulp.

"Yes." Zane's expression remained neutral. Joseph King could ruin everything.

Anubis leaned onto his forearms and stared at Fury. "I thought you were dead."

"I am." Fury's eyes bored into Anubis.

"Huh. Good to know my sources were correct." Ani smiled and had the balls to wink at one of the coldest killers ever to walk the earth.

"Don't fuck this up." Fury handed him his water bottle back and lifted out of the booth. The man walked out of the diner without a backward glance. Zane let out a breath. Fury wasn't going to report what he knew. He'd have his backup and work the plan to ensure Jewell was safe.

"Well, that went well." Thanatos chuckled and motioned the waiter over. He ordered enough for three people and then looked at Ani. The man shook his head and ordered a cheeseburger. Zane placed his order to go and waited for the angsty waiter to repeat the lengthy order before he left.

"So when do you start playing mouse to this fucker's cat?" Thanatos asked.

"Tonight." Jewell was going to have some choice words for his timing, but he'd try to mitigate any damage. Zane's mind wandered to the blue thong the woman was currently wearing. She'd been wanton with her teasing all morning. Hell, he'd sported wood all fucking morning, too.

Ani's eyes scanned the room. "Then let the games begin."

"Say what now?" Jewell's question shot back at him from where she sat behind her consoles.

"I have arranged for one of the offices on the lower levels to be converted into a bedroom for you. It is next to the gym, and I know you've showered there while I wasn't here. You'll be safe, and I won't need to worry about you while I'm taking care of business out there."

"Wow, I really thought you were different." Jewell closed her eyes and shook her head. Zane felt as if he had walked into a minefield. He was sure one wrong step here and that woman across the room would detonate. He'd seen it happen and he didn't want to be on the receiving end of it again.

"I'm going to be honest here and tell you I don't really understand that comment." Zane watched as she rubbed her forehead. Another sign of her frustration. Yeah, he'd stepped in it.

"*You* have decided for *me*, that it would be best if I stay here. Because if Vista is tracking *you*, you don't want to be distracted worrying about *me*." Jewell's finger pointed at herself and him with each emphasized word.

Zane nodded. He didn't want to piss her off even more.

"No. First, if Vista is tracking you, I am not on his radar. Second, we don't even know if he found the information that would lead him to you. Third, I thought you were different. Why would you unilaterally decide a course of action without consulting me? Didn't we have this huge blow up with my brothers about the exact thing? Damn it, when will people quit treating me like I can't make a fucking decision?"

"May I answer those questions or do you just want to rant?" Zane almost flinched at the glare she sent his way. The woman was shooting daggers that's for sure.

"Oh, by all means, explain those tactics. I dare you." She folded her arms across her chest and leaned back in her chair. The office door clicked open, and Alonzo walked in. He glanced up at Jewell and then over to Zane before he froze and bounced his eyes between them again. He swallowed hard, extended his arm and placed a piece of paper on Jewell's workstation. "I'll come back." He turned and left, shutting the door behind him.

"I'm waiting."

"First we don't know that Vista has found the information you left for him. No, you aren't a target, but if he doesn't find that information, everyone who works for Guardian, and I mean everyone, will have a target on their back. This guy is in pain. His stepbrother is dead. I'm sure he blames us; in his position, I would. So even though he doesn't know who you are, if you come into or leave this building you are a target. Period." Zane leaned forward and put his forearms on his knees. "Second, I didn't unilaterally decide to lock you in this facility. You've stayed here for days at a time without the benefit of a bed to sleep in. I need you here. If he takes me, my backup will get in contact with you, here. You need to be here to mobilize this place. I don't know what type of talent Vista was able to hire, and minutes will matter. We need to have you at the helm to make sure this guy doesn't pull a fast one and flit away after snuffing me out. I'm assuming you'd be able to track him if he gets on his computer again?"

Jewell's eyes narrowed, and she nodded, and he

continued, "Okay. I have a plan. One that will piss him off, but a mad hacker may make a mistake, right? Plus, if he thinks I'm the one who tracked him, he might not be as careful." Jewell nodded again. "Then please, be here, for me. Be ready. If you get that phone call, get your brothers on board and then you need to be here. I'll try to get him to come online."

"How?" Jewell's question told him he'd defused the bomb she was sitting on.

"Leave that to me."

"I don't like the sound of that." She uncrossed her arms and stared out the window of her office. Her people manned their stations in the theater setting. She shook her head. "I don't like the fact that you are out there and I'm in here."

"I know."

"I feel useless." She turned toward him. He saw the worry in her eyes and stood, heading over to her chair. He lowered until he was kneeling in front of her.

"You are the most precious thing in my life. I can't risk you walking out of this building when that bastard has the money and the means to hire goons to hurt the people who work here. You are the best there is. Get into that computer world of yours and find out who he hired and what he's planning on doing. I know if anyone can do it, you can."

"Promise me you'll be careful? If he is able to hurt you, I don't know what I would do." She placed her hand on his heart, and he covered it with his. He felt her love for him whether or not she could put that emotion into words.

"I have everything to live for. I love you, and I know you have feelings for me. I'm not going to let that guy take this away from us."

"When will this start?"

"Tonight."

Jewell pulled her bottom lip in and worried it. He put his thumb on her chin and pulled it out, leaning in to kiss the swollen flesh. "I haven't shown you the bedroom."

Jewell leaned her forehead against his. "Does the room have a lock?"

"As a matter of fact, it does."

Jewell pushed her chair away from him and stood. She glanced at the paper Alonzo had put on her desk and dropped it to the top of her workstation. "I'm through for the day. I think I need a nap if I'm working the night shift. I assume you'll be here during the day?"

Zane stood and nodded. "Good. You owe me one hell of an orgasm." She headed toward the door and glanced over her shoulder. "Are you coming?"

"Not yet, but I think it is inevitable." Zane adjusted his cock in his pants and buttoned his suit jacket to camouflage the tenting that he couldn't hide.

"Oh, not only is it inevitable, but it's guaranteed." Jewell winked and stepped out of her office.

The small office was at the end of the corridor past the temporary offices that lined the hall past the gym. They were used by returning teams, PSOs and new hires that had yet to be cleared at the higher levels. Zane put his finger on the pad, and the lock clicked open. He pushed the door open and held it, allowing Jewell to enter first. It was utilitarian at best, but it had a bed, her clothes from her locker in the gym and a small television. There were several bottles of water on the desk that had been pushed up against the wall along with a small coffee maker and a small box of coffee pods. That had to be Sonya's doing. Zane didn't think Jason would take the time for the creature comforts. Or maybe he would. He'd tended to believe the worst about her brothers based on the way she'd been worked when he was here previously. But he'd seen nothing but care and concern since he'd returned. Misguided, granted, but he'd have to give them all another chance.

Jewell shut the door and turned toward him. She dropped her purse onto the floor and started unbuttoning her shirt.

Zane caught her hands in his. "Oh, no. You don't get to tell me we aren't going to make love." The anger in her voice almost detracted from the fact that she'd said they'd be making love. He didn't think the words were misspoken. She always said what she meant, even if the timing was inappropriate.

"We will make love, but I have a present under these clothes. I get to unwrap it." He let her hands go and reached up to her hair, pulling the end of the tightly twisted bun out from where he'd watched her tuck it this morning. Her hair was so thick, and she'd wound it so tight that it was still damp when he unraveled it and let it fall past her shoulders. The faint smell of shampoo filled his senses.

He unbuttoned the tight cuffs of her long sleeve blouse. The tiny little buttons were a pain in the ass to unfasten, but he wasn't letting a bit of cloth and plastic deter him from his goal. His mind flashed to her gorgeous ass and that sky blue thong. He lowered to his knees and pulled the tail of her shirt out of her slacks. His hands traveled north under the material, sliding against her soft skin up to her ribcage. His thumbs caressed the bra that matched her thong and found her hardened nipples. He leaned forward and kissed her stomach through the material of her blouse. "I love you." He whispered the words. He did love her, but his words were said to the child he hoped and prayed she was carrying. It was selfish and insane, but the thought of a family was something he couldn't have dreamed of two years ago. Now, it was all he wanted.

Zane pulled his hands down her side and left the warm expanse of skin to reach up to unbutton her shirt. He kissed her where the material parted following the expanding opening of her shirt. He unhooked her slacks and unzipped them before he let them drop down her long, sexy legs to her feet. He removed her shoes and pulled the material away. He leaned back on his heels to admire the woman before him. Her hair floated over her shoulders, almost covering the blue lace of the bra she wore. Her breasts lifted in a rapid beat mirroring the pounding of the pulse in her neck.

He reached forward and placed his hands on her hips. They fit perfectly in the curve of her waist. He leaned forward and ran his tongue over the thin line of elastic lace that held the small triangle of blue material. Her hand cradled his head, and her fingers ran through his hair. He lowered and nuzzled the material out of his way. Both hands found purchase in his hair, and her fingers tightened when he spread her open so he could taste her.

He nudged her legs apart and brought her closer. His hands snaked through her legs, wrapping around them with his hands back on her hips. He was able to pull her closer to him and hold her there. He loved the taste of her, the way her thighs shook when he sucked her clit into his mouth and the jerk of her body when he released it. Her hands landed on his shoulders, and he felt her brace against them. He renewed his efforts, using the flat of his tongue to tease her before he sucked her clit into his mouth again. She hipped forward at the suction, and he tightened his hold and worked her until her fingernails dug into his shoulders through his shirt and jacket. He released her only to pull her back. He dropped one arm and used two fingers to enter her. His reward was a startled gasp. Her body stiffened. Every muscle contracted before she bucked against his face.

"Yes, God yes… Zane!" He continued to tease her sensitive skin until she drew away. He stood up while still holding her steady. Her bra and panties took seconds to remove before he laid her boneless body on the bed. Their eyes locked as he removed his clothes. The desire that filled her eyes made him feel bulletproof. His briefs dropped at the same time as she crooked her finger at him.

Zane crouched onto the bed and crawled up her body, stopping at her knees, hip, ribs, shoulder and neck to taste her. Her hands found purchase in his hair, and she pulled him up to her. The need of her kiss detonated inside him, sending shockwaves through his very soul. He centered himself between her legs. *Fuck! Condom!*

Zane pulled away from their kiss. Her arms clung to his neck preventing him from pulling away. "Babe, I need to get a condom." His pants were at the end of the bed. He had two in his wallet. She sighed but relaxed her grip. He found the condom and tore open the package. Jewell sat up and moved to the foot of the bed. She took the condom from him and rolled it down his cock. The sensation of her hands did little to alleviate the deep-seated need that thrummed through his body.

Jewell turned and positioned herself on her hands and knees. Sweet mother of god, he could not resist the invitation. He stepped forward bringing his shins up against the mattress. His hand shook as he extended it to caress the smooth round globes of her ass. She glanced over her shoulder at him. "I want you to take me, hard. I want to feel you inside me when you aren't here."

"I would never hurt you." Zane had hurt too many people in his life, he would never allow himself to bring the woman he loved harm.

"I know. But I love your cock deep inside of me. Take me. Make me yours." She dropped to her elbows and pushed back toward him. He grabbed her hips and found her core with the head of his cock. Jewell pushed back against him encasing the tip of his shaft in her tight heat. His eyes rolled back in his head, or maybe it just felt like it, because his brain definitely short-circuited. Zane's hips moved of their own accord. He couldn't stop.

Wouldn't stop. She met each thrust with her own, backing into him as he moved forward. Her staccato gasps filled the room. He reached under her with one hand and pulled her up onto her knees, bringing her back to his chest. His hand circled her neck possessively. Her hand covered his and held on. He snaked his other hand around her and split her sex. Her body shuddered against him when his fingers stroked her. He bent his knees and thrust deep inside her. Sex had never been like this before. Random fucks to get off couldn't compare to the need he had to protect and cherish this woman.

Zane lost the ability to assign meaning to his actions when Jewell lifted the hand he had around her neck and sucked two of his fingers into her mouth. The white-hot flash of desire that slammed into him lifted his balls tight against his body. He wasn't going to last, and he needed her to come before he did. His fingers added pressure to her clit with up and down strokes that coincided with the thrust of his hips. Jewell moaned around his fingers. Sensation took over, and Zane was consumed. He fought to keep them upright when his orgasm detonated like a five hundred pound bomb. The earth shook under his feet, his body fell forward, and it was a miracle that he braced himself when they both hit the mattress, or he would have suffocated Jewell. He continued to thrust through his orgasm. Her body bucked and tightened around his sensitive cock. Her muffled groan followed by huge gasps of air brought him back from one of the most fantastic orgasms of his life. Zane lunged up and over bringing him almost to the pillows. He pulled one of them down and flopped onto his back before he half pulled, half lifted Jewell up beside him. She tucked into his shoulder and brushed the hair out of her face. She draped her arm over his chest and patted him several times. "That was…"

"Epic?" He laughed at using her words from last night.

"Yeah, epic covers it." Her breathless chuckle fanned his sweat soaked skin. He covered her arm with is and rubbed his thumb over her soft skin.

"Zane?"

"Hmmm…"

"Tell me about you. I know you can't tell me much, but I don't know much about you and I… Well, you're important to me." She pulled away just a bit so she could look up at him. Well, he'd known this time would come. Hell, he'd practiced what he'd tell her, but that didn't make it any less complicated. He pulled the other pillow down and gave it to her and rolled to his side, so they faced each other.

He covered her hand with his and drew a deep breath. "I grew up in the midwest. Colorado. I was an only child. My mom died of cancer when I was twelve. My dad drank himself to death. He wasn't a bad man, he was just so incomplete without her that he was never the same after she passed. I was seventeen when he died. He loved her so much. Before he died, I'd talked him into signing my enlistment forms. We both knew I couldn't stay and he didn't want to live without her. I shipped off to Paris Island two weeks after he died."

Jewell turned her hand in his and squeezed it. He lifted their joined hand and kissed the back of hers. "I excelled at two things in the Marines, hand to hand combat and marksmanship. Following orders? Not so much." He laughed and shook his head, remembering the shit he got into because he thought he was all that. "But there was this Captain who was getting out. I respected the hell out of the man. He'd come out to my post and do post checks, and we started to talk. He was leaving the Corps to join Guardian. The guy sold me on the organization. I had six months left on my enlist-ment, so I figured why the fuck not. I mean, I wasn't going to make the Marines a career. I asked him if he thought they'd have any use for someone who's only skill was to fight and kill. He said he'd ask. He left shortly after that and I didn't hear a thing until three days before I was due to separate. A man showed up at the base and requested to speak to me. I was escorted to my CO's office, and I thought for sure I'd messed up royally. But the CO just left the office. The man was a recruiter for Guardian. He had my entire life in a file, down to the fights I got into at school. He told me he had a career path for me if I could pass the psych evals. I didn't even ask what it was. I just said yes." He was still grateful that Kannon hadn't forgotten him when he left the service and had mentioned his name to Guardian.

"They wanted you to be an assassin?"

Jewell's question brought him out of his memo-ries. He shook his head. "No, I was initially recruited to work with one of the teams assigned to overseas operations. After six months of train-ing, a different man pulled me from a team run and approached me. I knew this guy was someone important, and just looking at him I knew he was dangerous. He introduced himself as Demos and asked me if I'd rather work alone. To tell you the truth the man set every nerve I had on high alert. He was caged aggression and deadly.

"I asked him what he meant. He explained black door ops in very vague terms. Then he told me the training I'd done to this point with Guardian was toddler level compared to what they'd teach me."

"What did they teach you?"

She knew the answer, but she was asking him to admit it to her. He'd never told anyone about his life, and that is why he'd practiced what he'd say. When he started thinking about how to tell anyone about what he'd been, she'd hated him. He'd sit silently for hours watching her work while running scenarios through his mind, what he could say, what he couldn't. The thought that she'd be interested in him was a pipe dream, one he never believed he'd obtain. Yet, he found himself with her, naked not only physically, but emotionally. With Jewell's clearance level he could tell her intimate details of each assassination, but that isn't what she wanted. She wanted honesty and to have a piece of him he'd never given anyone. "They taught me how to kill.

Silently, alone and so no one could trace my actions."

Zane waited for any signs of judgment or revulsion, but none of those emotions crossed her face. She blinked at him and waited, so he continued. "I was damn good at it."

"What happened to make you leave?" Her hand squeezed his again. He rolled onto his back and gazed up at the ceiling. It had been a fucked up mission from the beginning. The man that had been targeted was the devil dressed in designer clothes. He'd been arrested fourteen times in three countries. Each time witnesses turned up dead or suddenly had amnesia. The evidence disappeared from secure holding areas, or charges were suddenly dropped. He was responsible for the deaths of thousands of people in the drug wars that ravaged the countries south of the United States. Zane's reconnaissance lasted for three months. During that time he witnessed the man rape, kill and then set fire to people. He couldn't get close enough to take him out. He'd seen the man walk up to a business associate and shove a gun in his mouth and blow the back of his head off. Again, he wasn't in a position to stop the insanity. All the while, the man's influence grew, and his organization continued to wreck lives and turn towns into graveyards. Then the bastard came to the United States, and Zane followed. He didn't have as many guards and had cleared the top floor of a plush New York hotel for his entourage. Zane saw the escorts arrive. He made the prostitute's bodyguard believe he was with the son of a bitch he'd been tracking. Getting up to the floor where the bastard lived was the hard part. Killing twelve of his men before he broke the bastard's neck was the fun part. And *that* was why he walked away. Of course, Guardian had recalled his ass. He didn't make them come looking for him. He drove down from New York and was in processing into the facility when Jacob got the intel on his assignment. The next eight months had been a necessary turning point in his life. He'd been debriefed, and he'd been confined while he'd gone through his evals. He knew the answers to give the docs, the ones that would override their concerns, but this time he didn't give them. This time he told them why he'd taken the bastard out where he did and how he did it. He was done. Unless someone was in danger, he refused to take any more life. He couldn't walk over that line again for fear that he'd never come back. They'd given him the eval twice, and he failed—twice.

He'd flown through the PSO training, but hadn't been called on to do more than babysitting spoiled rich kids. Then Jason King, the fucking Archangel himself, called him to his office and offered him an assignment. One he was told five others had failed to complete. His assignment's name was Jewell.

"Zane?" Jewell's fingers trailed over his jaw. He turned his head back to her. What had she asked? As if reading his mind, she repeated, "What happened to make you leave?"

He searched for a way to tell her, to explain the desperation he felt, the need to stop, the futility of taking out the minions of hell one by one, only to have legions take their place. "I couldn't do it anymore without losing me." He closed his eyes to prevent the emotion he was feeling from escaping in the form of a tear. Fuck, he'd never felt so raw, so exposed. But he'd opened himself to the woman he loved. Those simple words were the essence of his truth, the version he'd never told another.

Jewell lifted up onto her elbow and leaned over him. He slid his hand up her back and tangled his fingers in her fall of black hair. Her eyes held his and just before she lowered to kiss him she whispered, "I love the man you are. All of you, that man and this one."

He folded her into him. Their kiss wasn't one of demanding passion. It was soft, tender and truthful. It joined their souls, and he felt her words weave their way through his heart. The demons of his past had no place among them and by admitting his anguish and to a degree his weakness to her he'd exorcised them.

CHAPTER 23

Four days. Four fucking days that Zane had been trapesing from Guardian to work, to out of the way diners, restaurants, stopping to drop off laundry and then going back to his Guardian provided apartment. He was beginning to think that Jewell had buried the information too deep. He wondered if she should add more crumbs, he wouldn't question her on her decisions.

Zane used the stairs to get to his fifth-floor apartment. If someone was tracking him, he didn't want to seem too oblivious to his security, after all, he was supposed to be one of the best hackers in the world, and of course, he'd make sure he was safe. He'd varied his routes enough to make someone work to trail him. Not that anyone had. Ani and Thanatos had floated in and out of his daily treks. They'd never signaled that he had a tail, nor had he felt the presence of anyone watching him.

He glanced at the thread he'd trapped between the door jamb and the door before he left this morning. It was missing. Zane inserted the key into his deadbolt and unlocked it, then switched keys and unlocked the door itself. He put his keys in his pocket before he entered the apartment. Thanatos or Anubis could have entered the apartment. God knew none of them needed keys, but that was not in the plan unless something had gone wrong.

Zane closed the door and turned on the hall light. Thanatos stepped out of the shadows in the back of the room. "I must leave. My assignment has escalated. If I delay, more may die."

"Of course. Thank you for coming." Zane knew the longer Vista took in acting, the harder it would be for Thanatos and Anubis to remain.

"I have alerted Ani." Zane nodded his acknowledgment. "I will be back in three days' time if all goes well."

"Take care of yourself." Zane offered his hand, and the assassin took it. Zane watched the man leave and sat down in the semi-darkness of the living room. If Vista didn't make a move soon, he'd be forced to make a few more calls. He dropped his head back onto the chair and blew out a lungful of air. This playing bait shit sucked. He'd been trained to be on the offensive. If he had even the slightest glimmer of an idea of who this bastard was, he'd follow the fucker to the ends of the earth and make sure he never touched another keyboard.

His phone rang displaying the Guardian switchboard number. Zane swiped the face and answered. "Reynolds."

"Mr. Reynolds, this is Jewell. I've been monitoring that program you asked me to keep an eye on. It crashed about two minutes ago. All the divisions are screaming bloody murder."

"Thank you, Jewell, I'll be right in. Tell them to stop yelling at you."

"Do you think that will work?" The innocence in her voice was deceptive and made him smile.

"Doubtful, it never has worked for me." Zane ended the call and headed toward the office. Jewell had made contact or had found something that she needed him to see. It was their predetermined signal.

Jewell paced beside the dark web computer. The fucker. The son of a bitch. She glanced at the screen again. No. No this could not be happening. She sat down at the console and pulled the keyboard toward her and then stopped. No, she couldn't answer the fucker until Zane arrived. If he had eyes on Zane, then they would know he wasn't here yet. She and Zane had discussed this over and over again, but that bastard was... fuck! She threw the keyboard onto the ledge and pulled her legs up against her chest staring at the list of numbers. *"Fucking motherfucking son of a motherfucking bitch!"* Jewell's scream echoed around her filling her office with the frustration she felt.

"That was quite the rant." Jason's voice startled her. She spun around to find both him and Jacob standing at her door.

"Where's Zane?" He should have made it to the office before either of her brothers. His apartment was closer.

"Hasn't checked in yet. Maybe he ran into traffic." Jacob nodded toward the screen. "What is that?"

"That is a list of birthdates."

"Whose?" Jacob asked.

And wasn't that the question of the night? Jewell grit her teeth and answered, "Jason's, Yours, Jared's, Nicolas' and Zane's." She knew her brother's birthdates immediately but to identify Nicolas and Zane's she'd had to pull HR records. There were a couple others in the organization with the same birthdates, but it made sense the bastard was targeting the division chiefs.

"So he's keyed in on Zane?" Jason squatted down on his heels to look at the list of dates.

"Yeah. He had to have found the information I planted. He wouldn't know who he was out of the thousands of people we employ otherwise."

Her office door clicked, and all three heads spun around. Jared walked into the room. "Did you see Zane?" Jewell glanced down at the theater expecting to see him bounding up the stairs toward her office.

"No. What's going on?"

Jacob waved at the computer screen and brought Jared up to speed. Jared leaned over and then stood up again. "I may be asking a stupid question, but why is Zane's birthdate at the top?"

Jewell swung her head to the screen. All the other birthdates were in chronological order except Zane's. "Oh fuck. He's going after Zane first." The realization dawned just as Jewell's telephone rang. She grabbed at the receiver. "Zane?"

"They have him. I will follow and watch. I cannot engage." She didn't recognize the voice, it wasn't the assassin that was in Zane's apartment.

"I understand. Call me with the address so I can mobilize our response?" Her hands shook as she held the phone.

"I will." The phone line went dead. Jewell held it to her ear for several long seconds before she replaced it in its cradle.

"What the ever loving fuck is going on?"

Jason's question startled her so badly she jumped. "That was the person who is shadowing Zane. He said that Zane had been taken. He will call with the address of where when he could."

"Who?"

"Who is he working with?"

"He working with someone?"

All three questions bombarded her at the same

time. She nodded. "I don't know who, but someone he trusted. One was watching me until I barricaded myself here and the other is shadowing Zane. He didn't tell me who and I don't know their names."

"Zane is an assassin. Where in the hell would he pull favors from?" Jason looked at Jacob when he asked the question.

"He isn't an assassin any longer." Jewell's mind raced. He'd left that life before he lost himself. But he walked right back into the fire to protect her.

"Right." The contempt in Jacob's voice brought Jewell's head up and her anger back in full force.

"Don't you dare start talking shit about the man who is out there in danger because he wants me and this fucking organization to be safe. Say one more word Jacob, and I swear I will..." Jewell grabbed her hair and stamped her foot. "I'll fucking tell Jade to kick your ass!"

Jacob blinked at her tirade. "Contrary to popular belief, I am not afraid of Jade." He closed the distance between them and put his hand under Jewell's chin. "You really do care for this guy don't you?"

Jewell twisted away from her brother and faced the dark web computer. "I don't care for him." She turned and faced her family. "I love him."

Jared stuck his hand out toward Jacob. "Pay up, asshole."

Jacob hit Jared's hand. "I'd rather owe you the money than cheat you out of it. Now, how about we get our response teams together and find this motherfucking thorn in our side?"

"I want the same teams and investigators you used when we took down the Bratva if they are in town. I want the evidence, and I want the man. Alive if possible."

Jacob glanced at Jewell before he spoke. "If Zane is involved, alive might not be an option."

"He won't kill him unless someone else is in danger." Jewell automatically responded.

"You don't know that. His training would indicate otherwise." Jacob's voice sounded guarded.

"His training isn't who he is." She was sure of that fact. Zane was a decent human being, and her lover. She wouldn't believe otherwise.

"Get those teams alerted." Jason nodded toward the door.

Jewell watched them walk out. Jason's hand landed on her shoulder. "I chose Zane for this assignment because I believed he would die before he let anyone hurt you. I'm praying that doesn't happen."

"Me too."

"He will be a hard man to love." Jason pulled her in for a hug.

"No. He's easy to love, Jace." She leaned into him and let his warmth wrap around her.

CHAPTER 24

Unfortunately, the pain that threatened to split his skull in half wasn't unfamiliar. He'd been knocked unconscious before. What sucked was this time he allowed the buffoon to do it. Hell, he'd encouraged it. The man that followed him from his building to his car wasn't a professional. Zane had spotted him the instant he cleared the building's foyer. He played dumb and even dropped his keys by his car so the bastard could club him over the head.

He took stock of his injuries without moving. He knew better than to alert his captors that he was awake. He remained slumped forward allowing his body weight to pull against the rope that bound him to what felt like a wooden chair. Jesus, these guys were rank amateurs. One good slam against the wall and the flimsy chair he was tied to was kindling wood.

He could hear some mouth breather over in the corner. It was probably the goon that had been hired to bring him here. The room couldn't be that large. The first smart thing the bastard had done right and Zane would lay odds the dumbshit didn't know keeping him in a confined space would limit Zane's options. Not that it would matter. He could still kill the man in ten different ways. Not that it mattered, he only needed one.

Still, his head hurt like a motherfucker. Hopefully, the thug hadn't cracked his skull. Zane regulated his breathing and listened. There was a television playing in the corner of the room. It was almost muted. He couldn't understand the words, but the canned laugh track that punctuated the droning voices told him whoever was in the corner had shitty taste in programming.

Zane listened as a page crinkled when his guard turned a page of the newspaper he was reading. If Mr. Muscles was reading and distracted by the television, he wasn't watching his victim with any regularity. With that thought in mind, Zane opened his eyes slightly. The concrete floor under his chair had dark splatter stains on the portion he could see without moving. A dank smell permeated his senses. He was in a basement. The television was behind him and to his left. He glanced that way. *Well, fuck, that was not good.* In the corner, he could see the base of a large metal drum. There were twenty-pound bags of lye stacked next to it. Two that he could see. Somebody had a basic idea how to dispose of a body, and that meant someone other than the douchebag in the corner was involved.

He heard a door slam and then the echo of footsteps, but they moved away from the room he was being held. Mr. Muscles tensed when the door slammed. As the sound of the steps diminished, he sighed loudly and moved in his seat. He'd take the bored motherfucker out of his own misery in an instant if he could confirm Vista's identity and location.

Zane slowly pushed his weight forward and the ropes that bound him moved with him, loosening under the strain. He could probably work his way out of the binds without breaking the chair if his hands weren't zipped tied. He'd have to get his hands in front of him and stand to be able to slam his hands from above his head down to his abs pulling apart his arms to break the binds. Using the plastic restraints on anyone with even rudimentary training was a mistake.

The minutes ticked by. While he waited, Zane ran through the steps he'd take to kill the fucker reading the paper. One: Stand. Two: Swing the chair into the concrete block wall. Three: Lunge into Mr. Muscles and incapacitate him. Four: Slip his arms around his legs and stand. Five: Snap the zip ties and Six: Break Mr. Muscles' neck. Step six was thrown in just for the hell of it. The reality of his past meant that he would probably never run a tactical scenario where the final result wasn't death. Acting on that last step was the key to staying on this side of the black door. For Jewell, he'd let the man live. At least the mental exercise cleared away the lingering fog of unconsciousness, but it did little to alleviate the pain radiating through his head.

Even with a plan to escape in place, Zane sat still and waited. There was little he could do without knowing Vista's location. That fucker was his only concern; everything else was collateral noise. If he had to remain in this position all night, he would. The goon in the corner shifted, and the volume of the television rose to the point he could hear the sitcom. The noise almost obliterated the sound of a door opening and someone coming down the hall. No, there were two people. One heavy on his feet, the other... With him bound, even as poorly as he was, two could mean trouble. The steps stopped outside the door. He heard the sound of a key engage and then turn in a lock. Mr. Muscles stood and shuffled over to the door.

"Good, I got to fucking piss, and I'm..." The buffoon didn't have a chance to finish the statement. Zane heard the sound of a suppressed bullet hit flesh and then bodily fluid and brain matter splatter on the concrete wall behind him. A professional. Now shit was getting interesting.

"Why did you kill him?" Zane recognized a northeastern accent and a younger voice, not baritone, more tenor and it was shaking with emotion.

"He was dead the moment he agreed to be involved in this piss-poor plan. You hired me for a reason. I don't use rented meat to do my dirty work. What the fuck were you doing kidnapping this guy? You want him dead, I'll kill him. I won't let a brainless goon bring the cops to my door. You brought him to *my* safe house. I should fucking kill you, too." Zane noted the characteristics of the man talking. *No accent. Clear and brisk voice.* He heard the soft pad of footsteps and saw the black leather of expensive Italian shoes. Right, an assassin with dress sense. Just his fucking luck.

"He isn't awake yet. Do you think he is in a coma?"

"Shut up." The man's shoes were now next to the leg of Zane's chair.

"I know you're awake." The man planted the muzzle of his suppresser under Zane's chin and lifted his head. Zane blinked acting dazed. He crossed his eyes and blinked again before he rolled his eyes back into his head and let it fall off the barrel of the suppressor. He didn't look directly at either of the men, not wanting to let them know he was cognizant.

"Shit, his fucking brain is scrambled." North-east US said again.

"What information does he have that you needed him alive?" No accent asked.

"I don't want any questions answered. I want him awake so I can tell him how badly I'm going to fuck up his organization now that he isn't there to stop me."

"You have got to be fucking kidding me." No accent turned toward Northeast US. Zane could see his shoes move from between his eyelashes.

"What?"

"Do you think this is some sort of made for television event? You're paying me five million dollars to kill five men starting with this one, and you have nearly fucked everything up so you can get off by jacking your shit all over him? What the fuck kindergarten bullshit have I gotten myself into?"

"*He* is the bane of my existence. *He* is the one who is in charge of the intelligence gathering and computer security section. *He* is the reason I had to blow up *my* fucking safe house and the reason my brother had to die. I had to throw *him* off my tracks. I want him to know I have plans for his damn organization and those fucking bastards. I want them to hurt just as bad as I am hurting. They don't get to sit out there under his protective umbrella any longer. They are going to lose one of their own. They have no idea that I've already set the plan into motion. She'll be dead or wish she was by this time tomorrow."

Zane lifted his head, drawing both of their attention. There was no way the motherfucker was taking Jewell out. He'd kill the son of a bitch with his bare hands before that would happen. His eyes raked over the assassin that stood before him. "You're right. You don't know what you've gotten yourself into."

Northeast US snarled and lunged at him. No Accent caught him by the back of his hoodie and pulled him away. Northeast US was definitely Carter Lufkey. Older, pudgier, and greasier than his DMV picture, but him nonetheless. "Shut up! I won! I will destroy you, and there is nothing you can do about it." Lufkey spit at Zane, leaving a trail of saliva running down the side of his face.

Zane kept his eyes on the assassin and spoke clearly. "Fury, Anubis, Thanatos, Demos, Moriah, Lycos, Asp."

"What the fuck is he saying?" Carter screamed at No Accent.

"Shut up!" The hitman crossed over in front of Zane. Zane tracked him while keeping Lufkey in his peripheral vision. The hitman kept his weapon trained on Zane. The gun did not waiver. No Accent used his free hand to rub the back of his neck. They exchanged stares. Zane knew what his words were doing to the man in front of him.

No Accent suddenly moved and crossed the room to push Carter against the wall. "Why the fuck didn't you tell me?"

"Tell you what? I gave you the details. Five men, one at a time. I'll give you the other four's locations, and you take them out. You've never had a problem with the arrangement before."

"You are a complete idiot. If I didn't need this fucking money, I'd be out of here. That guy," He pointed toward Zane with his suppressed automatic, "Is spouting off names of assassins. Not hitmen like me, but the big boy assassins. You can't work in this business and not hear of them. If he knows about them, they may know about him, so you need to get the fuck out of here. I'll dispose of this guy and meet you at your place in Massachusetts. Wait for me there. If I have to hunt you down, I'm going to kill you just for the fun of it."

Carter Lufkey blanched, his pale face contorted with a mix of rage and crazy that left little doubt he'd carry through with his threat against Jewell. The bastard bolted out of the room like the hounds of hell were snapping at his balls.

Zane bunched his muscles to move, but the

hitman leveled his gun at Zane's temple. "Who are you? You aren't some computer geek, are you?"

Zane drew a breath and let it out slowly before he answered. "I have many names." Zane allowed the darkness he pushed down to come out to play. He rolled his eyes toward the hitman and presented him an evil grin. "If I tell you, I'll have to kill you."

"You are bound to a chair with a suppressed .45 at your temple, excuse me if I'm not afraid. What. Is. Your. Name?" The killer shoved the suppressor into Zane's skull, tearing the skin. Zane smiled and pushed his head into the weapon. The act shocked the fucker, and that told Zane the hired killer was weak. Coating his voice in an icy hate, Zane asked, "What makes you think you can kill me?"

"I know I can. You're going to die, like all the other men I've killed. One bullet through the brain. No one survives. Tell me your name."

Zane whispered his code name. The fucking idiot leaned in to hear it. It wasn't his first mistake, but it was his last. Zane pulled back, and head butted the fucker. His world spun from the pain, but he sprung to his feet, hitting the man's shoulder with his. Zane twisted violently, swinging the chair tied to his back into the hitman. The hitman slammed into the wall and grunted. Zane kept his momentum going forward. He pitched his body forward and followed the man toward the wall. Before he slammed into the cement, Zane twisted and crashed into the block wall. Sharp cracks of sound from the wooden chair splintering filled the small room. Zane felt the bindings loosen and shrugged violently. The ropes fell around his legs just as the killer lunged forward in a flying tackle toward Zane's knees. The impact dropped them both. They immediately rolled, each trying to gain the advantage. The hitman scurried to his knees searching for... The matte black of the weapon lay next to the barrel. It was to Zane's left. With his hands behind his back and sprawled out on the ground there was no way to snap the zip ties, so he improvised. Zane brought his knee up and struck out as the man leaped toward the weapon. His aim meant for the man's chest landed against the man's groin. The fucker collapsed next to him. Zane tucked into a ball, brought his arms around his legs and lurched to his feet. In one practiced motion, he lifted his arms above his head and then brought all his weight and strength down, pulling out as he did to break the plastic at his wrists. He stepped forward. A sharp tug on his shoulder blazed a trail of red hot pain through the haze of his adrenaline-soaked mind. Zane twisted and lunged backward. He felt his cheek explode with a lightening bolt of searing heat. His back hit low on the cement block wall. He flipped up, off balance. The assassin rolled on the ground and took aim. Zane kicked the fucker with all his strength, hoping to shatter ribs and puncture a lung. He dropped on top of the man and grappled for the gun. Zane's hand found the man's chin, and instinctively he pushed it up at the same time as his forearm deflected the weapon from its point blank aim. Three splats of gunfire chipped the cement block in front of Zane's face. He pushed his knee over the man's hand and weapon. With the weapon neutralized he cranked the bastard's head, severing his spinal cord.

"Freeze!"

Zane sat straddling the dead man. He leaned back and lifted his arms. He looked at the shoulder of his left arm. The darkness and quantity of blood soaking his shirt meant the fucker hadn't hit an artery. The Guardian team that entered the room wore helmet cams. From the months that he shadowed Jewell, he knew that she and her brothers were watching.

"Vista was here. He said he had plans in motion to take her out. She stays in that fucking building until we find the bastard."

Zane grabbed the hitman's weapon and checked the magazine. Three bullets left. He'd have two spares. He looked at the team lead and demanded, "Where the fuck are we?"

"Apartment building in Arlington."

"Is the perimeter secure?"

"Yes."

"Then the motherfucker is still in the building." They moved toward the door. Zane froze as the power died and the fire alarm blared. It was pitch black in the basement. The team lead pulled his night vision goggles off and yelled over the klaxon, "Archangel said to give you these."

Zane put them on and started out of the room again adjusting to the amplified ambient light. "Sir, the power for the entire grid is down. The teams outside are reporting the residents are exiting the building. They no longer have a cordon."

He grabbed the man's helmet cam and looked into the lens. "The hitman told him to go to his place in Massachusetts. Follow the vehicles from the building on the traffic cams. He's pissed and running, he might not think to deviate. Find that fucker."

Another team member handed Zane his com unit. He tucked the thing into his ear and dropped the receiver/transmitter into his pocket. "We have fifteen cars that have left the parking lot. Seven are heading north."

Jewell's voice set him in motion. "I need a fucking vehicle." He looked at the team leader.

"Sir!" A set of keys flew toward him from the other direction. He caught them in midair.

"Black Humvee outside to your left. Emergency weapons are in the tack box in the back. Keys are on the ring."

Zane called over his shoulder as he bolted out of the room, "Clear this building and make sure that fucker isn't laying low."

"Yes, sir!" The reply echoed off the walls of the hallway as he pounded down the dark corridor.

Zane reached the ground level and found the door to head out of the building. He threw the NVGs off as he burst out of the building. "Talk to me!"

"Head north. Get to the 495, if he is heading north he'll take 495 to 95." That was Jared's voice.

"We have the airports and bus stations covered.

Still tracking the vehicles. Three are still heading north. A blue Camaro, Grey SUV and white sedan." Jared answered his questions before he could ask them.

Jewell's voice came over the comms, "I have visual confirmation from traffic cams. Lufkey is in the SUV. He just got on the 495. Alerting local law enforcement."

"I'm three minutes behind him." Zane floored the tactical vehicle and ran a red light. He rammed the bumper of a small green car, sending the vehicle careening toward the side of the road and into another vehicle.

"They'll need an ambulance." Jared's voice floated past him. The accident was unfortunate, but Zane couldn't let that fucker get away. He raced past the vehicle in line to access the on-ramp and plowed his way between the on-ramp's cement embankment and the cars heading onto the interstate. He saw blue strobing lights behind him. "Tell those fuckers I'm not stopping."

"Local Law Enforcement has been apprised." Jared's calm voice came across again. Zane floored the vehicle and veered in and out of traffic. "On the 495. Where the fuck is he?"

"Five miles ahead of you in the passing lane.

LEOs are blocking his upcoming exits. That will clog the interstate and his escape route."

Zane veered over to the shoulder of the road and willed the Humvee to go faster. Pieces of tire treads, hubcaps, and assorted vehicle parts flew out from under his vehicle. He could see brake lights ahead in all lanes. He barreled down the shoulder of the road. "Is this lane clear? He was traveling at damn near one hundred miles an hour, if he hit anyone stalled on the road the chase would be over.

"You have a broken down vehicle three miles ahead." Zane immediately let off the gas and hit the brake. He needed the time to come to a stop without killing anyone. "Where the fuck is he?"

"Once you stop he will be a half mile up. Middle lane. He's still in the car." Zane skidded to a stop about ten feet from a minivan full of children. The woman who was attempting to change the tire looked up at him and then blanched. Zane didn't have time to explain the blood or the gun. He vaulted over her and ran like a madman down the shoulder of the road.

"Talk to me!" Zane slid over the hood of a vehicle and landed in the space between the far lane and the middle lane. The owner of the vehicle blew his horn and screamed at Zane. Zane popped up and started pounding pavement, his stride eating the space between him and Lufkey. His single-minded attention on reaching that bastard.

"Quarter mile. Wait, he's out of the car, and he's running. Get over a lane, and you'll see him."

Zane zagged between a semi truck and a bread truck and had eyes on the bastard. He wanted that fucker alive and shooting him now wasn't even on his mind. He was gaining on the out of shape punk. Lufkey darted looks over his shoulder as he tried to outrun Zane.

A flash of headlights in a side view mirror caught his attention. That was all Zane saw before the driver of a Mercedes opened the door to the luxury sedan. Carter picked that moment to look back at Zane. The kid didn't see the door open and ran full speed into it. The vehicle's door and the man collided springing forward and snapping back, landing Lufkey on his back in the road. Zane was close enough to see the fall and the blood that sprayed the side of the white truck beside the Mercedes. *No, no, no!* He slid to a stop beside Carter and dropped his weapon.

"I'm so sorry! I didn't... Oh my God! Is he dead? He has a gun!" The shrill wail of the woman's voice wasn't his concern. Lufkey was bleeding out. The corner of the top metal portion of the door over the driver's side window had torn Lufkey's carotid. Zane clamped his hand over the spurting bleed in a fruitless attempt to keep the fucker alive.

"Tell me where your computer is," Zane leaned down, moving his slick hand to try to stem the worst of the blood loss.

Lufkey grabbed Zane's hand. He pulled it away and whispered, "Fuck you." Zane reapplied pressure, but the man's eyes fixed and dilated on Zane. Lufkey's breathing stopped before the man's last exhale echoed through the turmoil on the 495. Zane sat back on his knees and took in the chaos surrounding him. People were running toward them. He reached back and picked up his weapon before he stood. The crowd that gathered parted. Zane walked between two vehicles and headed back to his.

"He died. I couldn't save him."

"We watched it happen." Traffic cams, of course. Zane nodded although Jared couldn't have known he acknowledged it.

"Jewell is working a way to track Vista's computer. Turn around and walk off the ramp about eight hundred feet ahead. LEOs will give you a ride to the hospital. We'll have one of our docs on standby." Jared's voice once again directing him.

"I'm not going to a hospital." Zane stopped and looked across the median at the vehicles driving the other direction.

"You are." That was Jewell's voice.

"I'm fine." Zane wanted to puke. The pain in his head had buried itself behind his eyes. Without the adrenaline packed chase, he was starting to feel the damage inflicted on his body.

"You've been shot."

He glanced down at his arm. He'd lost some blood. Either the bullet was still lodged in his bicep, or it was a graze. He didn't care to take off his shirt to find out. He took a deep breath to try to quell the nausea hitting him like a brick wall. "Been shot before."

Jewell hummed a noncommittal response. She changed the topic, and for that he was glad. "They ID'd the man Carter hired to kill you. We have an address. LEOs are there now, and some of Jared's people are en route. He has a computer. It is being brought in."

"Jewell, I didn't kill Lufkey. The hitman tried to

kill me. It was him or me." Zane turned and started walking toward the off ramp.

"I know. You aren't the man you used to be." Her voice was soft and reassuring. He saw the flash of blue strobe lights to his right at the apex of the exit Jared had directed him toward. He turned and walked that direction. Running tonight's events through his mind, he wasn't convinced.

CHAPTER 25

Jewell glanced out into her work center
again. She was waiting. Again. Waiting for
the computer, waiting for Zane, and waiting
for her brothers. Her phone rang at her console,
and she picked up the receiver.

"They didn't check the younger man's vehicle."
It was the same voice that had alerted her that
Zane had been taken and then again told her
where he was being held.

"What do you mean?" Jewell looked at the
license plate of the car Lufkey had driven. It was
registered to a Franklin Callaway. There was no
record of the man in any of the databases they'd
checked. It had to be Lufkey's car.

"Apartment building parking lot. 1975 Orange piece of shit Vega. I'll watch it until you show up."

"We're on it." Jewell was typing as she spoke, sending the information to Jared and a request to have the car impounded and any computer components brought to her immediately.

She hit send and listened carefully. She could hear traffic in the background, so she knew the man hadn't hung up. "Is he well?"

"Zane?"

"That is who you know him as."

"He was shot. He was still able to chase down the man we were after."

"You have closure then?"

"No. The perp died in a freak accident. We need his computer to find closure." Jewell didn't know why she told the man the truth, but he'd helped them, and Zane trusted him.

"I will stay until people come for the car. Treat him well. He is one of very few people in my world that I care about."

"I love him." Jewell felt the need to reassure the man.

"I know he loves you. He is one of the lucky ones."

"How so?"

"He still feels." The line went dead.

"Hey, who told you about the second vehicle?" Jared's head was buried in a folder as he opened her door and strode in.

Jewell blinked, clearing her mind and trying to process Jared's question. "What?" She didn't hear half of what he'd said.

"Who told you about the second vehicle?" A flurry of movement at the bottom of the theater caught both of their attention. Jason and Jacob bounded up the stairs.

"Jewell, how did you find out about another vehicle?" Jacob asked as he followed Jason through the open doorway.

"The person who was working with Zane. He called and told me that the men on scene had failed to secure the vehicle Carter arrived in."

"Fuck, we ran the plates of all the vehicles in the parking lot, right?" Jason asked as he flopped down in Zane's chair.

"Yes, we did, and we are in the process of cross-referencing them with the occupants of the building, but it wasn't a high priority. I think we all were focusing on the incoming computer. We would have figured it out, but it could have taken us hours." Jewell admitted the oversight. Her people were good, but there was only so much they could do in the time they'd been given.

"I'm not pointing fingers, just making sure we were working it." Jason leaned back in the chair. "I'll be glad when this nightmare is over."

A silent agreement covered the office. The memories of the events the Bratva and Vista had brought upon Guardian, and its members, rolled through Jewell's mind. She needed to find his computer and then she needed to get into his computer. If the bastard hadn't booby-trapped his system, she should be able to find a way in. Jewell leaned forward, suddenly exhausted. She'd been through an emotional wringer tonight. Her nerves were shot, and she needed... hell, she needed Zane.

"He is in-processing downstairs. He'll be here in a minute." Jacob spoke up breaking the heavy silence. Jewell turned her head and blinked at him. Had she said that out loud?

Jacob crossed in front of her and sat down on her workstation desktop. "I figured you were worried." Jewell nodded. She couldn't let her brothers see it, but she'd been terrified. The second they saw Zane on top of the dead man she'd been able to breathe. And then she couldn't. The blood that stained his shirt from both his arm and the blood that ran from the gash in his cheek were vivid on the video feed from the team's helmet cam. Bracing herself for him to be hurt and seeing it was two different things.

"We will need to debrief him, but after that, we'll give you two a little time alone," Jason added.

"Do we have an ETA on the computer?" Jewell asked because if she acknowledged the kindness of her brothers, she'd probably cry and *that* would piss her off and then she'd cry harder. She glanced down at the entranceway willing Zane to walk through it.

Jared looked at his watch. "Probably another thirty minutes out, and our guys should be at the car in about five minutes, give or take for traffic."

Jewell nodded. "He'll watch it until they get there."

"Did he say that?" Jacob picked up one of her pencils and frowned at the lack of eraser. He bounced his index finger against the mangled metal band. "You really need to start chewing gum or something." He turned and tossed the pencil into the wastebasket and raised his hands in victory when he sunk the shot.

"Five bucks says you can't make that again." Jared dared his brother.

"Oh, shit." Jason and Jewell said the words at the same time.

"Jinx! You owe me a coke!" Jewell laughed and pointed at Jason.

"Oh I see how it is, I get shot while the bosses play games." Zane stood at the door, and Jewell launched toward him. His 'oof' when she collided with him was followed by a strong one armed hug. The tears that she'd pushed away cascaded down her face. She buried her head into his chest. "Shhh… I'm fine. I love you." His whispered words were only for her.

Jewell squeezed him tighter and echoed his words against his chest.

One of her brothers cleared his throat. Jewell snuck her hand up between Zane's chest and her face and wiped at her tears. He held her until she took a step back and nodded her head. She glanced at his cheek and winced. "Holy shit is that a burn from a bullet!"

Zane lifted his right hand in a placating manner. "I'm fine."

"You're fine? You're *fine*?" Jewell could hear the hysteria in her voice and stopped, snapping her mouth shut.

Zane advanced on her and put his hand around

her neck, tipping her head up. He stared at her hard and nodded. "I'm alive. I'm a stubborn bastard, and nobody was keeping me from coming back to you."

"Not even his doctor." A tall blond man with blue eyes stood behind Zane. Jewell hadn't even seen the man come into the office.

"Is he your doctor? Why do you need a doctor?"

"He doesn't. That hard headed man has a concussion, a bullet hole and a bunch of other boo-boos, but he knows the drill. I, on the other hand, was called here."

Jason stood and extended his hand to the doctor. "Maliki. Thanks for coming in. If you can give us about a half hour, I'll meet with you in my office, and we can talk."

"No problem. I only followed him up here to make sure he didn't pass out halfway up the stairs." Maliki turned on his heel and left the office. That was when Jewell noticed the light flashing in the theater and an escort waiting for the doctor. Her people were hanging out in the break room until the visitor left. All monitors and screens had been blacked out. The fact that he wasn't cleared in her section spoke volumes.

"Zane, have a seat. We need to go over what

transpired tonight." Jared motioned toward his chair. Jewell watched carefully as Zane lowered slowly into the chair. He didn't flinch or grimace, but she could tell by the way he held his body he was sore.

"Start from the beginning." Jared leaned back against the wall and got comfortable.

"Jewell called me in, which meant something had happened?" He glanced over to her to fill in the blanks.

"Yeah, he popped up in the chat room." She nodded toward the screen.

"With what?"

"Birthdates. Yours, Jared's, Jacob's Nicolas' and Jason's." Zane squinted at her as if he was trying to decode the words.

Finally, he nodded and turned back to Jared. "As soon as I left the apartment building I knew the buffoon that the hitman took out was following me. I had to drop my keys to give him enough time to knock me the fuck out."

"Who was following you and reporting in to us?" Jacob's question was a logical one. Jewell knew Zane wasn't going to answer it the way her brother would like.

"A friend."

"Care to elaborate?" Jason asked.

Zane turned to him and stared at him for several seconds before he replied, "No."

Jared broke the silence with his next question. "What happened at the apartment building?"

"When I came around I was bound to a chair in that room. My arms were zip tied behind my back. The dick who crowned me was locked in the room with me. The man I killed took the hired muscle out within five seconds of opening the door. From what I could understand, Lufkey had hired the goon to kidnap me and the hitman didn't like anyone knowing where he was based or what he looked like."

"Common trend among hitmen, I hear." Jacob quipped.

"Probably," Zane admitted. "I acted like the fucker had clocked me harder than he did and I listened. Lufkey was off the deep end. He blamed me, or who he thought I was, for his brother's death."

"Fire inspector's report came in. The explosion was a result of a space heater and a damaged gas line. It had nothing to do with us. Although he also stated that there was no reason for the space heater to be plugged in and running. Personally, I believe Lufkey killed his brother and tried to solace his conscience with blaming us." Jewell listened to Jared's thoughts. She agreed with him. She'd read the report yesterday and had drawn the same conclusion.

"He admitted as much. Assuming I was Jewell, he said it was my fault he had to kill his brother. It takes all kinds of crazy. Anyway, he said they didn't get to sit under the protective umbrella I'd erected any longer. That he'd already set plans in motion to ensure you paid. He said you'd lose one of your own and that by this time tomorrow she'd be dead."

Jewell and her brothers exchanged dire glances before Jason asked, "Did he say Jewell's name?"

"No. He said she. No names."

"Fuck." Jason ran his hands over his face. "Jared, get ahold of Jasmine and Chad, make sure they are watching their six. Explain the threat. Jacob, call Chief and the Wonder Twins. I want mom and Frank protected at all times. Have them tell Joseph what is going on so he can ensure Ember is safe. Hell, tell Chief to keep Taty close. He probably knows about her by now. Adam and Keelee should be safe, but make sure they get the word, too. I know Tori and Faith have teams on them, but I want the team leaders notified to be hypervigilant. I'll call Gabriel and get word to him. Anna has been driving all over the city with Christian working issues for the shelter. She has an armed escort at all times, but they need to know."

"What about Jade?" Jewell interjected.

"She's undercover with the DEA. Do you think he'd be able to find any information about her?"

Jewell bit her bottom lip and worried it for a bit. Her mind processed all the variables, and none of it came out in a tidy bow. It was a ball of string with five ends. "I don't know. The birthdates he sent were all division chiefs. Why would he move from a major player to someone in our family? I don't know how he could extrapolate a bridge between the identified people and Jade. The Bratva was directing him when he went after Faith and Anna. Jasmine was also Bratva directed. I guess the question would be was he actually the one responsible for sending the Bratva after our families? If he was then it makes sense he'd look, if not and the Bratva was directing the attacks. I just don't know."

The silence of the room punctuated the end of her thoughts. There was no right answer, and everyone knew it. The bastard could have targeted any one of the women close to the leaders of this organization. Hell, for all Jewell knew Vista could have targeted any one of the women working for Guardian. It was like putting all your fingers in the holes in the dike and still needing your toes to keep the flood from coming.

"Zane, are you okay? Do I need to put people on you two tonight?" Jared asked, following his own train of thought.

Zane glanced over at Jewell and slowly shook his head. "We aren't going anywhere tonight. She'll have the computer to work on. I'm not making her leave. I'll stay too."

"There is the office we converted for her if you need to rest." Jared's suggestion earned him a glare from Zane that Jewell was certain could peel paint off the wall.

"Yeah, if looks could kill, my brother. Don't worry, Zane, I'll get a cot or bedroll brought up here. You'll need to crash sooner or later." Jacob spoke as he was heading toward the door.

"Thanks, I probably will." Zane acknowledging his weakness to her brothers meant he was hurting more than he told her when he'd come into the office.

"What are you going to do about Jade?" Jewell asked Jason as he stood.

"I'm going to call the DEA. She's deep undercover. If they yank her, it will negate over a year's worth of work. I don't have the authority to bring her home." He put his hands in his pockets and rocked back on his heels before he continued, "If I could I would."

"You know she can take care of herself." Jared put his hand on his brother's shoulder. "You can't control everything."

"No, but I can sure as hell try." Jason lifted a hand and headed out the door.

"I'm going to head back with him. We need to make sure everyone is safe, and then we need to talk with Maliki."

"Who is he?" Jewell asked taking a mental note to run his background.

"Dr. Maliki Blue. He's one unlucky man. He was in the wrong place at the wrong time and has had a rough road. I think he's worth trying to save." Jared glanced over at Zane. A smirk spread across his face. "I'm pretty happy with our salvage program." Jared used air quotes around the word salvage.

Zane chuckled. "Yeah, I'd say fuck you, but you're my boss."

"Eh... I'll give you that one. Besides, between the two of us," Jared moved his fingers between himself and Zane, "we both know *she's* the boss in this situation."

Zane laughed softly and leaned back in his chair, closing his eyes. "I'm in good hands then."

Jared turned to her and winked before he headed to the door. "Yep, pretty damn happy with the salvage program around here." He laughed to himself as the door shut.

Jewell made her way over to Zane and kneeled down beside his chair. Her hand settled on his thigh. The sensation of her warm palm resting on his leg sprung Zane's eyes open. He shifted in the chair without wincing too badly and dropped his chin to see her. "Are you really all right?" Her voice cracked slightly.

"Yeah, I'm okay. God knows I've been hurt worse." He gave a humorless chuckle and added, "Much worse."

Jewell laid her head on his thigh. She closed her eyes, preventing a tear from falling. Zane placed his hand gently on her head and stroked her soft hair. "I was so scared. I could see the blood from the video feed. And then you drove like a man possessed. I don't think I took a breath from the time your man called until... until you walked through that door."

"I was going to call from the hospital, but I'm guessing my cell phone is somewhere at the apartment building where I was being held."

Jewell nodded against his leg. "A vacant apartment's storage unit."

"Ani had my back."

"Ani is the guy working with you. He's an assassin, isn't he?" Jewell turned to look up at him.

"Yeah."

"He called three times. When you were taken. Then again with where you were being held, he knew it was the basement, but he didn't know exactly where in the basement, that is why it took so long to get to you. They cleared the units as they went until they got to you. Jared and Jacob said that was standard procedure."

"It is." Zane lifted his arm and repositioned his injured shoulder.

"I have to find out who he targeted," Jewell spoke more to herself than to Zane. If she concentrated on his threat, then she didn't have to remember the night's events, or how close she'd come to losing him.

"You will. You and your team are the best. You've beaten him at every turn. True, he got some digs in, but only because that fucker Kowalski gave him a way in." He frowned suddenly. "Wait. The pain pill I took is making me slow. You said Ani called you three times?"

"Yeah. Once when you were taken, once with your location, and once to tell us we didn't process Lufkey's vehicle. I'm assuming Lufkey took the hitman's car. Maybe it was closer to the building. Who knows why he drove the SUV away? We weren't looking for two vehicles, but we would have found it eventually."

"Was there anything in the car that he was trying to divert our attention from?"

"Don't know. My brothers showed up after that, and then you came in. I need to check, but I don't want to move." Zane's hand carded through her hair in a rhythmic pull. The warmth of her draped on his leg and the quiet hum of her systems wrapped around them. "I love you." Her words fell between them, soft and sure.

"I know you do, babe. I love you, too." Zane's voice softened.

"When did you know that you loved me?"

His hand paused its movement for a moment before it started again. "I guess fell in love with you in small steps. First, by watching you here interacting with your people and your family. I gave you a small piece of my heart each time I watched you put the mission before yourself. Every time you didn't eat or sleep because you were so damn focused on making Guardian's people and operations safe. A little more each time you suddenly didn't have any plans when one of your people needed to leave early or had a sick kid. I've watched you do too much with too little support and marveled at your drive and determination. When I figured out you hide your fear of being yourself behind your snark and sass, I knew I was in love. You are the most selfless person I've met. I love you for who you are."

Jewell's heart felt like it had swollen ten times its normal size. The irate red gash of a bullet burn over Zane's cheek, and the bruises that mottled the side his face with black, purple, green and yellow splotches couldn't hide the depth of emotion in his eyes. The gash where the man had hit him to knock him out wasn't as big as the furrow on his cheek, but the knot under it was the size of a golf ball. She reached up and traced his strong jaw with her finger. "And I love you for who you are, now, today. But I also understand that who you used to be will always be a part of you. I love that man just as much as I love the one here in front of me because I can't separate the two."

"You are one in a million." Zane ran his thumb over her cheek.

Jewell smiled and shook her head. "Nope, we are two in a million."

"Yeah, our crazies match up pretty well,, don't they?" Zane bopped her nose with his finger.

"They do." A buzz rattled through the quiet of the office. Jewell drew away from Zane's thigh and stood up. She bent over and swiped her lips across his. "If you need to sleep, go to the office downstairs." She headed to admit her technicians.

"I'm not leaving you. Besides, I have a concussion. I need someone to wake me up every couple of hours and make sure my brain is still functioning." Jewell paused before she opened the door. "I can do that."

"I know you can. Get the door. I'm not going to go to sleep for a while yet."

Jewell smiled at him because freaking out about his concussion he'd just reminded her of probably wasn't the best option at the moment. She turned to open her office door. Two of her techs walked into the office. One had a laptop, and the other had a desktop unit.

"Two? I thought it was just a laptop?" Still concerned for Zane, she glanced over her shoulder at the man she almost lost today. As much as she wanted to be with him, she had work to do. She needed to make sure whomever Vista had targeted was safe. Her mind flipped images of the strong women in her life through her mind. Her mom, Jasmine, Jade, Anna, Tori, Faith, and Tatyana were all strong independent women who needed her to find out what the bastard had planned. She couldn't fail.

With renewed determination she waited for her people to put the equipment down, Zane nodded acknowledging Alonzo and Brittany, who brought the computers into the office. Jewell motioned to the back workstation near where Zane sat. "Thanks, Britt, we'll take it from here." She glanced over at Zane. "You will let me know if you need anything." She wasn't going to put that statement up for debate. Zane nodded and leaned back in his chair. "If I fall asleep wake me up every two hours or so. Ask me some rudimentary questions and then let me go back to sleep."

"I'll call Jacob and have him put an expedited delivery on that cot." Jewell made a move toward the phone at her workstation. Brittany stopped at the door and spoke, "Jewell, I can get that arranged for you. I'll grab a couple of the guys and head over to that side of the house."

"That would be awesome. Thanks, Britt." Jewell really liked Brittany, she'd only been working at Guardian for just over a year, but she did a great job.

Jewell looked back over at Zane. He chuckled softly and waved his hand at the table where Alonzo was waiting. "Go, work, do the magic thing you do."

Jewell glanced at her workbench and then back to Zane who'd closed his eyes. She headed over to her computer and set a two-hour alarm before she returned to the other side of the office. She grabbed power cords and tossed one to Alonzo to power up the machines. "Where did the tower come from?" She lowered her voice, so she didn't wake Zane if he was already sleeping.

"The techs guys that had us sign the chain of custody forms said it came from a car in the parking lot of the apartment building. I'm assuming you know what that means."

"I do. This one could be Vista's primary."

"No shit?" Alonzo slid over and motioned her to the tower. "Then this one would be yours to crack. I'll take the laptop, and we'll meet in the middle?"

Jewell nodded instead of answering, her mind was already processing the steps she needed to take when the computer powered up. She grabbed an ESD bracelet and attached it to her work bench and her wrist. She threw one to Alonzo before she grounded herself to the workstation. She wasn't going to risk being careless. Building static electricity and not grounding herself could take out a board or a component and that shit wasn't going to happen. The computer in front of her was too damn valuable. Even though it didn't look like it. Jewell knew better than to judge a book by its cover or in this case a computer by its tower. She made fast work of the screws holding the plastic shell over the guts of the machine. When Alonzo helped her lift the casing, she damn near fainted. This *was* Vista's computer, it had to be. The hardware configurations were the absolute best of the best. She carefully examined the system and directed Alonzo to take pictures of everything. Before they tried to get into this beauty, she was going to document everything. Jewell bent over the system and punched the power button. It was time to match wits with one of the best hackers she'd ever worked against.

CHAPTER 26

Consciousness came slowly to Zane. The first thing that registered was Jewell laying against him. He lifted his head and winced. No, she wasn't laying against him, she was laying halfway on top of him. Slowly the aches and pains of his body sounded off in a roll call. Damn, he hated pain killers, but he took them if needed, especially when he knew he was safe. The post-sleep haze lingered longer than it should have. He'd chalk that up to the concussion. He blinked his eyes and focused on the office ceiling. Sleeping on the floor wasn't anything new to him. At least he had a foam pad and a sleeping bag as cushion this time. He flexed the hand of his good arm, the one Jewell was sleeping on. Millions of needles stabbed his nerves at the action.

Zane glanced up and across the room. The computers that Jewell and Alonzo had worked on last night were still there. Cables and wires dropped from the ceiling and attached to the larger system. It looked like a desktop version of Frankenstein's Monster. He blinked his eyes and tried to focus on the small digital clock on the far wall. Shit, it was either twelve noon or twelve midnight. There was no way of telling in Jewell's office. No windows or daylight could penetrate the bunker where her section was housed.

If it was midnight... no, it couldn't be midnight unless he'd slept almost twenty-four hours. It was close to eleven when he'd finished at the hospital. He glanced again at the workbench. Jewell had to have worked on that mess of electronics for hours, so he'd bet it was noon. Besides he could remember her waking him up once before he moved to the pallet and three times afterward. Damn painkillers, or maybe it was the concussion, but that deduction took way too long to make.

He moved again and regretted cursing the painkillers because he'd sure like one about now. Jewell moved suddenly and pushed off him. "Are you all right?" Her hair tumbled into her sleep-creased face.

"I'm fine. What time did you crash?" The blood rushed back to Zane's arm and the needle warfare waged against his nerve endings resurged with a vengeance. He fisted his hand hard and released it several times.

"Ummm… maybe at six? I set the alarm to wake you up at eight." She glanced at the digital clock and then at her computer. "I must have forgotten to set the alarm to wake you up at ten."

"Or you slept through it." He hated seeing the dark circles under her eyes.

"Well, there is that." She sat back on her butt and rubbed her neck. "The floor sucks."

"Yeah, did you get into his system?" He motioned toward her workbench.

"Yeah, that would be a big no. He has a one hundred key encryption on it."

"Which means we have nothing?" Zane barely suppressed a groan when he half pushed and half lifted himself into a sitting position.

Jewell covered her mouth as she yawned. She shook her head no and held up a finger of her other hand. Her entire body shook as she finished her wide yawn. "No, I got permission to plug the cipher program into Stampede."

"What in the world is Stampede?" Zane leaned back against the wall and rolled his neck.

"Well, it is a wild herd of running animals, or in this case, it is the supercomputer at The University of Texas. The thing is amazing. It exceeds five thousand teraflops. I mean like it is the seventh fastest computer in the world. Instead of months to crack the cipher, Stampede can do it in hours." She stood and held out a hand to him. Zane looked at it for a moment and readied himself for the pain that was coming. He grabbed her hand, and she moved to brace her legs herself before she let him use her as leverage and lifted off the floor. That time he didn't suppress the groan that escaped.

"Do you have more painkillers?" She leaned up and kissed him on the cheek. "I'd kiss you on the lips, but I have wicked morning breath." She wrinkled her nose and smiled at him before she spun and woke the computer screen over the workspace where Lufkey's computer was now located.

"See?" Jewell pointed to the screen. "It has half of them done in six hours. We should have access by," She glanced at the time on the monitor, "six tonight."

"Then you still have to find out what he was doing?" Zane's mind was starting to sharpen.

"Yeah." Jewell rubbed her eyes.

"Lufkey told me that 'she would be dead by this time tomorrow.' What time did the team storm the building?" His memory was a blur of events, but the timing had to be recorded.

Jewell walked across the room to her workstation and let her hands fly over the keyboard.

"Seven forty-eight," Jewell responded.

"Which means you'll have very little time to figure out what he's planning. Can that supercomputer go faster?"

He saw her shoulders drop at his question. "No."

"All right, so we do what we need to do to prep for when the cipher is cracked. Let's go get a shower, grab something to eat and swing by and talk to Jason to make sure the rest of the ladies are safe. Once we know he can't actually hurt anyone, you'll be able to concentrate on what you need to do."

Jewell drew a deep breath and nodded. She held her stomach and blanched. Zane was beside her in a second. "Are you all right?"

"Yeah, I've had an upset stomach for the last

couple days. Nothing to worry about." She smiled at him and grabbed his hand. "Nothing that coffee can't cure."

"Babe, do you think maybe it's time to use that pregnancy test you've been carrying around in your purse?" Zane pushed her hair back behind her ear and lifted her chin with his fingers. "Not acknowledging the possibility isn't good for you. You need to know and deal with the stress instead of playing the what-if game in your head."

"I promise you I'm not doing that. While I have looked at all the circumstances and possible outcomes, I've stuck strictly to facts, not extrapolations. Besides, it is too early for morning sickness. I've researched that." Jewell leaned into him and tucked up under his chin.

"Don't you want to know?" They were rocking slowly from side to side. Zane couldn't imagine going a day without feeling this woman against him.

"Yes. No. I don't know." She lifted her arms and wrapped them around his neck.

"Come on. Let's go grab a shower down at the gym and get some fresh clothes. Then we'll borrow one of your brother's private bathrooms. Hopefully, one of them will be needed somewhere else and won't be in their office." He kissed the top of her head. She nodded and pulled away from him.

"I really need a toothbrush, too." She held her hand over her mouth. "I had a candy bar about four this morning. I think my teeth may have grown fur."

Zane laughed and spun her around and pointed her to her workstation. "Check your statuses and then grab your purse so we can go find you a toothbrush."

"I can call Sonya and see what Jason's schedule is for the afternoon." Jewell checked her monitors as she spoke.

Zane smiled and held out his hand toward her when she looked over at him. "That sounds like a plan."

Zane hovered outside the bathroom door. He was dressed in sweats and a t-shirt that he'd borrowed from the training center. His bandaged arm and shoulder ached like a bitch, but he was clean and safe. He'd finally talked Jewell into using the pregnancy test that he'd seen in her purse. He wanted to know if they were pregnant. He didn't care one way or the other. Did he want a family? Hell, who knew... maybe? It wasn't something he'd ever thought he'd be able to have so he'd never really thought about it in any detail. What he did know was that he loved the woman who was probably quietly freaking out behind the bathroom door. He leaned against the door and tapped softly on the wood.

"Just a minute." He couldn't read anything by her tone. He shook his head. He'd bet she hadn't even used the test yet. The door opened, and she slipped through it. There was nothing in her hand.

"Did you decide not to find out?"

"No, I found out." She pulled her bottom lip into her mouth and bit down.

Zane lifted his hand and pulled her lip away from her teeth. He dropped his head and kissed her swollen bottom lip. "Are we pregnant?"

"No, we're not pregnant." She drew a long breath in and released it in a shuddering sigh.

"Are you... upset?" Zane had to ask because he wasn't sure how to gauge her expression right now.

"No. Yes." She lifted her eyes to him. "Maybe?"

Zane saw a myriad of emotions displayed. He chuckled softly and pulled her into him. "We have the rest of our lives to decide when we want to start a family." Zane put a kiss on the top of her head. "Besides, I didn't want to deal with your brothers at a shotgun wedding."

Jewell laughed. It was a light, carefree sound. "This is the twenty-first century. Shotgun weddings are out of vogue."

"Tell me you don't think they would have circled the wagons."

"Oh, they would have tried." She slipped her arm through his and led him toward Jason's office door. "But I have a secret weapon that is guaranteed to make them back up and think before they act like cavemen."

"Really, and what would that be?" Zane stopped and asked before he opened the door.

She lifted up on her toes and kissed him softly. "You."

CHAPTER 27

Zane was right, she did feel more centered. The few hours of sleep she'd had last night in Zane's arms were the best she'd had in days. Knowing that she wasn't pregnant also took a weight off her shoulders, one she didn't really know had settled upon her. Did she want to have a baby? Yes, definitely—someday. Did she want a life with Zane? Absolutely. Did they have miles to go before either would happen? Probably. But those were variables she was happy accepting.

Jewell stared at the screen. Stampede had all but the last three digits of the cipher solved. Alonzo was ready to assist her and Zane was seated in his chair with his tablet. She watched as Stampede dropped another digit. Jewell added it to

Lufkey's computer. *Two more you bastard.* Two more and she'd have access to the fucker's system. She had a plan of attack. She'd work the first five most recent programs to have been opened. Alonzo would hit the man's email before he started on his internet usage and history. Yvette, one of her best white hat hackers, would work the next five programs. There was no need for any more people, the three of them would be able to dissect the system, and with Guardian's proprietary programs, they'd shred any remaining safeguards and gain access in a quick, efficient bloodletting.

Stampede dropped the last digit, and all three of them attacked their keyboards. She didn't hear or see anything but the screen in front of her. The first three programs were tracking programs, each more complex than the last. Guardian's GPS coordinates were installed in all three. There were others. Jewell copied them and dropped them into Guardian's system and threw the locations up on the theater screen. Her brothers and Zane were down at the bottom of the steps. She didn't need to hear their discussion, it wouldn't help her access the information faster, and in fact, their presence would just distract her.

She found a set of three more coordinates and

dragged them across the systems and populated them on the same screen as the first coordinates. She scoured the programs one more time and then dropped them for the fourth program. Jewell looked at the program with awe. The son of a bitch had built a system to hack governmental agencies. Not just the simple ones like the Department of Energy, but he had hacked the Department of Treasury, the Department of Justice, Homeland Security to include Immigrations and Customs Enforcement. The long-line algorithm that ran the base of the program was frankly beyond Jewell's comprehension. The one thing that stood out was, while Vista had been using the program, he wasn't the one who developed it. The language was too advanced and too smooth. Jewell would dig into who'd written it later. She sent the list of hacked agencies to the theater and started pulling information out of the system. She traced the hack to the files that were pulled and started sending them out. She didn't take the time to look at what she was extracting. She couldn't. File after file was sent to systems at the front of the theater. Her people would do as directed by her brothers and the brains that moved Guardian. What she was doing now was a search and recovery operation and time was of the essence. She'd get the information to the people who knew what to do with it.

Time ceased to exist as she became laser focused on the fourth program. She pulled the last cache of files out and sent them down and didn't miss a beat as she opened the next program. The file was a media metadata storage unit. Jewell searched the files. It didn't have the video or the photographs, but it had information on the media. She cleared that file quickly and then started searching the hard drive for partitioned material. Yvette was almost done with the recent files and would be jumping over to help Alonzo with tracing the man's internet history, now that they had access to his programs they could find out what he was doing on the Dark Net and who he contacted. Anything that could help determine what Vista was doing would benefit the agencies he'd hacked.

Jewell paused when she found a photo and video cache. An eerie sense of foreboding hit her because of the way the photos had been hidden. Whatever the reason, whatever was here important enough for Vista to strip the photos from the metadata pointing to them and hide them in a partitioned area of his hard drive. Jewell highlighted and grabbed all of the photos and cast them to the screen. The largest files and most obvious programs were shredded out first because they had everything. Now they needed to comb through the detritus and find out what the man had hidden.

She heard her office door open and rolled her shoulders at the interruption. She heard Zane sit down in his chair. The only other sounds were of the tapping of keyboards, the clicks of their mice and the hum of the systems that filled her office. Jewell jumped when a bottle of water appeared beside her. She glared at the offending object and then at the man who placed it there.

"You three have been at this for over five hours," Zane answered her unspoken question.

"Five hours? The deadline?" She glanced out at the theater, but the screens were dark.

"Your brothers have the information they needed." Zane's voice held that distant, polite tone he'd used when he was watching over her the first time. The sudden cessation of keystrokes made her glance over at Alonzo and Yvette. They looked at Zane with the same concern and questions she had.

"Who? Who did they target?" Jewell's stomach

dropped, not wanting to know the answer but needing to hear it anyway.

"Jade."

Jewell's stomach flipped, and she covered her mouth with her hand. Zane pulled her from her chair and hugged her close. Jewell pulled away to cling to a portion of her sanity and not fall apart in Zane's arms. She glanced at Alonzo and Yvette. "You've done enough for tonight. We have the information we needed. We can sift through this tomorrow. Thank you."

"I hope it was enough." Alonzo put his hand on her arm and smiled as he waited for Yvette to come out from behind the workbench.

"Thank you. I'm sure my brothers are doing everything they can do." She looked at Zane, who nodded in agreement.

When the door clicked shut she buried herself into his strong chest. "Did they get to her in time?"

"Jason has alerted the Attorney General. They are waiting for their agent to make contact. He has established check-in times. If they send someone in and there hasn't been a compromise, they endanger the team. If something has happened already, the agent won't make his check-in call.

That will alert them to move in. Until then, we have to wait."

"How long until he checks in?" She needed to make sure Jade was all right. Her sister was one of the toughest people she knew, but she was still alone and in a dangerous situation.

Zane drew a deep breath before he answered. "Next week."

Jewell shook her head in disbelief. "Jason can't be willing to wait that long!"

"He wasn't until the DEA explained the ramifications of making contact." Zane grabbed her water bottle off the workstation and opened it, handing it to her. Jewell put it back down, not in the least interested in the damn water.

"What ramifications? What could be more important than the life of my sister and their agent?"

"The lives of at least thirty women and children. Jason wouldn't say more. He probably said too much, but he knew you'd have questions. He also asked me to ask you not to hack the DEA and to wait like the rest of the family."

Jewell chuffed out a lungful of air. "He knows me."

"He does. He also asked me if I wanted to go to

the ranch with you. He assumed you would want to be with your mom and Jasmine when they found out."

"Yeah, I do. I can hook into the system from the comms facility at the ranch and monitor things here. When do we leave?"

"Jason put a plane on standby for us. As soon as you want." Zane bent down and kissed her softly on the lips. "You have to believe she will be all right."

"If anyone will be, it would be Jade." Jewell glanced at the computer that they'd been working on.

"I've heard that about ten times now between you and your brothers. I take it she's a tough cookie?"

"The toughest." She melted against Zane and breathed in his scent.

"If she is anything like you, she'll find a way to adapt and overcome any obstacle." Zane held her hand as he walked her to her station. "Log out of this system. We have a flight to catch."

Jewell didn't even hesitate to do as he asked. She logged out of her systems and grabbed her purse from her desk. As the left the office, she turned out the lights and looked down over the people who were working the missions, operations orders and background investigations that Guardian required. Her people helped make the organization one of the best security entities in the world. She was proud of what she'd accomplished, but it was also time for a change. She'd had an idea for a couple of weeks now, and it had firmed up over the last week. She'd talk to Jason when she got settled at the ranch.

Jewell grabbed Zane's hand and started down the stairs. This wasn't her life anymore. It was a very important piece of it, but there was so much more now. So much more.

CHAPTER 28

Zane watched out the right side of the window as the plane landed. The sky was a brilliant blue with large white clouds spotting the expanse of the horizon. They had both fallen asleep right after take-off. Turbulence over Minnesota jarred him awake. His shoulder and arm throbbed and ached, but he'd do it all over again if it meant Jewell was safe.

The specter of Vista was still looming. Jewell's sister now bore the brunt of the bastard's venom. He put his hand on Jewell's thigh, grounding himself to the fact that she was safe. As much of a bastard as it made him, Zane was glad Jewell's destiny was no longer tied to that bastard. He hated that her sister was still in jeopardy. Zane had immediately volunteered to go in and bring her out. Wherever 'in' was. From what he gathered, her brothers didn't know, and the DEA wasn't sharing. He'd go in and get her if only to stop Jewell from worrying and of course to protect her sister. Jason had turned his offer down flat.

Jason King amazed him. The almost unimaginable stress that man carried on his shoulders had been amplified tenfold, specifically because he didn't have control of this mission. Zane couldn't imagine how the man felt. He must be swimming in a feeling of impotence. Speaking from experience, he didn't envy that man.

The landing gear engaged. The flight attendant shook his head when Zane motioned to Jewell asking if he should wake her up, but the sound of the wheels lowering roused her from her sleep anyway. She rubbed her eyes and yawned before stretching like a cat and sitting up. "Are we there?"

"Landing."

"Hmmm… what time is it?" Jewell flopped onto his good shoulder and yawned again.

Zane glanced at his watch. "Six."

Jewell jumped and pulled away from him. "Oh good. Dinner is at six-thirty. My mom's cooking is the best and Aunt Betty makes the best pies and cobblers." She damn near bounced in her seat as she spoke. He hadn't seen her this animated since she'd played in the video game tournament. Zane chuckled as she described her mom's chicken and dumplings. "And she doesn't make the thin noodle-like dumplings, she makes the thick fluffy ones and oh, my God, they melt in your mouth and are heaven on earth."

The plane touched down and taxied toward a small hanger. They disembarked and walked out into what Zane would describe as the middle of a high tech western movie. He could hear cattle calling to each other and to his right the tops of giant wind turbines could be seen over the rolling hills. There were solar panels on the roofs of the outlying buildings that were obviously part of the training complex that Jewell had described to him. When he looked to the right, he was in an epic cowboy adventure, complete with animals and sound effects. If he did an about face, there was no doubt a paramilitary entity had set up a training facility. His eyes were drawn to a structure that had at least ten different antennas mounted to the roof. It was impossible to determine the purpose of the other structures, but by the looks of things, the complex was substantial.

Two men waited at the edge of the tarmac. As they approached the men's loose stature altered. He could sense the body language change from 'welcome' to 'who the fuck are you.'

As they got closer, Zane could see they were twins. Twins that rivaled his height and bulk and they were warriors. He could sense the battle scars even though he couldn't see them.

They glanced at him and then looked a Jewell. They moved their eyes and heads at the exact same time. Freaky as fuck but... really cool too. "Jewell." The one on the right said.

"Dixon, Drake. How have you been?" Jewell left his side and hugged the man that spoke and then the other.

"Been better."

"Have you heard anything?" Jewell fumbled with her phone, looking at the screen. The one who was speaking put his hand on hers. "Nothing yet."

The silent one swallowed hard and looked away. "I'm Zane Reynolds." He extended his hand toward the silent one. The man measured Zane the way Zane had measured them as he approached.

Finally, he extended his hand. "Drake."

Jewell slipped her arm through Zane's and

tilted her head until it lay on his bicep. "Guys, Zane's my..." She turned and looked at Zane and broke into laughter. "Hell, boyfriend is such a teenager's term."

"Try lover." The one that had to be Dixon deadpanned.

"But I wouldn't say that in front of Frank or your mom," Drake added.

"Or any of her brothers," Zane chimed in.

Both of the twin's faces split into identical grins, and both said, "True that." Zane chuckled to himself as they did a coordinated turn and started down a cement pathway.

Jewell leaned into him as they walked. They stepped off the cement and followed a graveled pathway around a large rolling hill. Zane schooled his expression as he took in what he hadn't seen when they landed. They walked as a loose group toward a freaking mansion made of logs. Judging from the outside, the thing had to be at least six thousand square feet of living space. Not that Zane was an engineer, but he'd learned to understand architecture, and this building was a work of art. As they turned the corner and walked along the front of the house, a massive porch gave the imposing structure a welcoming appearance. There was a man sitting on the porch in an old-fashioned swing. Jewell made a small squealing noise and bolted up the stairs. The tall, lean and hard looking cowboy stood and wrapped her into his arms. Zane could hear a mumbled conversation but stood back at the top of the stairs to give them their private moment.

Jewell turned toward him and extended her hand. Zane walked over. As he did the gravity of the situation hit him. *Fuck, he was meeting Jewell's stepfather.* That was heavy on many levels. Zane extended his hand. "Sir, I'm Zane Reynolds."

The weathered face didn't change expressions. Zane felt the weight of the cowboy's stare before the man extended his hand. "Frank Marshall. I'm Jewell's stepdad."

"I'm sorry to be meeting you under the circumstances, sir, but I want you to know we would have met regardless. I'm in love with Jewell, and I won't hide that fact."

The old cowboy cocked his head and considered Zane. Finally, he nodded. "Fair enough." He hugged Jewell before he moved even with Zane. "Hurt her, and you'll deal with me." The words were quiet, intended for just the two of them. He clapped Zane on his injured shoulder as he walked by. Zane blanched but held firm. The old man couldn't know he'd been shot in the shoulder... or did he?

"Your mom is in the kitchen with Betty. She heard you were coming and started cooking. Get yourself settled and cleaned up. Dinner is in fifteen minutes. Don't be late." Frank Marshall nodded at the twins, who fell into step after him.

Zane exhaled heavily and rolled his shoulder. Fuck that was uncomfortable. "So, did I pass?" He turned toward Jewell, who stood with a wide smile on her face.

"Oh, you passed. Frank told me that Jason, Jacob, and Jared had each called him and told him you were the right man for me."

"Oh, thank God. So let's get cleaned up because I'm not about to piss that man off and make him wait for dinner."

Jewell laughed and took his hand, leading him into the most impressive foyer he'd ever seen. The antler light fixture was easily six foot across and hung from over a massive stairway. But the thing that drew his attention was the fireplace in the grand room. He could park a 4x4 truck in the fire box. Zane held Jewell's hand as he gaped at the country style opulence. "So... your mom married well."

Jewell laughed at his remark. "She married for love, but it was cool that Frank could take care of her. Let's go, we have only a few minutes to make it to dinner." She motioned toward the stairs, and Zane followed like a puppy.

"This is your room." Jewell pointed toward the door and then motioned toward the adjoining room. "That's mine." She leaned up and whispered, "There is an adjoining door. We are taking over Jasmine and Jade's rooms."

"Are you sure your mom will be okay with that?"

"I'm not worried about my mom. Frank? He's the one I'd worry about. Go. Wash up and then knock on my door. I'll escort you to the grand inquisition."

Zane watched her disappear through her door and entered the huge bedroom. He glanced over the massive bed, built-in dresser and exposed log wall to the huge window. The rolling green pastures were dotted with cattle and contrasted against the vivid blue of the expansive skyline. A snick of metal drew his attention. He pivoted and watched Jewell enter his room from hers. She grinned at him and pointed at the bathroom. "There should be everything you need in there. Mom is good about restocking the bathrooms with new stuff. They never know who will be stopping in or passing through."

Zane shook his head and lifted his hand, pulling a beckoning finger toward her. Her eyebrows rose in question, but she followed his unspoken direction and approached him. He pulled her into him and took her lips. The fresh taste of mint burst across the delicious taste of the woman to whom he'd given his heart.

She pulled away and shook her head. "Go, get cleaned up, or we will be late for dinner, and that will piss Frank off. The man has like two rules and being late for dinner is breaking one of them. Dinner time around here is almost sacred."

Zane took off his suit jacket and laid it on the bed before he undid his cufflinks and rolled up his shirt sleeves. "Why is that?"

"Mom says it is because everyone can be together, if only for that short time. The needs of the ranch and the complex are pretty demanding, but for an hour every night, Frank has everyone check-in and makes sure they have everything they need."

"Does he run the training complex, too?" Zane asked around the toothbrush in his mouth.

"No, Chief oversees the entire complex. Under him, Dixon and Drake take care of the day to day training requirements, running the ancillary programs, rotating people in and out and recruiting trainers. Adam is in charge of the hospital and rehab area. But Frank treats all those guys like his sons. He's just that way." Jewell sat on his bed when he came back out to the bedroom. Fuck, he'd rather just pull her down onto that soft looking mattress and forget dinner. But he still needed to meet her mother and deal with the inevitable questions.

"Well then, lead the way." Zane started to roll down his shirt sleeves when she placed her hand on his.

"Leave them rolled up. Everyone else will be in jeans and work clothes. Be comfortable. I love you and they will, too. "

Zane didn't try to prevent the puff of laughter that her comment forced out of him. "Frank doesn't seem to be on the 'glad Zane's dating his stepdaughter' bandwagon."

"That's just his outside layer. Inside he's as soft as a marshmallow." Jewell stood on her tiptoes and brushed her lips against his. "Don't tell me my big, bad assassin is afraid of a sixty-year-old cowboy?" Her eyes danced with laughter when she tilted her head and looked up at him.

Zane snapped his fingers and pointed at her. "You see *that's* the dilemma. I can't kill him."

"No, I agree. That would be rude." Jewell quipped right back at him.

"Right? So my options are limited."

"You could try talking to him." Jewell headed toward the door to the bedroom.

"Been there, done that, got the cold shoulder." Zane followed her as he spoke.

"Does that bother you?" She paused and looked over her shoulder.

"If it were anyone else, I wouldn't give it a second thought, but I want your people to accept me."

"My people will, but even if they didn't, they aren't who you are in love with." Jewell's smile spread across her face. Zane reminded himself to never let her know how that expression melted him. He'd do anything to keep her this happy.

"True." Zane reached out, and Jewell took his hand. "Let's get the inquisition over." Zane sighed dramatically.

"Stop worrying." She laughed when he rolled his eyes and tugged him along the hallway and down the grand staircase.

Zane could smell the food as soon as they left the bedroom. He sure as hell hoped it tasted as good as it smelled. When they stepped into the dining room, all conversation ceased. Jewell pulled away and darted over to an older woman, wrapping her in a hug. He swept the room, noting how many people were gathered around the table, and catalogued the entrances and exits to include the windows. His eyes landed on Fury for a millisecond before he noticed the very pregnant woman next to him. A man with an eye patch and a beautiful blonde woman, plus the twins were all seated around the table. Frank nodded at him, and he nodded back before he turned to take in the reunion of mother and daughter.

Jewell pulled back and reached her hand out. "Zane, this is my mom. Mom, this is Zane Reynolds."

The woman's warm, welcoming expression eased a bit the tension he'd been carrying. "Zane, it is good to meet you. I'm Amanda. Jason and Joseph have told me so much about you. Thank you for everything you've done to keep my family safe." He didn't expect the hug that enveloped him. He tensed slightly and glanced at Jewell although he had no idea why.

"I would do anything to make sure Jewell was safe." Zane's voice was low and intended for her mom's ears only.

"I know. Take good care of my girl." She pulled away and gestured toward the table. "Please sit down. We need to eat while the food's hot."

"That would be my preference." Frank's gruff voice from the head of the table earned a low rumble of laughter from everyone who was seated.

Zane was seated between Jewell and her mom. He pulled out both ladies' chairs and situated them before he took his seat. As if by some imaginary cue everyone at the table dropped their heads and folded their hands. Well, everyone except Joseph, who stared directly at Zane.

"Father God, thank you once again for the bounty of our lives, for the food at this table and the people who surround it." A round of Amens flanked Frank's prayer, and then a coordinated type of chaos erupted. Dish after dish of food was passed around the table. Zane took a sample of everything and even put a scoop of a fresh chopped vegetable salad on Jewell's plate after she'd passed the dish without taking any. She cocked her eyebrow at him. He put a second scoop on her plate. She smiled and nudged him with her shoulder. Zane turned to pass the dish to Amanda. The woman's expression arrested Zane's movements for a moment. Zane didn't know for sure, but he thought he saw tears misting her eyes. But the moment passed when Jewell handed him a dish of homemade biscuits.

"So, Zane, where are your people from?" Frank asked before he took a bite of his chicken.

"I don't have any people. I grew up in several areas, but none that I call home." Zane was going to be completely honest with the man until he bumped up against his previous life, then he'd hedge the truth.

"What do you do for Guardian?" Zane's head swiveled to the blonde woman across from him.

"Hi, I'm Adam Cassidy, and this is my wife, Keelee. She's Frank's daughter and has his penchant for asking direct questions." The man's smile seemed to take the sting out of the comment because the woman scrunched her nose at him and smiled as she turned back to Zane.

"It is a pleasure to meet you, and I'm a personal security officer." Zane was happy to tell them the truth, or at least the most recent version of the truth.

"Is that how you met Jewell?" The very pregnant redhead sitting next to Fury asked. When Zane turned toward her, she gave him a little wave. "Hi, I'm Ember. I believe you've met my husband, Joseph."

Zane nodded at Fury because he'd never be able to think of the man as anyone else. "A pleasure. Yes, ma'am, I met Jewell last year when there was a perceived threat to some of the people who worked at Guardian. We've worked together since then."

"How long have you worked with Guardian?" Amanda asked as she passed one of the twins the bowl of mashed potatoes... again. Damn those two could eat.

"Since I left the service, over twelve years now."

"Oh, then you must know my daughters Jade and Jasmine?" Zane sensed the twins and Jewell tense more than saw it happen. Fury was out of his line of sight, but no doubt that man was waiting for him to respond. From the innocent way she asked, he doubted Amanda knew Jade could be in jeopardy.

"I'm sorry, no. I just recently transferred into the field. I was used in other areas before that."

Jewell slid her hand on his thigh and glanced over at the twins. "Where's Chief?"

"He and Taty work on her rehab Monday, Wednesday and Friday nights. It's when the clinic is available. She's getting some of her mobility back in her shoulder, but the arm is still weak." The one he thought was Drake spoke because his brother had just taken a huge bite off of the chicken leg he held in his hand.

A tinny cry broke through a small speaker on the sideboard. "And that would be Miss Elizabeth waking up from her nap." The man who introduced himself as Adam chuckled as his wife gulped her drink while she was standing up.

"Yeah, she wouldn't go down this afternoon. There are new puppies at the barn, and she wore them out. I'll be right back." Keelee darted through the door before anyone could respond.

"So, Zane, do you ride?" Frank was wiping his plate with half a buttered biscuit. Zane nodded before he swallowed the food he had in his mouth. "Yes, sir. I learned how to ride in the service. We were required to be in places a Humvee couldn't take us. I've also ridden for pleasure."

Frank nodded and leaned back in his chair. His gaze lingered on Zane. "So, son, what are your intentions toward my daughter?"

The iced tea Jewell had been drinking sprayed across the table. Dixon and Drake broke out in laughter, and a smile even tugged on Joseph's lips. Zane put down his fork and knife and leaned in so he could see the man over Jewell, who was now trying to wipe up her mess.

Adam laughed and held up his hands in a gesture of surrender. "I've had this conversation with him. Good luck, my friend."

Zane drew his attention away from the man across from him back to Frank before he spoke, "I love her, and I have loved her for a long time now. She is my forever. My intentions past those facts are private and are none of your business."

Jewell turned toward him, her eyes as huge as saucers. She slowly swiveled her head back toward Frank. Zane watched the older man now that the people around the table were motionless and silent.

Frank sucked his teeth, making a 'tsking' sound, and leaned forward on his forearms and glared down the table at Zane. "Son, Jason told me you had balls the size of coconuts, glad to see you have the sense to pull them out and use them when you need to." He looked at Joseph and nodded toward Zane. "You know him?"

Joseph raised an eyebrow at the older man and nodded once.

"You figure he's good enough for your sister?"

Zane didn't know whether he was more annoyed at the conversation about him, going on around him, or more curious as to Fury's answer.

Joseph swung his eyes to Zane and then back to Frank. He lifted his chin again.

"Huh." Frank stood and leaned over to Amanda kissing her on the cheek. "Good dinner, hun." He glanced at the twins on the way out of the dining room. They'd somehow cleared their plates in record time. Frank stopped as he hit the arched doorway. "You drink Scotch?" Zane nodded. "I'll pour." Frank meandered out of the room.

"I think that means he wants you to go with him." Jewell nudged him as she whispered, her radiant smile flashed at him.

Dixon and Drake stood at the same time and stepped around their chairs in unison. Freaky. Zane really wasn't sure he'd ever get used to that shit. One of them, he'd given up on figuring out which one was which, motioned toward him. "Come on. Never a good idea to keep him waiting."

Adam wiped his lips and dropped his napkin. "I'm heading back to the clinic after I go see my girls. I have rounds to make. It was good to meet you, Zane."

Zane replied in kind and glanced at Fury as he stood. He paused, half standing. For just a second he could have sworn Fury was smiling. But the expression was so fleeting Zane wondered if he'd seen it or not. He bent down and pressed a soft kiss on Jewell's lips. "If I don't come back, send in a search party." Her laughter followed him out of the door.

CHAPTER 29

Jewell sat on Zane's bed and brushed her hair out. She'd helped her mom and Keelee clear the table and do the dishes. Joseph and Ember had retired after dinner. Ember got tired easily now, and Joseph was a hovering, doting ball of nerves. After dinner, she'd passed Frank's study and heard laughter, so she was pretty sure Zane didn't need rescuing. She smiled to herself. The man was amazing on so many levels. He'd recreated himself. His choices in his life had cost him, and she was amazed that he was able to stop, take a step back and realize he didn't want to be the person he'd become any longer. He was rock solid, and that gave her a sense of security that she didn't know she'd been missing.

The door opened silently. She smiled as he entered. "You didn't need a search party?"

Zane chuckled and started taking off his shirt as he crossed the room. "No, I seemed to have made it through the evening relatively unscathed."

His dress shirt slid off his shoulders, pulling Jewell's eyes to the taut muscles that moved and shifted as he undid his belt, button, and zipper. Jewell leaned forward and crawled across the mattress that separated them. Zane froze as she approached. She liked the lust that filled his eyes. She did that to him. He chose her. Jewell felt liberated at the thought. He wanted her. Her, the computer nerd. She sat on her heels and reached out, grabbing the waistband of his boxers and pulled him closer to the bed.

Jewell leaned forward and licked one of his nipples. His entire body tightened, and he stopped breathing. She pulled the brown disk into her mouth and teased the tightening nub. He groaned a low and desperate sound. Jewell licked her way to the other side of his chest as she pushed his pants and boxers down his thighs. His long, hard cock felt like the softest velvet in her hand as she stroked up his iron-hard shaft. She sucked his other nipple into her mouth and thumbed his slit, spreading the dew drop of come that had formed at the tip around the crown of his cock.

"Babe, that feels so good." Zane's hands cupped the back of her head, and his hips thrust forward into her hand. Jewell bit down slightly, causing Zane to suck in a lungful of air. She pulled away and laid down on her back, dropping her head off the mattress of the bed. She'd only done this once before.

She scooted over until Zane's cock and balls were directly over her face. She reached up and stroked his cock while she licked and sucked on his balls. Jewell lost track of time, instead focused on the man above her.

He tapped her arm and whispered in a hoarse plea, "Babe, you need to stop, or I'll shoot."

Jewell tilted her head so she could see him. "I want that." Before he could respond, she pulled his cock down and sucked the head into her mouth.

"Fuck!" Zane dropped down over, her bracing himself on his hands by her hips. His hips thrust forward slightly moving his cock deeper down her throat. She moaned at the sensation of him taking his pleasure. His tempo increased, but he didn't thrust any deeper. Jewell wrapped her hands around the back of his thighs and pulled him in, sending his cock down her throat. Her gag reflex triggered, and he pulled out, but she grabbed his thighs and drew him back. Zane finally got the message and started to fuck her mouth. She moaned against his flesh.

"Oh, God. I'm..." Zane didn't finish his words. His thrusts lost their tempo, and he pushed deeper, cutting off her air when he came. Jewell gasped for air around his cock when he started to withdraw. She braced against his thighs to keep him in her mouth as she sucked the length of his cock. He shivered violently and pulled away. "Too sensitive." His gravelly voice was breathless.

Jewell lifted her head up onto the bed and scooted to the center so he could lie down. Zane flopped onto the bed, his arm landing over her waist. The mattress stopped most of the momentum, but she still bounced when he collapsed. She laughed at him and ran her hand over his arm that corralled her.

"God, that was amazing," Zane spoke into the pillow, which muffled his words, but that's what Jewell believed he said.

"Glad you enjoyed yourself." She turned to him

and snuggled up next to him. He pulled her in, turning onto his side as he did.

"Not bad for starters." Zane lowered his lips to hers.

"Not bad?" Jewell laughed and tried to pull away.

"Okay, unbelievably good for starters." Zane's strong arms brought her close, and he lowered his head to her breast. The man's tongue needed to be registered as a deadly weapon because what he could do with it was insane. She arched into him. His hand trailed down the length of her body, pausing to tickle, tease or trace. He rolled her onto her back while continuing his sensuous onslaught. His touches lifted her higher, pulling that delicious heat and tension to her core. Jewell's body reacted to Zane. Her senses were swamped with his smell, with the sensations of his touch and kisses. The crinkle of a condom wrapper drifted through the overwhelming awareness of... him. Zane had wrapped his essence around her until she didn't know how she could breathe without him being here, in her arms. She grabbed his biceps when he centered over her.

His eyes locked with hers. "I love you."

The honesty of his words laid her bare. She slid

her hand up to his shoulders. "You are the most amazing man I know. I love you. All of you, your past, who you are now and whoever you will become."

Zane entered her as his lips descended onto hers. Jewell lifted her hips, begging for his heat. He enveloped her in his arms, cradling her against his chest. She wrapped her arms around his neck and her legs around his. The passion, awareness, and emotion of their lovemaking brought tears to her eyes. Zane kissed her tears away and held her as if she was precious. The intimacy devastated anything she'd ever experienced. The man who'd sat behind her and quietly made his way into her life had filled it to capacity. He found the dark, lonely places and filled them with meaning, love, and hope. Jewell arched into him and shattered against the steady rhythm of his strokes. She allowed the crescendo of their lovemaking to carry her as he crested and crashed with her.

Zane carefully pulled out of her and disposed of the condom before he enfolded her in his arms. She pulled the sheet over them and snuggled up next to him. She melted into him and breathed a sigh of contentment. Zane's presence in her life had forced her out of the protective shell she'd built. A self-imposed chain link fence of programs and systems that blocked people from getting too close. He'd found a way past her defenses and deposited himself into her heart. She smiled against his warm skin. She was loved.

EPILOGUE

Drake tamped down the gut-wrenching dread that had been hounding him since he and Dixon had found out Jade's cover may have been compromised. He glanced over at his brother, who was sitting as still as a statue in the same position he'd assumed when they'd entered the secure communications room. They hadn't been called into the teleconference with the Administrator of the Drug Enforcement Agency, but they were here and so far no one had asked why. He had a feeling Chief knew, but the others had no clue. Joseph, Jewell, her man Zane and Chief also sat around the conference room table.

Jason's voice came across the speaker. "We will go live in two minutes. I'm muting all participants.

The DEA does not need to hear any reaction other than mine."

Jewell looked over at Zane. "I don't like the sound of that." Drake agreed with her. It sounded like Jason was expecting bad news. He sat still and impassive, mimicking his brother's pose. He could feel the tension and concern rolling off his brother.

"Mr. King, I've heard from our agent." A voice Drake didn't recognize came across the speaker.

"And?" Jason's voice was clipped and icy.

"There seems to be a complication. Your agent hasn't been in direct contact with our agent in over two months."

Drake jumped up at the same time as everyone else in the room bolted to their feet. Zane held out his hands. "Quiet, we don't want to miss what is said."

"You damn well better explain yourself, and quickly." Jason's voice cracked like a whip across the room.

"They were separated, as was expected. From our research it was discovered some of the women who are brought in are used as labor, the men are the front of the organization. Your agent told our man she would give him the designated sign if she were in distress. She has yet to give that sign."

Drake's insides sank. Jade would never give a distress signal. If there was one thing he and Dixon had learned about her, it was that she believed she was invincible.

"So you don't know if she is alive or dead." The question snapped both his and Dixon's heads toward the speaker.

"Our agent sees her occasionally when the women are moved from one area of the compound to the other. Again, she has not sent him the distress signal or tried to make contact."

"When was the last time he physically saw her?" Jason bit out the question.

"Two weeks ago."

"Again, you don't know if she is alive or dead." Drake felt the rage that was conveyed in Jason's growled statement. He felt it boiling under his skin like a poison.

"You are correct. I do not."

Drake glanced at Dixon at the exact time his brother glanced at him. There was no way they weren't going after Jade. They would get her back, and they'd kill anyone who stood in their way.

"I contacted the Department of Justice and the

Secretary of State when your office started giving me the runaround. Guardian has been given permission to go in and extract our agent and take down the compound." Jason's clipped statement gave Drake hope. Guardian being in charge of the operation gave Jade more of a chance than if the FBI got involved. They sure as fuck didn't need another Waco incident.

"I was advised of that this morning. I can't say as I am pleased. Two years' worth of undercover operations will be ruined if it isn't handled –."

Jason's rage tore through the man's whine, "Guardian has assumed this case. I want every shred of information you have, immediately. Failure to comply is not an option unless you want the POTUS involved."

Drake swept the room. Joseph was unreadable as were Chief and Zane. Jewell had tears in her eyes, but she was holding strong. Dixon shifted next to him. He cast his brother a questioning look. A minuscule shake of his head forestalled any further communication. They would talk when they were alone.

Jason's commanding timber interrupted his thoughts. "I've hung up on the fucking administrator of the fucking DEA. Jewell, I need you and

Zane back here immediately. Dixon and Drake, you are the only pilots at the ranch. Get the G6 fueled and get them here, now."

"We are going after her." Dixon barked at the speaker, surprising everyone except Drake.

"You won't be involved in this operation, I need you at the ranch." Jason's dismissal sounded distracted.

"Bullshit! We are involved. Either you use us, or we'll go get her ourselves." Drake added his thoughts to his brother's outburst.

Joseph looked at Zane. "Jason, I can't leave Ember, she is going to download any day now. Use Zane and the Twins. They have the expertise you need. If you go in with a whole team, you'll put everyone at risk. Have the teams standby until they can find Jade and make sure there are no other hostages."

Drake listened to Jason exhale, and then silence descended. Finally, he spoke, "Double D, get Jewell and Zane to DC. Jacob, Jared, and I will plan the op. Chief, I'll want you on standby, but I need someone to keep the complex running while we go get Jade."

"Roger that." Chief acknowledged the charge

he'd been given. He motioned to the twins. "I need to see you."

Dixon felt the rage building under his skin. He knew Drake could feel it too. There was no way in hell they wouldn't be included in the mission. His brother nudged him, and he glanced up. Joseph and Chief stood before them. Jewell and Zane were nowhere to be seen. Well, fuck.

"You better clear your heads or Jason will take you both out of the mission." Joseph stared at him and then at Drake.

"Roger, that." They both answered at the same time.

"I need to be with Jewell when she tells mom what is going on. Keep me informed. I don't give a flying fuck what time it is, I want immediate updates."

"You got it." Chief turned back toward where he and Drake were standing after Joseph ghosted out of the room.

"Keep your head in the game. I'm assuming they believe you want to help because she's a King and part of your extended family."

Dixon nodded at the same time as Drake. They hadn't told anyone about the night they'd shared with Jade. Nothing happened between them, but their time with her had changed them both, and before either one could spend any more time with her she was assigned this undercover gig.

"We need to file a flight plan, get the plane fueled, do a pre-check and get in the air." Drake rattled off the immediate tasks at hand.

Chief leveled his stare at them for several long seconds before he nodded once. "Roger that. Be safe and go get your woman."

To read Jade's Story, Click Here!

The End

Guardian Defenders Series

Gabriel

Maliki

John

Jeremiah

Guardian Security Shadow World

Anubis (Guardian Shadow World Book 1)

Asp (Guardian Shadow World Book 2)

Lycos (Guardian Shadow World Book 3)

Thanatos (Guardian Shadow World Book 4)

Tempest (Guardian Shadow World Book 5)

Smoke (Guardian Shadow World Book 6)

Reaper (Guardian Shadow World Book 7)

Hope City

Hope City - Brock

HOPE CITY - Brody- Book 3

Hope City - Ryker - Book 5

Hope City - Killian - Book 8

STAND ALONE NOVELS

SEAL Forever - Silver SEALs

A Heart's Desire - Stand Alone

Hot SEAL, Single Malt (SEALs in Paradise)

Hot SEAL, Savannah Nights (SEALs in Paradise)

ABOUT THE AUTHOR

USA Today and Amazon Bestselling Author, Kris Michaels is the alter ego of a happily married wife and mother. She writes romance, usually with characters from military and law enforcement backgrounds.